The Science Fiction Bestiary

Nine Stories of Science Fiction

Edited by

Robert Silverberg

THOMAS NELSON INC.
New York   Camden

First edition

Library of Congress Catalog Card Number: 70–160148
International Standard Book Number: 0–8407–6172–4
Manufactured in the United States of America

Acknowledgments

"The Hurkle Is a Happy Beast," by Theodore Sturgeon, copyright 1949 by Mystery House, Inc. Reprinted by permission of Robert P. Mills, Ltd., agent for the author.

"Grandpa," by James H. Schmitz, copyright 1955 by Street & Smith Publications, Inc. Reprinted by permission of the author and his agents, Scott Meredith Literary Agency, Inc., 580 Fifth Avenue, New York, New York 10036.

"The Blue Giraffe," by L. Sprague de Camp, copyright 1939 by Street & Smith Publications, Inc. Reprinted by permission of the author.

"The Preserving Machine," by Philip K. Dick, copyright 1953 by Mercury Publications, Inc. Reprinted by permission of the author and his agents, Scott Meredith Literary Agency, Inc.

Contents

Introduction

In medieval times one of the favorite literary forms was the *bestiary*—the encyclopedic description of animals—real, rumored, or imaginary. The author of a bestiary tried not only to describe and classify the species he discussed, but also to present the animals in short narratives that could be used for moral and religious instruction. Thus the lion was offered as a symbol for royal courage, the ant for industriousness, the tortoise for perseverance. Through the pages of the bestiaries wandered these familiar creatures, as well as a good many whose existence was, at best, highly uncertain—unicorns, griffins, basilisks, dragons, and the like.

Modern zoology has taken a lot of the fun out of compiling bestiaries. We know that our planet is inhabited by many strange and wonderful creatures, yes, aardvarks and pangolins and platypuses and anteaters, but we also have become aware that such marvelous monstrosities as the phoenix, the roc, and the chimera are not to be found even in the most remote corners of the world. Fortunately, writers of science fiction have stepped in to fill this vacuum in the department of unnatural history. Across the pages of science-fiction magazines have marched some of the unlikeliest, most fanciful animals created by the human imagination since the heyday of the twelfth-century bestiary compilers.

The first writer who consciously specialized in extraterrestrial zoology was the lamented Stanley G. Weinbaum. In his brief career during the middle 1930's he spawned an astonishing host of startling animals, several of which you will encounter in the present volume. Weinbaum's success inspired others to contribute their share of zoological marvels, and so, collected here for your delight and amazement, we find gnurrs, hurkles, hokas, bach bugs, and a blue giraffe, to name just a few of the fantastic fauna that have been uncovered by the dedicated researches of the science-fictionists in stories reprinted now. I regret that this book could not have been twice as long as it is; for each remarkable beast you meet here, two or three equally astounding ones had to remain unsung, imprisoned—for the time being—in the crumbling files of old science-fiction magazines.

ROBERT SILVERBERG

The Hurkle
Is a Happy Beast

By Theodore Sturgeon

Ted Sturgeon has been writing science fiction somewhat more than thirty years, which is an odd thing to have to say about a youthful-looking man who, just a few months ago, was proudly displaying his brand-new baby to me at a Los Angeles party. But, like so many of the great science-fiction writers, Sturgeon got a supernaturally early start at his trade, and was already a major figure in the field at an age when most young men are just beginning to make their first vague plans for a career.

His work has always been marked by charm, grace, wit, and eloquence—qualities not as widespread in science fiction as they ought to be. Sturgeon's irrepressible warmth and gaiety are well displayed in this tale of hurkles, first published over twenty years ago but plainly the product of a writer who even then was a grand master.

Lirht *is either* in a different universal plane or in another island galaxy. Perhaps these terms mean the same thing. The fact remains that Lirht is

11

a planet with three moons (one of which is unknown) and a sun, which is as important in its universe as is ours.

Lirht is inhabited by gwik, its dominant race, and by several less highly developed species which, for purposes of this narrative, can be ignored. Except, of course, for the hurkle. The hurkle are highly regarded by the gwik as pets, in spite of the fact that a hurkle is so affectionate that it can have no loyalty.

The prettiest of the hurkle are blue.

Now, on Lirht, in its greatest city, there was trouble, the nature of which does not matter to us, and a gwik named Hvov, whom you may immediately forget, blew up a building which was important for reasons we cannot understand. This event caused great excitement, and gwik left their homes and factories and strubles and streamed toward the center of town, which is how a certain laboratory door was left open.

In times of such huge confusion, the little things go on. During the "Ten Days that Shook the World" the cafés and theaters of Moscow and Petrograd remained open, people fell in love, sued each other, died, shed sweat and tears; and some of these were tears of laughter. So on Lirht, while the decisions on the fate of the miserable Hvov were being formulated, gwik still fardled, funted, and fupped. The great central hewton still beat out its mighty pulse, and in the anams the corsons grew. . . .

Into the above-mentioned laboratory, which had been left open through the circumstances described, wandered a hurkle kitten. It was very happy to find itself there; but then, the hurkle is a happy beast. It prowled about fearlessly—it could become invisible if frightened—and it glowed at the legs of the tables and at the glittering, racked walls. It moved sinuously, humping its back and arching along on the floor. Its front and rear legs were stiff and straight as the legs of a chair; the middle pair had two sets of knees, one bending forward, one back. It was engineered as ingeniously as a scorpion, and it was exceedingly blue.

Occupying almost a quarter of the laboratory was a huge and intricate machine, unhoused, showing the signs of development projects the galaxies over— temporary hookups from one component to another, cables terminating in spring clips, measuring devices standing about on small tables near the main work. The kitten regarded the machine with curiosity and friendly intent, sending a wave of radiations outward which were its glow or purr. It arched daintily around to the other side, stepping delicately but firmly on a floor switch.

Immediately there was a rushing, humming sound, like small birds chasing large mosquitoes, and parts of the machine began to get warm. The kitten watched curiously, and saw, high up inside the clutter of coils and wires, the most entrancing muzziness it had ever seen. It was like heat-flicker over a fallow field; it was like a smoke-vortex; it was like red neon lights on a wet pavement. To the hurkle kitten's senses, that red-orange flicker was also like the smell of catnip to a cat, or anise to a terrestrial terrier.

It reared up toward the glow, hooked its forelegs over a busbar—fortunately there was no ground potential—and drew itself upward. It climbed from transformer to power-pack, skittered up a variable condenser—the setting of which was changed thereby—disappeared momentarily as it felt the bite of a hot tube, and finally teetered on the edge of the glow.

The glow hovered in midair in a sort of cabinet, which was surrounded by heavy coils embodying tens of thousands of turns of small wire and great loops of bus. One side, the front, of the cabinet was open, and the kitten hung there fascinated, rocking back and forth to the rhythm of some unheard music it made to contrast this sourceless flame. Back and forth, back and forth it rocked and wove, riding a wave of delicious, compelling sensation. And once, just once, it moved its center of gravity too far from its point of support. Too far—far enough. It tumbled into the cabinet, into the flame.

One muggy, mid-June day a teacher, whose name was Stott and whose duties were to teach seven subjects to forty moppets in a very small town, was writing on a blackboard. He was writing the word Madagascar, and the air was so sticky and warm that he could feel his undershirt pasting and unpasting itself on his shoulder blade with each round "a" he wrote.

Behind him there was a sudden rustle from the moist seventh-graders. His schooled reflexes kept him from turning from the board until he had finished what he was doing, by which time the room was in a young uproar. Stott about-faced, opened his mouth, closed it again. A thing like this would require more than a routine reprimand.

His forty-odd charges were writhing and squirming in an extraordinary fashion, and the sound they made, a sort of whimpering giggle, was unique. He looked at one pupil after another. Here a hand was busily scratching a nape; there a boy was digging guiltily under his shirt; yonder a scrubbed and shining damsel violently worried her scalp.

Knowing the value of individual attack, Stott intoned, "Hubert, what seems to be the trouble?"

The room immediately quieted, though diminished scrabblings continued. "Nothin', Mister Stott," quavered Hubert.

Stott flicked his gaze from side to side. Wherever it rested, the scratching stopped and was replaced by agonized control. In its wake was rubbing and twitching. Stott glared, and idly thumbed a lower left rib. Someone snickered. Before he could identify the source, Stott was suddenly aware of an intense itching. He checked the impulse to go after it, knotted his jaw, and swore to himself that he wouldn't scratch as long as he was out there, front and center. "The class will—" he began tautly, and then stopped.

There was a—a *something* on the sill of the open window. He blinked and looked again. It was a translucent, bluish cloud which was almost nothing at all. It was less than a something should be, but it was indeed more than a nothing. If he stretched his imagination just a little, he might make out the outlines of an arched creature with too many legs; but of course that was ridiculous.

He looked away from it and scowled at his class. He had had two unfortunate experiences with stink bombs, and in the back of his mind was the thought of having seen once, in a trick-store window, a product called "itching powder." Could this be it, this terrible itch? He knew better, however, than to accuse anyone yet; if he was wrong, there was no point in giving the little geniuses any extra-curricular notions.

He tried again. "The cl—" He swallowed. This itch was . . . "The class will—" He noticed that one head, then another and another, were turning toward the window. He realized that if the class got too interested in what he thought he saw on the window sill, he'd have a panic on his hands. He fumbled for his ruler and rapped twice on the desk. His control was not what it should have been at the moment; he struck far too hard, and the reports were like gunshots. The class turned to him as one; and behind them the thing on the window sill appeared with great distinctness.

It was blue—a truly beautiful blue. It had a small spherical head and an almost identical knob at the other end. There were four stiff, straight legs, a long sinuous body, and two central limbs with a boneless look about them. On the side of the head were four pairs of eyes, of graduated sizes. It teetered there for perhaps ten seconds, and then, without a sound, leapt through the window and was gone.

Mr. Stott, pale and shaking, closed his eyes. His knees trembled and weakened, and a delicate, dewy mustache of perspiration appeared on his upper lip. He clutched at the desk and forced his eyes open; and then, flooding him with relief, pealing into his terror, swinging his control back to him, the bell rang to end the class and the school day.

"Dismissed," he mumbled, and sat down. The class

picked up and left, changing itself from a twittering pattern of rows to a rowdy kaleidoscope around the bottleneck doorway. Mr. Stott slumped down in his chair, noticing that the dreadful itch was gone, had been gone since he had made that thunderclap with the ruler.

Now, Mr. Stott was a man of method. Mr. Stott prided himself on his ability to teach his charges to use their powers of observation and all the machinery of logic at their command. Perhaps, then, he had more of both at his command—after he recovered himself—than could be expected of an ordinary man.

He sat and stared at the open window, not seeing the sun-swept lawns outside. And after going over these events a half dozen times, he fixed on two important facts:

First, that the animal he had seen, or thought he had seen, had six legs.

Second, that the animal was of such nature as to make anyone who had not seen it believe he was out of his mind.

These two thoughts had their corollaries:

First, that every animal he had ever seen which had six legs was an insect, and

Second, that if anything were to be done about this fantastic creature, he had better do it by himself. And whatever action he took must be taken immediately. He imagined the windows being kept shut to keep the thing out—in this heat—and he cowered away from the thought. He imagined the effect of such a monstrosity if it bounded into the midst of a classroom full of children in their early teens, and he recoiled. No; there could be no delay in this matter.

He went to the window and examined the sill. Nothing. There was nothing to be seen outside, either. He stood thoughtfully for a moment, pulling on his lower lip and thinking hard. Then he went downstairs to borrow five pounds of DDT powder from the janitor for an "experiment." He got a wide, flat wooden box and an electric fan, and set them up on a table he pushed close to the window. Then he sat down to wait, in case, just in case the blue beast returned.

When the hurkle kitten fell into the flame, it braced itself for a fall at least as far as the floor of the cabinet. Its shock was tremendous, then, when it found itself so braced and already resting on a surface. It looked around, panting with fright, its invisibility reflex in full operation.

The cabinet was gone. The flame was gone. The laboratory with its windows, lit by the orange Lirhtian sky, its ranks of shining equipment, its hulking, complex machine—all were gone.

The hurkle kitten sprawled in an open area, a sort of lawn. No colors were right; everything seemed half-lit, filmy, out-of-focus. There were trees, but not low and flat and bushy like honest Lirhtian trees, but with straight naked trunks and leaves like a portle's tooth. The different atmospheric gases had colors; clouds of fading, changing faint colors obscured and revealed everything. The kitten twitched its cafmors and ruddled its kump, right there where it stood; for no amount of early training could overcome a shock like this.

It gathered itself together and tried to move; and then it got its second shock. Instead of arching over inchwormwise, it floated into the air and came down three times as far as it had ever jumped in its life.

It cowered on the dreamlike grass, darting glances all about, under, and up. It was lonely and terrified and felt very much put upon. It saw its shadow through the shifting haze, and the sight terrified it even more, for it had no shadow when it was frightened on Lirht. Everything here was all backwards and wrong way up; it got more visible, instead of less, when it was frightened; its legs didn't work right, it couldn't see properly, and there wasn't a single solitary malapek to be throdded anywhere. It thought it heard some music; happily, that sounded all right inside its round head, though somehow it didn't resonate as well as it had.

It tried, with extreme caution, to move again. This time its trajectory was shorter and more controlled. It tried a small, grounded pace, and was quite successful. Then it bobbed for a moment, seesawing on its flexible middle pair of legs, and, with utter abandon, flung itself skyward. It went up perhaps fifteen feet, turning end over end, and landed with its stiff forefeet in the turf.

It was completely delighted with this sensation. It gathered itself together, gryting with joy, and leapt up again. This time it made more distance than altitude, and bounced two long, happy bounces as it landed.

Its fears were gone in the exploration of this delicious new freedom of motion. The hurkle, as has been said before, is a happy beast. It curvetted and sailed, soared and somersaulted, and at last brought up against a brick wall with stunning and unpleasant results. It was learning, the hard way, a distinction between weight and mass. The effect was slight but painful. It drew back and stared forlornly at the bricks. Just when it was beginning to feel friendly again . . .

It looked upward, and saw what appeared to be an opening in the wall some eight feet above the ground. Overcome by a spirit of high adventure, it sprang upward and came to rest on a window sill—a feat of which it was very proud. It crouched there, preening itself, and looked inside.

It saw a most pleasing vista. More than forty amusingly ugly animals, apparently imprisoned by their lower extremities in individual stalls, bowed and nodded and mumbled. At the far end of the room stood a taller, more slender monster with a naked head—naked compared with those of the trapped ones, which were covered with hair like a mawson's egg. A few moments' study showed the kitten that in reality only one side of the heads was hairy; the tall one turned around and began making tracks in the end wall, and its head proved to be hairy on the other side too.

The hurkle kitten found this vastly entertaining. It began to radiate what was, on Lirht, a purr, or glow. In this fantastic place it was not visible; instead, the trapped animals began to respond with most curious writhings and squirmings and susurrant rubbings of their hides with their claws. This pleased the kitten even more, for it loved to be noticed, and it redoubled the glow. The receptive motions of the animals became almost frantic.

Then the tall one turned around again. It made a

curious sound or two. Then it picked up a stick from the platform before it and brought it down with a horrible crash.

The sudden noise frightened the hurkle kitten half out of its wits. It went invisible; but its visibility system was reversed here, and it was suddenly out-standingly evident. It turned and leapt outside, and before it reached the ground, a loud metallic shrilling pursued it. There were gabblings and shufflings from the room, which added force to the kitten's consum-ing terror. It scrambled to a low growth of shrub-bery and concealed itself among the leaves.

Very soon, however, its irrepressible good nature returned. It lay relaxed, watching the slight move-ment of the stems and leaves—some of them may have been flowers—in a slight breeze. A winged crea-ture came humming and dancing about one of the blossoms. The kitten rested on one of its middle legs, shot the other out and caught the creature in flight. The thing promptly jabbed the kitten's foot with a sharp black probe. This the kitten ignored. It ate the thing, and belched. It lay still for a few minutes, savoring the sensation of the bee in its clarfel. The experiment was suddenly not a success. It ate the bee twice more and then gave it up as a bad job.

It turned its attention again to the window, won-dering what those racks of animals might be up to now. It seemed very quiet up there. . . . Boldly the kitten came from hiding and launched itself at the window again. It was pleased with itself; it was get-ting quite proficient at precision leaps in this mad place. Preening itself, it balanced on the window sill and looked inside.

Surprisingly, all the smaller animals were gone.

The larger one was huddled behind the shelf at the end of the room. The kitten and the animal watched each other for a long moment. The animal leaned down and stuck something into the wall.

Immediately there was a mechanical humming sound and something on a platform near the window began to revolve. The next thing the kitten knew it was enveloped in a cloud of pungent dust.

It choked and became as visible as it was frightened, which was very. For a long moment it was incapable of motion; gradually, however, it became conscious of a poignant, painfully penetrating sensation which thrilled it to the core. It gave itself up to the feeling. Wave after wave of agonized ecstasy rolled over it, and it began to dance to the waves. It glowed brilliantly, though the emanation served only to make the animal in the room scratch hysterically.

The hurkle felt strange, transported. It turned and leapt high into the air, out from the building.

Mr. Stott stopped scratching. Disheveled indeed, he went to the window and watched the odd sight of the blue beast, quite invisible now, but coated with dust, so that it was like a bubble in a fog. It bounced across the lawn in huge floating leaps, leaving behind it diminishing patches of white powder in the grass. He smacked his hands, one on the other, and smirking, withdrew to straighten up. He had saved the earth from battle, murder, and bloodshed, forever, but he did not know that. No one ever found out what he had done. So he lived a long and happy life.

And the hurkle kitten?

It bounded off through the long shadows, and

vanished in a copse of bushes. There it dug itself a shallow pit, working drowsily, more and more slowly. And at last it sank down and lay motionless, thinking strange thoughts, making strange music, and racked by strange sensations. Soon even its slightest movements ceased, and it stretched out stiffly, motionless. . . .

For about two weeks. At the end of that time, the hurkle, no longer a kitten, was possessed of a fine, healthy litter of just under two hundred young. Perhaps it was the DDT, and perhaps it was a new variety of radiation that the hurkle received from the terrestrial sky, but they were all parthenogenetic females, even as you and I.

And the humans? Oh, we *bred* so! And how happy we were!

But the humans had the slidy itch, and the scratchy itch, and the prickly or tingly or titillative paraesthetic formication. And there wasn't a thing they could do about it.

So they left.

Isn't this a lovely place?

Grandpa

By James H. Schmitz

James Schmitz lives in California, has been writing science fiction since 1943, and enjoys an enthusiastic following among knowledgeable readers. They admire his supple style and his inventive mind, which often turns to complex stories of political intrigue in the far galaxies, or to ingenious depictions of life on other worlds. "Grandpa" is one of his most successful stories, a delicious portrayal of an alien creature.

A green-winged, downy thing as big as a hen fluttered along the hillside to a point directly above Cord's head and hovered there, twenty feet above him. Cord, a fifteen-year-old human being, leaned back against a skipboat parked on the equator of a world that had known human beings for only the past four Earth years, and eyed the thing speculatively. The thing was, in the free and easy terminology of the Sutang Colonial Team, a swamp bug. Concealed in the downy fur back of the bug's head was a second, smaller, semiparasitical thing, classed as a bug rider.

The bug itself looked like a new species to Cord. Its parasite might or might not turn out to be another unknown. Cord was a natural research man; his first glimpse of the odd flying team had sent endless curi-

24

osities thrilling through him. How did that particular phenomenon tick, and why? What fascinating things, once you'd learned about it, could you get it to *do*?

Normally, he was hampered by circumstances in carrying out any such investigation. The Colonial Team was a practical, hardworking outfit—two thousand people who'd been given twenty years to size up and tame down the brand-new world of Sutang to the point where a hundred thousand colonists could be settled on it, in reasonable safety and comfort. Even junior colonial students like Cord were expected to confine their curiosity to the pattern of research set up by the station to which they were attached. Cord's inclination toward independent experiments had got him into disfavor with his immediate superiors before this.

He sent a casual glance in the direction of the Yoger Bay Colonial Station behind him. No signs of human activity about that low, fortresslike bulk in the hill. Its central lock was still closed. In fifteen minutes, it was scheduled to be opened to let out the Planetary Regent, who was inspecting the Yoger Bay Station and its principal activities today.

Fifteen minutes was time enough to find out something about the new bug, Cord decided.

But he'd have to collect it first.

He slid out one of the two handguns holstered at his side. This one was his own property: a Vanadian projectile weapon. Cord thumbed it to position for anesthetic small-game missiles and brought the hovering swamp bug down, drilled neatly and microscopically through the head.

As the bug hit the ground, the rider left its back. A

tiny scarlet demon, round and bouncy as a rubber ball, it shot toward Cord in three long hops, mouth wide to sink home inch-long, venom-dripping fangs. Rather breathlessly, Cord triggered the gun again and knocked it out in mid-leap. A new species, all right! Most bug riders were harmless plant-eaters, mere suckers of vegetable juice—

"*Cord!*" A feminine voice.

Cord swore softly. He hadn't heard the central lock click open. She must have come around from the other side of the station.

"Hi, Grayan!" he shouted innocently without looking around. "Come see what I got! New species!"

Grayan Mahoney, a slender, black-haired girl two years older than he, came trotting down the hillside toward him. She was Sutang's star colonial student, and the station manager, Nirmond, indicated from time to time that she was a fine example for Cord to pattern his own behavior on. In spite of that, she and Cord were good friends, but she bossed him around considerably.

"Cord, you dope!" she scowled as she came up. "Quit acting like a collector! If the Regent came out now, you'd be sunk. Nirmond's been telling her about you!"

"Telling her what?" Cord asked, startled.

"For one," Grayan reported, "that you don't keep up on your assigned work. Two, that you sneak off on one-man expeditions of your own at least once a month and have to be rescued—"

"Nobody," Cord interrupted hotly, "has had to rescue me yet!"

"How's Nirmond to know you're alive and healthy when you just drop out of sight for a week?" Grayan countered. "Three," she resumed, checking the items off on slim fingertips, "he complained that you keep private zoological gardens of unidentified and possibly deadly vermin in the woods back of the station. And four . . . well, Nirmond simply doesn't want the responsibility for you any more!" She held up the four fingers significantly.

"Golly!" gulped Cord, dismayed. Summed up tersely like that, his record *didn't* look too good.

"Golly is right! I keep warning you! Now Nirmond wants the Regent to send you back to Vanadia—and there's a starship coming in to New Venus forty-eight hours from now!" New Venus was the Colonial Team's main settlement on the opposite side of Sutang.

"What'll I do?"

"Start acting like you had good sense mainly." Grayan grinned suddenly. "I talked to the Regent, too—Nirmond isn't rid of you yet! But if you louse up on our tour of the Bay Farms today, you'll be off the Team for good!"

She turned to go. "You might as well put the skip-boat back; we're not using it. Nirmond's driving us down to the edge of the Bay in a treadcar, and we'll take a raft from there. Don't let them know I warned you!"

Cord looked after her, slightly stunned. He hadn't realized his reputation had become as bad as all that! To Grayan, whose family had served on Colonial Teams for the past four generations, nothing worse was imaginable than to be dismissed and sent back ignominiously to one's own homeworld. Much to his surprise, Cord was discovering now that he felt exactly the same way about it!

Leaving his newly bagged specimens to revive by themselves and flutter off again, he hurriedly flew the skipboat around the station and rolled it back into its stall.

Three rafts lay moored just offshore in the marshy cove, at the edge of which Nirmond had stopped the treadcar. They looked somewhat like exceptionally broad-brimmed, well-worn sugarloaf hats floating out there, green and leathery. Or like lily pads twenty-five feet across, with the upper section of a big, gray-green pineapple growing from the center of each. Plant animals of some sort. Sutang was too new to have had its phyla sorted out into anything remotely like an orderly classification. The rafts were a local oddity which had been investigated and could be regarded as harmless and moderately useful. Their usefulness lay in the fact that they were employed as a rather slow means of transportation about the shallow, swampy waters of the Yoger Bay. That was as far as the Team's interest in them went at present.

The Regent had stood up from the back seat of the car, where she was sitting next to Cord. There were only four in the party; Grayan was up front with Nirmond.

"Are those our vehicles?" The Regent sounded amused.

Nirmond grinned, a little sourly. "Don't underestimate them, Dane! They could become an important economic factor in this region in time. But, as a matter of fact, these three are smaller than I like to use." He was peering about the reedy edges of the cove. "There's a regular monster parked here usually—"

Grayan turned to Cord. "Maybe Cord knows where Grandpa is hiding."

It was well meant, but Cord had been hoping nobody would ask him about Grandpa. Now they all looked at him.

"Oh, you want Grandpa?" he said, somewhat flustered. "Well, I left him . . . I mean I saw him a couple of weeks ago about a mile south from here—"

Grayan sighed. Nirmond grunted and told the Regent, "The rafts tend to stay wherever they're left, providing it's shallow and muddy. They use a hairroot system to draw chemicals and microscopic nourishment directly from the bottom of the bay. Well—Grayan, would you like to drive us there?"

Cord settled back unhappily as the treadcar lurched into motion. Nirmond suspected he'd used Grandpa for one of his unauthorized tours of the area, and Nirmond was quite right.

"I understand you're an expert with these rafts, Cord," Dane said from beside him. "Grayan told me we couldn't find a better steersman, or pilot, or whatever you call it, for our trip today."

"I can handle them," Cord said, perspiring. "They don't give you any trouble!" He didn't feel he'd made a good impression on the Regent so far. Dane was a young, handsome-looking woman with an easy way of talking and laughing, but she wasn't the head of the Sutang Colonial Team for nothing. She looked quite capable of shipping out anybody whose record wasn't up to par.

"There's one big advantage our beasties have over a skipboat, too," Nirmond remarked from the front seat. "You don't have to worry about a snapper trying to climb on board with you!" He went on to describe the stinging ribbon-tentacles the rafts spread around them under water to discourage creatures that might make a meal off their tender underparts. The snappers and two or three other active and aggressive species of the Bay hadn't yet learned it was foolish to attack armed human beings in a boat, but they would skitter hurriedly out of the path of a leisurely perambulating raft.

Cord was happy to be ignored for the moment. The Regent, Nirmond and Grayan were all Earth people, which was true of most of the members of the Team; and Earth people made him uncomfortable, particularly in groups. Vanadia, his own homeworld, had barely graduated from the status of Earth colony itself, which might explain the difference. All the Earth people he'd met so far seemed dedicated to what Grayan Mahoney called the Big Picture, while Nirmond usually spoke of it as "Our Purpose Here." They acted strictly in accordance with their Team Regulations—sometimes, in Cord's opinion, quite insanely. Because now and then the Regulations didn't quite cover a new situation and then somebody was likely to get killed. In which case the Regulations would be modified promptly, but Earth people didn't seem otherwise disturbed by such events.

Grayan had tried to explain it to Cord:

"We can't really ever *know* in advance what a new world is going to be like! And once we're there, there's too much to do, in the time we've got, to study it inch by inch. You get your job done, and you take a chance. But if you stick by the Regulations you've got the best chances of surviving anybody's been able to figure out for you—"

Cord felt he preferred to just use good sense and not let Regulations or the job get him into a situation he couldn't figure out for himself.

To which Grayan replied impatiently that he hadn't yet got the Big Picture—

The treadcar swung around and stopped, and Grayan stood up in the front seat, pointing. "That's Grandpa, over there!"

Dane also stood up and whistled softly, apparently impressed by Grandpa's fifty-foot spread. Cord looked around in surprise. He was pretty sure this was several hundred yards from the spot where he'd left the big raft two weeks ago; and as Nirmond said, they didn't usually move about by themselves.

Puzzled, he followed the others down a narrow path to the water, hemmed in by tree-sized reeds. Now and then he got a glimpse of Grandpa's swimming platform, the rim of which just touched the shore. Then the path opened out, and he saw the whole raft lying in sunlit, shallow water; and he stopped short, startled.

Nirmond was about to step up on the platform, ahead of Dane.

"Wait!" Cord shouted. His voice sounded squeaky with alarm. "Stop!"

He came running forward.

They had frozen where they stood, looked around swiftly, then glanced back at Cord coming up. They were well trained.

"What's the matter, Cord?" Nirmond's voice was quiet and urgent.

"Don't get on that raft—it's changed!" Cord's voice sounded wobbly, even to himself. "Maybe it's not even Grandpa—"

He saw he was wrong on the last point before he'd finished the sentence. Scattered along the rim of the raft were discolored spots left by a variety of heat-guns, one of which had been his own. It was the way you goaded the sluggish and mindless things into motion. Cord pointed at the cone-shaped central projection. "There—his head! He's sprouting!"

"Sprouting?" the station manager repeated uncomprehendingly. Grandpa's head, as befitted his girth, was almost twelve feet high and equally wide. It was armor-plated like the back of a saurian to keep off plant-suckers, but two weeks ago it had been an otherwise featureless knob, like those on all other rafts. Now scores of long, kinky, leafless vines had grown out from all surfaces of the cone, like green wires. Some were drawn up like tightly coiled springs, others trailed limply to the platform and over it. The top of the cone was dotted with angry red buds, rather like pimples, which hadn't been there before either. Grandpa looked unhealthy.

"Well," Nirmond said, "so it is. Sprouting!" Grayan made a choked sound. Nirmond glanced at Cord as if puzzled. "Is that all that was bothering you, Cord?"

"Well, sure!" Cord began excitedly. He hadn't caught the significance of the word "all"; his hackles were still up, and he was shaking. "None of them ever—"

Then he stopped. He could tell by their faces that they hadn't got it. Or rather, that they'd got it all right but simply weren't going to let it change their plans. The rafts were classified as harmless, according to the Regulations. Until proved otherwise, they would continue to be regarded as harmless. You didn't waste time quibbling with the Regulations—apparently

even if you were the Planetary Regent. You didn't feel
you had the time to waste.

He tried again. "Look—" he began. What he
wanted to tell them was that Grandpa with one unknown factor added wasn't Grandpa any more. He
was an unpredictable, oversized lifeform, to be
investigated with cautious thoroughness till you
knew what the unknown factor meant.

But it was no use. They knew all that. He stared at
them helplessly. "I—"

Dane turned to Nirmond. "Perhaps you'd better
check," she said. She didn't add, "—to reassure the
boy!" but that was what she meant.

Cord felt himself flushing terribly. They thought
he was scared—which he was—and they were feeling
sorry for him, which they had no right to do. But
there was nothing he could say or do now except
watched Nirmond walk steadily across the platform.
Grandpa shivered slightly a few times, but the rafts
always did that when someone first stepped on them.
The station manager stopped before one of the kinky
sprouts, touched it and then gave it a tug. He reached
up and poked at the lowest of the budlike growths.
"Odd-looking things!" he called back. He gave Cord
another glance. "Well, everything seems harmless
enough, Cord. Coming aboard, everyone?"

It was like dreaming a dream in which you yelled
and yelled at people and couldn't make them hear
you! Cord stepped up stiff-legged on the platform behind Dane and Grayan. He knew exactly what would
have happened if he'd hesitated even a moment. One
of them would have said in a friendly voice, careful
not to let it sound too contemptuous: "You don't have
to come along if you don't want to, Cord!"

Grayan had unholstered her heat-gun and was ready to start Grandpa moving out into the channels of the Yoger Bay.

Cord hauled out his own heat-gun and said roughly, "I was to do that!"

"All right, Cord." She gave him a brief, impersonal smile, as if he were someone she'd met for the first time that day, and stood aside.

They were so infuriatingly polite! He was, Cord decided, as good as on his way back to Vanadia right now.

For a while, Cord almost hoped that something awesome and catastrophic would happen promptly to teach the Team people a lesson. But nothing did. As always, Grandpa shook himself vaguely and experimentally when he felt the heat on one edge of the platform and then decided to withdraw from it, all of which was standard procedure. Under the water, out of sight, were the raft's working sections: short, thick leaf-structures shaped like paddles and designed to work as such, along with the slimy nettle-streamers which kept the vegetarians of the Yoger Bay away, and a jungle of hair roots through which Grandpa sucked nourishments from the mud and the sluggish waters of the Bay, and with which he also anchored himself.

The paddles started churning, the platform quivered, the hair roots were hauled out of the mud; and Grandpa was on his ponderous way.

Cord switched off the heat, reholstered his gun, and stood up. Once in motion, the rafts tended to keep traveling unhurriedly for quite a while. To stop them, you gave them a touch of heat along their leading edge; and they could be turned in any direction by using the gun lightly on the opposite side of the platform.

It was simple enough. Cord didn't look at the others. He was still burning inside. He watched the reed beds move past and open out, giving him glimpses of the misty, yellow and green and blue expanse of the brackish Bay ahead. Behind the mist, to the west, were the Yoger Straits, tricky and ugly water when the tides were running; and beyond the Straits lay the open sea, the great Zlanti Deep, which was another world entirely and one of which he hadn't seen much as yet.

Suddenly he was sick with the full realization that he wasn't likely to see any more of it now! Vanadia was a pleasant enough planet; but the wildness and strangeness were long gone from it. It wasn't Sutang.

Grayan called from beside Dane, "What's the best route from here into the farms, Cord?"

"The big channel to the right," he answered. He added somewhat sullenly, "We're headed for it!"

Grayan came over to him. "The Regent doesn't want to see all of it," she said, lowering her voice. "The algae and plankton beds first. Then as much of the mutated grains as we can show her in about three hours. Steer for the ones that have been doing best, and you'll keep Nirmond happy!"

She gave him a conspiratorial wink. Cord looked after her uncertainly. You couldn't tell from her behavior that anything was wrong. Maybe—

He had a flare of hope. It was hard not to like the Team people, even when they were being rock-headed about their Regulations. Perhaps it was that purpose that gave them their vitality and drive, even though it made them remorseless about themselves and everyone else. Anyway, the day wasn't over yet. He might still redeem himself in the Regent's opinion. Something might happen—

Cord had a sudden cheerful, if improbable, vision of some Bay monster plunging up on the raft with snapping jaws, and of himself alertly blowing out what passed for the monster's brains before anyone else—Nirmond, in particular—was even aware of the threat. The Bay monsters shunned Grandpa, of course, but there might be ways of tempting one of them.

So far, Cord realized, he'd been letting his feelings control him. It was time to start thinking!

Grandpa first. So he'd sprouted—green vines and red buds, purpose unknown, but with no change observable in his behavior-patterns otherwise. He was the biggest raft in this end of the Bay, though all of them had been growing steadily in the two years since Cord had first seen one. Sutang's seasons changed slowly; its year was somewhat more than five Earth years long. The first Team members to land here hadn't yet seen a full year pass.

Grandpa then was showing a seasonal change. The other rafts, not quite so far developed, would be reacting similarly a little later. Plant animals—they might be blossoming, preparing to propagate.

"Grayan," he called, "how do the rafts get started? When they're small, I mean."

Grayan looked pleased; and Cord's hopes went up a little more. Grayan was on his side again anyway!

"Nobody knows yet," she said. "We were just talking about it. About half of the coastal marsh-fauna of the continent seems to go through a preliminary larval stage in the sea." She nodded at the red buds on the raft's cone. "It *looks* as if Grandpa is going to produce flowers and let the wind or ride take the seeds out through the Straits."

It made sense. It also knocked out Cord's still half-held hope that the change in Grandpa might turn out to be drastic enough, in some way, to justify his reluctance to get on board. Cord studied Grandpa's armored head carefully once more—unwilling to give up that hope entirely. There were a series of vertical gummy black slits between the armor plates, which hadn't been in evidence two weeks ago either. It looked as if Grandpa were beginning to come apart at the seams. Which might indicate that the rafts, big as they grew to be, didn't outlive a full seasonal cycle, but came to flower at about this time of Sutang's year and died. However, it was a safe bet that Grandpa wasn't going to collapse into senile decay before they completed their trip today.

Cord gave up on Grandpa. The other notion returned to him—Perhaps he could coax an obliging Bay monster into action that would show the Regent he was no sissy!

Because the monsters were there, all right.

Kneeling at the edge of the platform and peering down into the wine-colored, clear water of the deep channel they were moving through, Cord could see a fair selection of them at almost any moment.

Some five or six snappers, for one thing. Like big, flattened crayfish, chocolate-brown mostly, with green and red spots on their carapaced backs. In some areas they were so thick you'd wonder what they found to live on, except that they ate almost anything, down to chewing up the mud in which they squatted. However, they preferred their food in large chunks and alive, which was one reason you didn't go swimming in the Bay. They would attack a boat on occasion; but the excited manner in which the ones he saw were scuttling off toward the edges of the channel showed they wanted to have nothing to do with a big moving raft.

Dotted across the bottom were two-foot round holes which looked vacant at the moment. Normally, Cord knew, there would be a head filling each of those holes. The heads consisted mainly of triple sets of jaws, held open patiently like so many traps to grab at anything that came within range of the long, wormlike bodies behind the heads. But Grandpa's passage, waving his stingers like transparent pennants through the water, had scared the worms out of sight, too.

Otherwise, mostly schools of small stuff—and then a flash of wicked scarlet, off to the left behind the raft, darting out from the reeds! Turning its needle-nose into their wake.

Cord watched it without moving. He knew that creature, though it was rare in the Bay and hadn't been classified. Swift, vicious—alert enough to snap swamp bugs out of the air as they fluttered across the surface. And he'd tantalized one with fishing tackle once into leaping up on a moored raft, where it had flung itself about furiously until he was able to shoot it.

No fishing tackle. A handkerchief might just do it, if he cared to risk an arm—

"What fantastic creatures!" Dane's voice just behind him.

"Yellowheads," said Nirmond. "They've got a high utility rating. Keep down the bugs."

Cord stood up casually. It was no time for tricks!

The reed bed to their right was thick with yellowheads, a colony of them. Vaguely froggy things, man-
sized and better. Of all the creatures he'd discovered
in the Bay, Cord liked them least. The flabby, sacklike
bodies clung with four thin limbs to the upper sections of the twenty-foot reeds that lined the channel.
They hardly ever moved, but their huge, bulging eyes
seemed to take in everything that went on about
them. Every so often, a downy swamp bug came close
enough; and a yellowhead would open its vertical,
enormous, tooth-lined slash of a mouth, extend the
whole front of its face like a bellows in a flashing
strike; and the bug would be gone. They might be
useful, but Cord hated them.

"Ten years from now we should know what the
cycle of coastal life is like," Nirmond said. "When we
set up the Yoger Bay Station there were no yellowheads here. They came the following year. Still with
traces of the oceanic larval form; but the metamorphosis was almost complete. About twelve inches
long—"

Dane remarked that the same pattern was dupli-
cated endlessly elsewhere. The Regent was inspecting
the yellowhead colony with field glasses; she put them
down now, looked at Cord and smiled. "How far to
the farms?"

"About twenty minutes."

"The key," Nirmond said, "seems to be the Zlanti
Basin. It must be almost a soup of life in spring."

"It is," nodded Dane, who had been here in Sutang's
spring, four Earth years ago. "It's beginning to look as
if the Basin alone might justify colonization. The
question is still"—she gestured toward the yellowheads—"how do creatures like that get there?"

They walked off toward the other side of the raft, arguing about ocean currents. Cord might have followed. But something splashed back of them, off to the left and not too far back. He stayed, watching.

After a moment, he saw the big yellowhead. It had slipped down from its reedy perch, which was what had caused the splash. Almost submerged at the water line, it stared after the raft with huge pale-green eyes. To Cord, it seemed to look directly at him. In that moment, he knew for the first time why he didn't like yellowheads. There was something very like intelligence in that look, an alien calculation. In creatures like that, intelligence seemed out of place. What use could they have for it?

A little shiver went over him when it sank completely under the water and he realized it intended to swim after the raft. But it was mostly excitement. He had never seen a yellowhead come down out of the reeds before. The obliging monster he'd been looking for might be presenting itself in an unexpected way.

Half a minute later, he watched it again, swimming awkwardly far down. It had no immediate intention of boarding at any rate. Cord saw it come into the area of the raft's trailing stingers. It maneuvered its way between them with curiously human swimming motions, and went out of sight under the platform.

He stood up, wondering what it meant. The yellowhead had appeared to know about the stingers; there had been an air of purpose in every move of its approach. He was tempted to tell the others about it, but there was the moment of triumph he could have if it suddenly came slobbering up over the edge of the platform and he nailed it before their eyes.

It was almost time anyway to turn the raft in toward the farms. If nothing happened before then—

He watched. Almost five minutes, but no sign of the yellowhead. Still wondering, a little uneasy, he gave Grandpa a calculated needling of heat.

After a moment, he repeated it. Then he drew a deep breath and forgot all about the yellowhead.

"Nirmond!" he called sharply.

The three of them were standing near the center of the platform, next to the big armored cone, looking ahead at the farms. They glanced around.

"What's the matter now, Cord?"

Cord couldn't say it for a moment. He was suddenly, terribly scared again. Something had gone wrong!

"The raft won't turn!" he told them.

"Give it a real burn this time!" Nirmond said.

Cord glanced up at him. Nirmond, standing a few steps in front of Dane and Grayan as if he wanted to protect them, had begun to look a little strained, and no wonder. Cord already had pressed the gun to three different points on the platform; but Grandpa appeared to have developed a sudden anesthesia for heat. They kept moving out steadily toward the center of the Bay.

Now Cord held his breath, switched the heat on full and let Grandpa have it. A six-inch patch on the platform blistered up instantly, turned brown, then black—

Grandpa stopped dead. Just like that.

"That's right! Keep burn——" Nirmond didn't finish his order.

A giant shudder. Cord staggered back toward the

water. Then the whole edge of the raft came curling up behind him and went down again, smacking the Bay with a sound like a cannon shot. He flew forward off his feet, hit the platform face down and flattened himself against it. It swelled up beneath him. Two more enormous slaps and joltings. Then quiet. He looked round for the others.

He lay within twelve feet of the central cone. Some twenty or thirty of the mysterious new vines the cone had sprouted were stretched out stiffly toward him now, like so many thin green fingers. They couldn't quite reach him. The nearest tip was still ten inches from his shoes.

But Grandpa had caught the others, all three of them. They were tumbled together at the foot of the cone, wrapped in a stiff network of green vegetable ropes, and they didn't move.

Cord drew his feet up cautiously, prepared for another earthquake reaction. But nothing happened. Then he discovered that Grandpa was back in motion on his previous course. The heatgun had vanished. Gently, he took out the Vanadian gun.

"Cord? It didn't get you?" It was the Regent.

"No," he said, keeping his voice low. He realized suddenly he'd simply assumed they were all dead. Now he felt sick and shaky.

"What are you doing?"

Cord looked at Grandpa's big armor-plated head with a certain hunger. The cones were hollowed out inside; the station's lab had decided their chief function was to keep enough air trapped under the rafts to float them. But in that central section was also the organ that controlled Grandpa's overall reactions.

He said softly, "I got a gun and twelve heavy-duty explosive bullets. Two of them will blow that cone apart."

"No good, Cord!" the pain-racked voice told him. "If the thing sinks, we'll die anyway. You have anesthetic charges for that gun of yours?"

He stared at her back. "Yes."

"Give Nirmond and the girl a shot each, before you do anything else. Directly into the spine, if you can. But don't come any closer—"

Somehow, Cord couldn't argue with that voice. He stood up carefully. The gun made two soft spitting sounds.

"All right," he said hoarsely. "What do I do now?"

Dane was silent a moment. "I'm sorry, Cord. I can't tell you that. I'll tell you what I can—"

She paused for some seconds again. "This thing didn't try to kill us, Cord. It could have easily. It's incredibly strong. I saw it break Nirmond's legs. But as soon as we stopped moving, it just held us. They were both unconscious then—"

"You've got that to go on. It was trying to pitch you within reach of its vines or tendrils, or whatever they are, wasn't it?"

"I think so," Cord said shakily. That was what had happened, of course; and at any moment Grandpa might try again.

"Now it's feeding us some sort of anesthetic of its own through those vines. Tiny thorns. A sort of numbness—" Dane's voice trailed off a moment. Then she said clearly, "Look, Cord—it seems we're food it's storing up! You get that?"

"Yes," he said.

"Seeding time for the rafts. There are analogues. Live food for its seed probably; not for the raft. One couldn't have counted on that. Cord?"

"Yes. I'm here."

"I want," said Dane, "to stay awake as long as I can. But there's really just one other thing—this raft's going somewhere. To some particularly favorable location. And that might be very near shore. You might make it in then; otherwise it's up to you. But keep your head and wait for a chance. No heroics, understand?"

"Sure, I understand," Cord told her. He realized then that he was talking reassuringly, as if it weren't the Planetary Regent but someone like Grayan.

"Nirmond's the worst," Dane said. "The girl was knocked unconscious at once. If it weren't for my arm—But, if we can get help in five hours or so, everything should be all right. Let me know if anything happens, Cord."

"I will," Cord said gently again. Then he sighted his gun carefully at a point between Dane's shoulder blades, and the anesthetic chamber made its soft, spitting sound once more. Dane's taut body relaxed slowly, and that was all.

There was no point Cord could see in letting her stay awake; because they weren't going anywhere near shore.

The reed beds and the channels were already behind them, and Grandpa hadn't changed direction by the fraction of a degree. He was moving out into the open Bay—and he was picking up company!

So far, Cord could count seven big rafts within two miles of them; and on the three that were closest he could make out a sprouting of new green vines. All of them were traveling in a straight direction; and the common point they were all headed for appeared to be the roaring center of the Yoger Straits, now some three miles away!

Behind the Straits, the cold Zlanti Deep—the rolling fogs, and the open sea! It might be seeding time for the rafts, but it looked as if they weren't going to distribute their seeds in the Bay—

For a human being, Cord was a fine swimmer. He had a gun and he had a knife, in spite of what Dane had said; he might have stood a chance among the killers of the Bay. But it would be a very small chance, at best. And it wasn't, he thought, as if there weren't still other possibilities. He was going to keep his head.

Except by accident, of course, nobody was going to come looking for them in time to do any good. If anyone did look, it would be around the Bay Farms. There were a number of rafts moored there; and it would be assumed they'd used one of them. Now and then something unexpected happened and somebody simply vanished—by the time it was figured out just what had happened on this occasion, it would be much too late.

Neither was anybody likely to notice within the next few hours that the rafts had started migrating out of the swamps through the Yoger Straits. There was a small weather station a little inland, on the north side of the Straits, which used a helicopter occasionally. It was about as improbable, Cord decided dismally, that they'd use it in the right spot just now as it would be for a jet transport to happen to come in low enough to spot them.

The fact that it was up to him, as the Regent had

said, sank in a little more after that! Cord had never felt so lonely.

Simply because he was going to try it sooner or later, he carried out an experiment next that he knew couldn't work. He opened the gun's anesthetic chamber and counted out fifty pellets—rather hurriedly because he didn't particularly want to think of what he might be using them for eventually. There were around three hundred charges left in the chamber then; and in the next few minutes Cord carefully planted a third of them in Grandpa's head.

He stopped after that. A whale might have showed signs of somnolence under a lesser load. Grandpa paddled on undisturbed. Perhaps he had become a little numb in spots, but his cells weren't equipped to distribute the soporific effect of that type of drug.

There wasn't anything else Cord could think of doing before they reached the Straits. At the rate they were moving, he calculated that would happen in something less than an hour; and if they did pass through the Straits, he was going to risk a swim. He didn't think Dane would have disapproved, under the circumstances. If the raft simply carried them all out into the foggy vastness of the Zlanti Deep, there would be no practical chance of survival left at all.

Meanwhile, Grandpa was definitely picking up speed. And there were other changes going on—minor ones, but still a little awe-inspiring to Cord. The pimply-looking red buds that dotted the upper part of the cone were opening out gradually. From the center of most of them protruded now something like a thin, wet, scarlet worm: a worm that twisted weakly, extended itself by an inch or so, rested and twisted again, and stretched up a little farther, groping into

the air. The vertical black slits between the armor
plates looked somehow deeper and wider than they
had been even some minutes ago; a dark, thick liquid
dripped slowly from several of them.

Under other circumstances Cord knew he would
have been fascinated by these developments in
Grandpa. As it was, they drew his suspicious attention only because he didn't know what they meant.

Then something quite horrible happened suddenly.
Grayan started moaning loudly and terribly and
twisted almost completely around. Afterwards, Cord
knew it hadn't been a second before he stopped her
struggles and the sounds together with another anesthetic pellet; but the vines had tightened their grip
on her first, not flexibly but like the digging, bony
green talons of some monstrous bird of prey. If Dane
hadn't warned him—

White and sweating, Cord put his gun down slowly
while the vines relaxed again. Grayan didn't seem to
have suffered any additional harm; and she would
certainly have been the first to point out that his
murderous rage might have been as intelligently directed against a machine. But for some moments
Cord continued to luxuriate furiously in the thought
that, at any instant he chose, he could still turn the
raft very quickly into a ripped and exploded mess of
sinking vegetation.

Instead, and more sensibly, he gave both Dane and
Nirmond another shot, to prevent a similar occur-
rence with them. The contents of two such pellets,
he knew, would keep any human being torpid for at
least four hours. Five shots—

Cord withdrew his mind hastily from the direction
it was turning into; but it wouldn't stay withdrawn.

The thought kept coming up again; until at last he had to recognize it:

Five shots would leave the three of them completely unconscious, whatever else might happen to them, until they either died from other causes or were given a counteracting agent.

Shocked, he told himself he couldn't do it. It was exactly like killing them.

But then, quite steadily, he found himself raising the gun once more, to bring the total charge for each of the three Team people up to five. And if it was the first time in the last four years Cord had felt like crying, it also seemed to him that he had begun to understand what was meant by using your head—along with other things.

Barely thirty minutes later, he watched a raft as big as the one he rode go sliding into the foaming white waters of the Straits a few hundred yards ahead, and dart off abruptly at an angle, caught by one of the swirling currents. It pitched and spun, made some headway, and was swept aside again. And then it righted itself once more. Not like some blindly animated vegetable, Cord thought, but like a creature that struggled with intelligent purpose to maintain its chosen direction.

At least, they seemed practically unsinkable—

Knife in hand, he flattened himself against the platform as the Straits roared just ahead. When the platform jolted and tilted up beneath him, he rammed the knife all the way into it and hung on. Cold water rushed suddenly over him, and Grandpa shuddered like a laboring engine. In the middle of it all, Cord had the horrified notion that the raft might release its unconscious human prisoners in its struggle with

the Straits. But he underestimated Grandpa in that.
Grandpa also hung on.

Abruptly, it was over. They were riding a long
swell, and there were three other rafts not far away.
The Straits had swept them together, but they seemed
to have no interest in one another's company. As
Cord stood up shakily and began to strip off his
clothes, they were visibly drawing apart again. The
platform of one of them was half-submerged; it must
have lost too much of the air that held it afloat and,
like a small ship, it was foundering.

From this point, it was only a two-mile swim to the
shore north of the Straits, and another mile inland
from there to the Straits Head Station. He didn't
know about the current; but the distance didn't seem
too much, and he couldn't bring himself to leave
knife and gun behind. The Bay creatures loved
warmth and mud, they didn't venture beyond the
Straits. But Zlanti Deep bred its own killers, though
they weren't often observed so close to shore.

Things were beginning to look rather hopeful.

Thin, crying voices drifted overhead, like the voices
of curious cats, as Cord knotted his clothes into a
tight bundle, shoes inside. He looked up. There were
four of them circling there; magnified seagoing
swamp bugs, each carrying an unseen rider. Probably harmless scavengers—but the ten-foot wing-
spread was impressive. Uneasily, Cord remembered
the venomously carnivorous rider he'd left lying beside the station.

One of them dipped lazily and came sliding down
toward him. It soared overhead and came back, to
hover about the raft's cone.

The bug rider that directed the mindless flier

hadn't been interested in him at all! Grandpa was baiting it!

Cord stared in fascination. The top of the cone was alive now with a softly wriggling mass of the scarlet, wormlike extrusions that had started sprouting before the raft left the Bay. Presumably, they looked enticingly edible to the bug rider.

The flier settled with an airy fluttering and touched the cone. Like a trap springing shut, the green vines flashed up and around it, crumpling the brittle wings, almost vanishing into the long soft body—

Barely a second later, Grandpa made another catch, this one from the sea itself. Cord had a fleeting glimpse of something like a small, rubbery seal that flung itself out of the water upon the edge of the raft, with a suggestion of desperate haste—and was flipped on instantly against the cone where the vines clamped it down beside the flier's body.

It wasn't the enormous ease with which the unexpected kill was accomplished that left Cord standing there, completely shocked. It was the shattering of his hopes to swim to shore from here. Fifty yards away, the creature from which the rubbery thing had been fleeing showed briefly on the surface, as it turned away from the raft; and the glance was all he needed. The ivory-white body and gaping jaws were similar enough to those of the sharks of Earth to indicate the pursuer's nature. The important difference was that, wherever the white hunters of the Zlanti Deep went, they went by the thousands.

Stunned by that incredible piece of bad luck, still clutching his bundled clothes, Cord stared toward shore. Knowing what to look for, he could spot the telltale roilings of the surface now—the long, ivory gleams that flashed through the swells and vanished again. Shoals of smaller things burst into the air in sprays of glittering desperation and fell back.

He would have been snapped up like a drowning fly before he'd covered a twentieth of that distance!

But almost another full minute passed before the realization of the finality of his defeat really sank in.

Grandpa was beginning to eat!

Each of the dark slits down the sides of the cone was a mouth. So far only one of them was in operating condition, and the raft wasn't able to open that one very wide as yet. The first morsel had been fed into, however: the bug rider the vines had plucked out of the flier's downy neck fur. It took Grandpa several minutes to work it out of sight, small as it was. But it was a start.

Cord didn't feel quite sane any more. He sat there, clutching his bundle of clothes and only vaguely aware of the fact that he was shivering steadily under the cold spray that touched him now and then, while he followed Grandpa's activities attentively. He decided it would be at least some hours before one of that black set of mouths grew flexible and vigorous enough to dispose of a human being. Under the circumstances, it couldn't make much difference to the other human beings here; but the moment Grandpa reached for the first of them would also be the moment he finally blew the raft to pieces. The white hunters were cleaner eaters, at any rate; and that was about the extent to which he could still control what was going to happen.

Meanwhile, there was the very faint chance that the weather station's helicopter might spot them—

Meanwhile also, in a weary and horrified fascination, he kept debating the mystery of what could have produced such a nightmarish change in the rafts. He could guess where they were going by now; there were scattered strings of them stretching back to the Straits or roughly parallel to their own course, and the direction was that of the plankton-swarming pool of the Zlanti Basin, a thousand miles to the north. Given time, even mobile lily pads like the rafts had been could make that trip for the benefit of their seedlings. But nothing in their structure explained the sudden change into alert and capable carnivores.

He watched the rubbery little seal-thing being hauled up to a mouth next. The vines broke its neck; and the mouth took it in up to the shoulders and then went on working patiently at what was still a trifle too large a bite. Meanwhile, there were more thin cat cries overhead; and a few minutes later, two more sea bugs were trapped almost simultaneously and added to the larder. Grandpa dropped the dead seal-thing and fed himself another bug rider. The second rider left its mount with a sudden hop, sank its teeth viciously into one of the vines that caught it again, and was promptly battered to death against the platform.

Cord felt a resurge of unreasoning hatred against Grandpa. Killing a bug was about equal to cutting a branch from a tree; they had almost no life-awareness. But the rider had aroused his partisanship because of its appearance of intelligent action—and it was in fact closer to the human scale in that feature than to the monstrous life-form that had, mechanically, but quite successfully, trapped both it and the human beings. Then his thoughts had drifted again;

and he found himself speculating vaguely on the curious symbiosis in which the nerve systems of two creatures as dissimilar as the bugs and their riders could be linked so closely that they functioned as one organism.

Suddenly an expression of vast and stunned surprise appeared on his face.

Why—now he knew!

Cord stood up hurriedly, shaking with excitement, the whole plan complete in his mind. And a dozen long vines snaked instantly in the direction of his sudden motion, and groped for him, taut and stretching. They couldn't reach him, but their savagely alert reaction froze Cord briefly where he was. The platform was shuddering under his feet, as if in irritation at his inaccessibility; but it couldn't be tilted up suddenly here to throw him within the grasp of the vines, as it could around the edges.

Still, it was a warning! Cord sidled gingerly around the cone till he had gained the position he wanted, which was on the forward half of the raft. And then he waited. Waited long minutes, quite motionless, until his heart stopped pounding and the irregular angry shivering of the surface of the raft-thing died away, and the last vine tendril had stopped its blind groping. It might help a lot if, for a second or two after he next started moving, Grandpa wasn't too aware of his exact whereabouts.

He looked back once to check how far they had gone by now beyond the Straits Head Station. It couldn't, he decided, be even an hour behind them. Which was close enough, by the most pessimistic count—if everything else worked out all right! He didn't try to think out in detail what that "everything else" could include, because there were factors that simply couldn't be calculated in advance. And he had an uneasy feeling that speculating too vividly about them might make him almost incapable of carrying out his plan.

At last, moving carefully, Cord took the knife in his left hand but left the gun holstered. He raised the tightly knotted bundle of clothes slowly over his head, balanced in his right hand. With a long, smooth motion he tossed the bundle back across the cone, almost to the opposite edge of the platform.

It hit with a soggy thump. Almost immediately, the whole far edge of the raft buckled and flapped up to toss the strange object to the reaching vines.

Simultaneously, Cord was racing forward. For a moment, his attempt to divert Grandpa's attention seemed completely successful—then he was pitched to his knees as the platform came up.

He was within eight feet of the edge. As it slapped down again, he threw himself desperately forward.

An instant later, he was knifing down through cold, clear water, just ahead of the raft, then twisting and coming up again.

The raft was passing over him. Clouds of tiny sea creatures scattered through its dark jungle of feeding roots. Cord jerked back from a broad, wavering streak of glassy greenness, which was a stinger, and felt a burning jolt on his side, which meant he'd been touched lightly by another. He bumped on blindly through the slimy black tangles of hair roots that covered the bottom of the raft; then green half-light passed over him, and he burst up into the central bubble under the cone.

Half-light and foul, hot air. Water slapped around him, dragging him away again—nothing to hang on to here! Then above him, to his right, molded against the interior curve of the cone as if it had grown there from the start, the froglike, man-sized shape of the yellowhead.

The raft rider—

Cord reached up and caught Grandpa's symbiotic partner and guide by a flabby hind leg, pulled himself half out of the water and struck twice with the knife, fast while the pale-green eyes were still opening.

He'd thought the yellowhead might need a second or so to detach itself from its host, as the bug riders usually did, before it tried to defend itself. This one merely turned its head; the mouth slashed down and clamped on Cord's left arm above the elbow. His right hand sank the knife through one staring eye, and the yellowhead jerked away, pulling the knife from his grasp.

Sliding down, he wrapped both hands around the slimy leg and hauled with all his weight. For a moment more, the yellowhead hung on. Then the countless neural extensions that connected it now with the raft came free in a succession of sucking, tearing sounds; and Cord and the yellowhead splashed into the water together.

Black tangle of roots again—and two more electric burns suddenly across his back and legs! Strangling, Cord let go. Below him, for a moment, a body was turning over and over with oddly human motions; then a solid wall of water thrust him up and aside, as something big and white struck the turning body and went on.

Cord broke the surface twelve feet behind the raft. And that would have been that, if Grandpa hadn't already been slowing down.

After two tries, he floundered back up on the platform and lay there gasping and coughing awhile. There were no indications that his presence was resented now. A few vine tips twitched uneasily, as if trying to remember previous functions, when he came limping up presently to make sure his three companions were still breathing; but Cord never noticed that.

They were still breathing; and he knew better than to waste time trying to help them himself. He took Grayan's heat-gun from its holster. Grandpa had come to a full stop.

Cord hadn't had time to become completely sane again, or he might have worried now whether Grandpa, violently sundered from his controlling partner, was still capable of motion on his own. Instead, he determined the approximate direction of the Straits Head Station, selected a corresponding spot on the platform and gave Grandpa a light tap of heat.

Nothing happened immediately. Cord sighed patiently and stepped up the heat a little.

Grandpa shuddered gently. Cord stood up.

Slowly and hesitatingly at first, then with steadfast—though now again brainless—purpose, Grandpa began paddling back toward the Straits Head Station.

The Blue Giraffe

BY L. SPRAGUE DE CAMP

Tall, distinguished-looking Sprague de Camp, scholarly by nature and rather formidable of mien, is another of science fiction's long-time pillars. He was part of a gifted crew of young men who swept into science fiction all at once, in the late 1930's, and transformed it from dreary hackwork into the stimulating literary form we cherish today—a crew whose members included such writers as Theodore Sturgeon, Isaac Asimov, Robert Heinlein, A. E. van Vogt, and Lester del Rey. Through the decades that followed, de Camp maintained his position among these formidable competitors, and his distinctive brand of erudite and sparkling fiction has never lost its popularity. "The Blue Giraffe," which dates from 1939, is a good example of the kind of story that won de Camp his high reputation.

*A*thelstan Cuff was, to put it very mildly, astonished that his son should be crying. It wasn't that he had exaggerated ideas about Peter's stoicism, but the fact was that Peter never cried. He was, for a twelve-year-old boy, self-possessed to the point of grimness. And now he was undeniably sniffling. It must be something jolly well awful.

Cuff pushed aside the pile of manuscript he had

been reading. He was the editor of *Biological Review;* a stoutish Englishman with prematurely white hair, prominent blue eyes, and a complexion that could have been used for painting box cars. He looked a little like a lobster who had been boiled once and was determined not to repeat the experience.

"What's wrong, old man?" he asked.

Peter wiped his eyes and looked at his father calculatingly. Cuff sometimes wished that Peter wasn't so damned rational. A spot of boyish unreasonableness would be welcome at times.

"Come on, old fella, out with it. What's the good of having a father if you can't tell him things?"

Peter finally got it out. "Some of the guys—" He stopped to blow his nose. Cuff winced slightly at the "guys." His one regret about coming to America was the language his son picked up. As he didn't believe in pestering Peter all the time, he had to suffer in silence.

"Some of the guys say you aren't really my father."

It had come, thought Cuff, as it was bound to sooner or later. He shouldn't have put off telling the boy for so long.

"What do you mean, old man?" he stalled.

"They say," *sniff*, "I'm just a 'dopted boy."

Cuff forced out, "So what?" The despised Americanism seemed to be the only thing that covered the situation.

"What do you mean, 'so what'?"

"I mean just that. What of it? It doesn't make a particle of difference to your mother or me, I assure you. So why should it to you?"

Peter thought. "Could you send me away some time, on account of I was only 'dopted?"

"Oh, so that's what's worrying you? The answer is no. Legally you're just as much our son as if . . . as anyone is anybody's son. But whatever gave you the idea we'd ever send you away? I'd like to see that chap who could get you away from us."

"Oh, I just wondered."

"Well, you can stop wondering. We don't want to, and we couldn't if we did. It's perfectly all right, I tell you. Lots of people start out as adopted children, and it doesn't make any difference to anybody. You wouldn't get upset if somebody tried to make fun of you because you had two eyes and a nose, would you?"

Peter had recovered his composure. "How did it happen?"

"It's quite a story. I'll tell you, if you like."

Peter only nodded.

"I've told you," said Athelstan Cuff, "about how before I came to America I worked for some years in South Africa. I've told you about how I used to work with elephants and lions and things, and about how I transplanted some white rhino from Swaziland to the Kruger Park. But I've never told you about the blue giraffe—"

In the 1940's the various South African governments were considering the problem of a park that would be not merely a game preserve available to tourists, but a completely wild area in which no people other than scientists and wardens would be allowed. They finally agreed on the Okavango River Delta in Ngamiland, as the only area that was sufficiently large and at the same time thinly populated. The reasons for its sparse population were simple enough: nobody likes to settle down in a place when he is likely to find his house and farm under three feet of water some fine morning. And it is irritating to set out to fish in a well-known lake only to find that the lake has turned into a grassy plain, around the edges of which the mopane trees are already springing up.

So the Batawana, in whose reserve the Delta lay, were mostly willing to leave this capricious stretch of swamp and jungle to the elephant and the lion. The few Batawana who did live in and around the Delta were bought out and moved. The Crown Office of the Bechuanaland Protectorate got around its own rules against alienation of tribal lands by taking a perpetual lease on the Delta and surrounding territory from the Batawana, and named the whole area Jan Smuts Park.

When Athelstan Cuff got off the train at Francistown in September of 1976, a pelting spring rain was making the platform smoke. A tall black in khaki loomed out of the grayness, and said: "You are Mr. Cuff, from Cape Town? I'm George Mtengeni, the warden at Smuts. Mr. Opdyck wrote me you were coming. The Park's car is out this way."

Cuff followed. He'd heard of George Mtengeni. The man wasn't a Chwana at all, but a Zulu from near Durban. When the Park had been set up, the Batawana had thought that the warden ought to be a Tawana. But the Makoba, feeling chesty about their independence from their former masters, the Batawana, had insisted on his being one of their nation. Finally the Crown Office in disgust had hired an outsider. Mtengeni had the very dark skin and narrow nose found in so many of the Kaffir Bantu. Cuff guessed that he probably had a low opinion of the Chwana people in general and the Batawana in particular.

They got into the car. Mtengeni said: "I hope you don't mind coming way out here like this. It's too bad that you couldn't come before the rains started; the pans they are all full by now."

"So?" said Cuff. "What's the Mababe this year?" He referred to the depression known variously as Mababe Lake, Swamp, or Pan, depending on whether at a given time it contained much, little, or no water.

"The Mababe, it is a lake, a fine lake full of drowned trees and hippo. I think the Okavango is shifting north again. That means Lake Ngami it will dry up again."

"So it will. But look here, what's all this business about a blue giraffe? Your letter was dashed uninformative."

Mtengeni showed his white teeth. "It appeared on the edge of the Mopane Forest seventeen months ago. That was just the beginning. There have been other things since. If I'd told you more, you would have written the Crown Office saying that their warden was having a nervous breakdown. Me, I'm sorry to drag you into this, but the Crown Office keeps saying they can't spare a man to investigate."

"Oh, quite all right, quite," answered Cuff. "I was glad to get away from Cape Town anyway. And we haven't had a mystery since old Hickey disappeared."

"Since who disappeared? You know me, I can't keep up with things out in the wilds."

"Oh, that was many years ago. Before your time, or mine for that matter. Hickey was a scientist who set out into the Kalahari with a truck and a Xosa assistant, and disappeared. Men flew all over the Kalahari looking for him, but never found a trace, and the sand had blown over his tire tracks. Jolly odd, it was."

The rain poured down steadily as they wallowed along the dirt road. Ahead, beyond the gray curtain, lay the vast plains of northern Bechuanaland with their great pans. And beyond the plains were, allegedly, a blue giraffe, and other things.

The spidery steelwork of the tower hummed as they climbed. At the top, Mtengeni said: "You can look over that way . . . west . . . to the other side of the forest. That's about twenty miles."

Cuff screwed up his eyes at the eyepieces. "Jolly good 'scope you've got here. But it's too hazy beyond the forest to see anything."

"It always is, unless we have a high wind. That's the edge of the swamps."

"Dashed if I see how you can patrol such a big area all by yourself."

"Oh, these Bechuana they don't give much trouble. They are honest. Even I have to admit that they have some good qualities. Anyway, you can't get far into the Delta without getting lost in the swamps. There are ways, but then, I only know them. I'll show them to you, but please don't tell these Bechuana about them. Look, Mr. Cuff, there's our blue giraffe."

Cuff started. Mtengeni was evidently the kind of man who would announce an earthquake as casually as the morning mail.

Several hundred yards from the tower half a dozen

giraffes were moving slowly through the brush, feeding on the tops of the scrubby trees. Cuff swung the telescope on them. In the middle of the herd was the blue one. Cuff blinked and looked again. There was no doubt about it; the animal was as brilliant a blue as if somebody had gone over it with paint. Athelstan Cuff suspected that that was what somebody *had* done. He said as much to Mtengeni.

The warden shrugged. "That, it would be a peculiar kind of amusement. Not to say risky. Do you see anything funny about the others?"

Cuff looked again. "Yes . . . by Jove, one of 'em's got a beard like a goat; only it must be six feet long, at least. Now look here, George, what's all this leading up to?"

"I don't know myself. Tomorrow, if you like, I'll show you one of those ways into the Delta. But that, it's quite a walk, so we'd better take supplies for two or three days."

As they drove toward the Tamalakane, they passed four Batawana, sad-looking reddish-brown men in a mixture of native and European clothes. Mtengeni slowed the car and looked at them suspiciously as they passed, but there was no evidence that they had been poaching.

He said: "Ever since their Makoba slaves were freed, they've been going on a . . . decline, I suppose you would call it. They are too dignified to work."

They got out at the river. "We can't drive across the ford this time of year," explained the warden, locking the car. "But there's a rapid a little way down, where we can wade."

They walked down the trail, adjusting their packs.

There wasn't much to see. The view was shut off by the tall soft-bodied swamp plants. The only sound was the hum of insects. The air was hot and steamy already, though the sun had been up only half an hour. The flies drew blood when they bit, but the men were used to that. They simply slapped and waited for the next bite.

Ahead there was a deep gurgling noise, like a fog-horn with water in its works. Cuff said: "How are your hippo doing this year?"

"Pretty good. There are some in particular that I want you to see. Ah, here we are."

They had come in sight of a stretch of calm water. In the foreground a hippopotamus repeated its fog-horn bellow. Cuff saw others, of which only the eyes, ears, and nostrils were visible. One of them was mov-ing; Cuff could make out the little V-shaped wakes pointing back from its nearly submerged head. It reached the shallows and lumbered out, dripping noisily.

Cuff blinked. "Must be something wrong with my eyes."

"No," said Mtengeni. "That hippo she is one of those I wanted you to see."

The hippopotamus was green with pink spots.

She spied the men, grunted suspiciously, and slid back into the water.

"I still don't believe it," said Cuff. "Dash it, man, that's impossible."

"You will see many more things," said Mtengeni. "Shall we go on?"

They found the rapid and struggled across; then walked along what might, by some stretch of the imagination, be called a trail. There was little sound other than their sucking footfalls, the hum of insects, and the occasional screech of a bird or the crashing of a buck through the reeds.

They walked for some hours. Then Mtengeni said: "Be careful. There is a rhino near."

Cuff wondered how the devil the Zulu knew, but he was careful. Presently they came on a clear space in which the rhinoceros was browsing.

The animal couldn't see them at that distance, and there was no wind to carry their smell. It must have heard them, though, for it left off its feeding and snorted, once, like a locomotive. It had two heads.

It trotted toward them sniffing.

The men got out their rifles. "My God!" said Athelstan Cuff. "Hope we don't have to shoot him. My God!"

"I don't think so," said the warden. "That's Tweedle. I know him. If he gets too close, give him one at the base of the horn and he . . . he will run."

"Tweedle?"

"Yes. The right head is Tweedledum and the left is Tweedledee," said Mtengeni solemnly. "The whole rhino I call Tweedle."

The rhinoceros kept coming. Mtengeni said: "Watch this." He waved his hat and shouted: "Go away! *Footsack!*"

Tweedle stopped and snorted again. Then he began to circle like a waltzing mouse. Round and round he spun.

"We might as well go on," said Mtengeni. "He will keep that up for hours. You see Tweedledum is fierce,

but Tweedledee, he is peaceful, even cowardly. So
when I yell at Tweedle, Tweedledum wants to charge
us, but Tweedledee, he wants to run away. So the
right legs go forward and the left legs go back, and
Tweedle, he goes in circles. It takes him some time
to agree on a policy."

"*Whew!*" said Athelstan Cuff. "I say, have you got
any more things like this in your zoo?"

"Oh, yes, lots. That's what I hope you'll do something about."

Do something about this! Cuff wondered whether
this was touching evidence of the native's faith in
the white's omniscience, or whether Mtengeni had
gotten him there for the cynical amusement of
watching him run in useless circles. Mtengeni himself gave no sign of what he was thinking.

Cuff said: "I can't understand, George, why somebody hasn't looked into this before."

Mtengeni shrugged. "Me, I've tried to get somebody to, but the government won't send anybody, and
the scientific expeditions, there haven't been any of
them for years. I don't know why."

"I can guess," said Cuff. "In the old days people
even in the so-called civilized countries expected
travel to be a jolly rugged proposition, so they didn't
mind putting up with a few extra hardships on trek.
But now that you can ride or fly almost anywhere on
soft cushions, people won't put themselves out to get
to a really uncomfortable and out-of-the-way place
like Ngamiland."

Over the swampy smell came another, of carrion.
Mtengeni pointed to the carcass of a waterbuck fawn,
which the scavengers had apparently not discovered
yet.

"That's why I want you to stop this whatever-it-is," he said. There was real concern in his voice.

"What do you mean, George?"

"Do you see its legs?"

Cuff looked. The forelegs were only half as long as the hind ones.

"That buck," said the Zulu. "It naturally couldn't live long. All over the Park, freaks like this they are being born. Most of them don't live. In ten years more, maybe twenty, all my animals will have died out because of this. Then my job, where is it?"

They stopped at sunset. Cuff was glad to. It had been some time since he'd done fifteen miles in one day, and he dreaded the morrow's stiffness. He looked at his map and tried to figure out where he was. But the cartographers had never seriously tried to keep track of the changes in the Okavango's multifarious branches, and had simply plastered the whole Delta with little blue dashes with tufts of blue lines sticking up from them, meaning simply "swamp." In all directions the country was a monotonous alternation of land and water. The two elements were inextricably mixed.

The Zulu was looking for a dry spot free of snakes. Cuff heard him suddenly shout *"Footsack!"* and throw a clod at a log. The log opened a pair of jaws, hissed angrily, and slid into the water.

"We'll have to have a good fire," said Mtengeni, hunting for dry wood. "We don't want a croc or hippo wandering into our tent by mistake."

After supper they set the automatic bug-sprayer going, inflated their mattresses, and tried to sleep. A lion roared somewhere in the west. That sound no

African, native or Africander, likes to hear when he is on foot at night. But the men were not worried; lions avoided the swampy areas. The mosquitoes presented a more immediate problem.

Many hours later, Athelstan Cuff heard Mtengeni getting up.

The warden said: "I just remembered a high spot half a mile from here, where there's plenty of firewood. Me, I'm going out to get some."

Cuff listened to Mtengeni's retreating steps in the soft ground; then to his own breathing. Then he listened to something else. It sounded like a human yell.

He got up and pulled on his boots quickly. He fumbled around for the flashlight, but Mtengeni had taken it with him.

The yell came again.

Cuff found his rifle and cartridge belt in the dark and went out. There was enough starlight to walk by if you were careful. The fire was nearly out. The yells seemed to come from a direction opposite to that in which Mtengeni had gone. They were high-pitched, like a woman's screams.

He walked in their direction, stumbling over irregularities in the ground and now and then stepping up to his calves in unexpected water. The yells were plainer now. They weren't in English. Something was also snorting.

He found the place. There was a small tree, in the branches of which somebody was perched. Below the tree a noisy bulk moved around. Cuff caught the outline of a sweeping horn, and knew he had to deal with a buffalo.

He hated to shoot. For a Park official to kill one of

his charges simply wasn't done. Besides, he couldn't see to aim for a vital spot, and he didn't care to try to dodge a wounded buffalo in the dark. They could move with race-horse speed through the heaviest growth.

On the other hand, he couldn't leave even a poor fool of a native woman treed. The buffalo, if it was really angry, would wait for days until its victim weakened and fell. Or it would butt the tree until the victim was shaken out. Or it would rear up and try to hook the victim out with its horns.

Athelstan Cuff shot the buffalo. The buffalo staggered about a bit and collapsed.

The victim climbed down swiftly, pouring out a flood of thanks in Xosa. It was very bad Xosa, even worse than the Englishman's. Cuff wondered what she was doing here, nearly a thousand miles from where the Maxosa lived. He assumed that she was a native, though it was too dark to see. He asked her if she spoke English, but she didn't seem to understand the question, so he made shift with the Bantu dialect.

"*Uveli phi na?*" he asked sternly. "Where do you come from? Don't you know that nobody is allowed in the Park without special permission?"

"*Izwe kamafene wabantu,*" she replied.

"What? Never heard of the place. Land of the baboon people, indeed! What are you?"

"*Ingwamza.*"

"You're a white stork? Are you trying to be funny?"

"I didn't say I was a white stork. Ingwamza's my name."

"I don't care about your name. I want to know what you *are*."

"*Umfene umfazi.*"

Cuff controlled his exasperation. "All right, all right, you're a baboon woman. I don't care what clan you belong to. What's your tribe? Batawana, Bamangwato, Bangwaketse, Barolong, Herero, or what? Don't try to tell me you're a Xosa; no Xosa ever used an accent like that."

"*Amafene abantu.*"

"What the devil are the baboon people?"

"People who live in the Park."

Cuff resisted the impulse to pull out two handfuls of hair by the roots. "But I tell you nobody lives in the Park! It isn't allowed! Come now, where do you really come from and what's your native language and why are you trying to talk Xosa?"

"I told you, I live in the Park. And I speak Xosa because all we *amafene abantu* speak it. That's the language Mqhavi taught us."

"Who is Mqhavi?"

"The man who taught us to speak Xosa."

Cuff gave up. "Come along, you're going to see the warden. Perhaps he can make some sense out of your gabble. And you'd better have a good reason for trespassing, my good woman, or it'll go hard with you. Especially as it resulted in the killing of a good buffalo." He started off toward the camp, making sure that Ingwamza followed him closely.

The first thing he discovered was that he couldn't see the light of any fire to guide him back. Either he'd come farther than he thought, or the fire had died altogether while Mtengeni was getting wood. He kept on for a quarter of an hour in what he thought was the right direction. Then he stopped. He had, he realized, not the vaguest idea of where he was.

He turned. "*Sibaphi na?*" he snapped. "Where are we?"

"In the Park."

Cuff began to wonder whether he'd ever succeed in delivering this native woman to Mtengeni before he strangled her with his bare hands. "I know we're in the Park," he snarled. "But *where* in the Park?"

"I don't know exactly. Somewhere near my people's land."

"That doesn't do me any good. Look: I left the warden's camp when I heard you yell. I want to get back to it. Now how do I do it?"

"Where is the warden's camp?"

"I don't know, stupid. If I did I'd go there."

"If you don't know where it is, how do you expect me to guide you thither? I don't know either."

Cuff made strangled noises in his throat. Inwardly he had to admit that she had him there, which only made him madder. Finally he said: "Never mind, suppose you take me to your people. Maybe they have somebody with some sense."

"Very well," said the native woman, and she set off at a rapid pace, Cuff stumbling after her vague outline. He began to wonder if maybe she wasn't right about living in the Park. She seemed to know where she was going.

"Wait," he said. He ought to write a note to Mtengeni, explaining what he was up to, and stick it on a tree for the warden to find. But there was no pencil or paper in his pockets. He didn't even have a match safe or a cigarette lighter. He'd taken all those things out of his pockets when he'd lain down.

They went on a way, Cuff pondering on how to get

in touch with Mtengeni. He didn't want himself and
the warden to spend a week chasing each other
around the Delta. Perhaps it would be better to stay
where they were and build a fire—but again, he had
no matches, and didn't see much prospect of making
a fire by rubbing sticks in this damned damp country.

Ingwamza said: "Stop. There are buffalo ahead."

Cuff listened and heard faintly the sound of snapping grass stems as the animals fed.

She continued: "We'll have to wait until it gets
light. Then maybe they'll go way. If they don't, we
can circle around them, but I couldn't find the way
around in the dark."

They found the highest point they could and settled down to wait. Something with legs had crawled
inside Cuff's shirt. He mashed it with a slap.

He strained his eyes into the dark. It was impossible to tell how far away the buffalo were. Overhead
a nightjar brought its wings together with a single
startling clap. Cuff told his nerves to behave themselves. He wished he had a smoke.

The sky began to lighten. Gradually Cuff was able
to make out the black bulks moving among the reeds.
They were at least two hundred yards away. He'd
have preferred that they were at twice the distance,
but it was better than stumbling right on them.

It became lighter and lighter. Cuff never took his
eyes off the buffalo. There was something queer about
the nearest one. It had six legs.

Cuff turned to Ingwamza and started to whisper:
"What kind of buffalo do you call—" Then he gave a
yell of pure horror and jumped back. His rifle went
off, tearing a hole in his boot.

He had just gotten his first good look at the native woman in the rapidly waxing dawn. Ingwamza's head was that of an overgrown chacma baboon.

The buffalo stampeded through the feathery papyrus. Cuff and Ingwamza stood looking at each other. Then Cuff looked at his right foot. Blood was running out of the jagged hole in the leather.

"What's the matter? Why did you shoot yourself?" asked Ingwamza.

Cuff couldn't think of an answer to that one. He sat down and took off his boot. The foot felt numb, but there seemed to be no harm done aside from a piece of skin the size of a sixpence gouged out of the margin. Still, you never knew what sort of horrible infection might result from a trifling wound in these swamps. He tied his foot up with his handkerchief and put his boot back on.

"Just an accident," he said. "Keep going, Ingwamza."

Ingwamza went, Cuff limping behind. The sun would rise any minute now. It was light enough to make out colors. Cuff saw that Ingwamza, in describing herself as a baboon-woman, had been quite literal, despite the size, general proportions, and posture of a human being. Her body, but for the greenish-yellow hair and the short tail, might have passed for that of a human being, if you weren't too particular. But the astonishing head with its long bluish muzzle gave her the appearance of an Egyptian animal-headed god. Cuff wondered vaguely if the 'fene abantu were a race of man-monkey hybrids. That was impossible, of course. But he'd seen so many impossible things in the last couple of days.

She looked back at him. "We shall arrive in an hour or two. I'm sleepy." She yawned. Cuff repressed a shudder at the sight of four canine teeth big enough for a leopard. Ingwamza could tear the throat out of a man with those fangs as easily as biting the end off a banana. And he'd been using his most hectoring colonial-administrator tone on her in the dark! He made a resolve never to speak harshly to anybody he couldn't see.

Ingwamza pointed to a carroty baobab against the sky. "*Izwe kamagene wabantu.*" They had to wade a little stream to get there. A six-foot monitor lizard walked across their path, saw them, and disappeared with a scuttle.

The *'fene abantu* lived in a village much like that of any Bantu people, but the circular thatched huts were smaller and cruder. Baboon people ran out to peer at Cuff and to feel his clothes. He gripped his rifle tightly. They didn't act hostile, but it gave you a dashed funny feeling. The males were larger than the females, with even longer muzzles and bigger tusks.

In the center of the village sat a big *umfene umntu* scratching himself in front of the biggest hut. Ingwamza said. "This is my father, the chief. His name is Indlovu." To the baboon-man she told of her rescue.

The chief was the only *umfene umntu* that Cuff had seen who wore anything. What he wore was a necktie. The necktie had been a gaudy thing once.

The chief got up and made a speech, the gist of which was that Cuff had done a great thing, and that Cuff would be their guest until his wound healed. Cuff had a chance to observe the difficulties that the *'fene*

abantu had with the Xosa tongue. The clicks were
blurred, and they stumbled badly over the lip-smack.
With those mouths, he could see how they might.

But he was only mildly interested. His foot was hurt-
ing like the very devil. He was glad when they led him
into a hut so he could take off his boot. The hut was
practically unfurnished. Cuff asked the *'fene abantu*
if he might have some of the straw used for thatch-
ing. They seemed puzzled by his request, but com-
plied, and he made himself a bed of sorts. He hated
sleeping on the ground, especially on ground infested
with arthropodal life. He hated vermin, and knew he
was in for an intimate acquaintance with them.

He had nothing to bandage his foot with, except
the one handkerchief, which was now thoroughly
blood-soaked. He'd have to wash and dry it before it
would be fit to use again. And where in the Okavango
Delta could he find water fit to wash the handkerchief in? Of course he could boil the water. In what?
He was relieved and amazed when his questions
brought forth the fact that there was a large iron pot
in the village, obtained from God knew where.

The wound had clotted satisfactorily, and he dis-
lodged the handkerchief with infinite care from the
scab. While his water was boiling, the chief, Indlovu,
came in and talked to him. The pain in his foot had
subsided for the moment, and he was able to realize
what an extraordinary thing he had come across,
and to give Indlovu his full attention. He plied Indlovu with questions.

The chief explained what he knew about himself
and his people. It seemed that he was the first of the
race; all the others were his descendants. Not only

Ingwamza but all the other *amafene abafazi* were his daughters. Ingwamza was merely the last. He was old now. He was hazy about dates, but Cuff got the impression that these beings had a shorter life span than human beings, and matured much more quickly. If they were in fact baboons, that was natural enough.

Indlovu didn't remember having had any parents. The earliest he remembered was being led around by Mqhavi. Stanley H. Mqhavi had been a black man, and worked for the machine man, who had been a pink man like Cuff. He had had a machine up on the edge of the Chobe Swamp. His name had been Heeky.

Of course, Hickey! thought Cuff. Now, he was getting somewhere. Hickey had disappeared by simply running his truck up to Ngamiland without bothering to tell anybody where he was going. That had been before the Park had been established; before Cuff had come out from England. Mqhair must have been his Xosa assistant. His thoughts raced ahead of Indlovu's words.

Indlovu went on to tell about how Heeky had died, and how Mqhavi, not knowing how to run the machine, had taken him, Indlovu, and his now numerous progeny in an attempt to find his way back to civilization. He had gotten lost in the Delta. Then he had cut his foot somehow, and gotten sick, very sick. Cuff had come out from England. Mqhavi must have Mqhavi, had gotten well he had been very weak. So he had settled down with Indlovu and his family. They already walked upright and spoke Xosa, which Mqhavi had taught them. Cuff got the idea that the early family relationships among the 'fene abantu had of necessity involved close inbreeding. Mqhavi had taught them all he knew, and then died, after warning them not to go within a mile of the machine, which, as far as they knew, was still up at the Chobe Swamp.

Cuff thought, that blasted machine is an electronic tube of some sort, built to throw short waves of the length to affect animal genes. Probably Indlovu represented one of Hickey's early experiments. Then Hickey had died, and—left the thing going. He didn't know how it got power; some solar system, perhaps.

Suppose Hickey had died while the thing was turned on. Mqhavi might have dragged his body out and left the door open. He might have been afraid to try to turn it off, or he might not have thought of it. So every animal that passed that doorway got a dose of the rays, and begat monstrous offspring. These super-baboons were one example; whether an accidental or a controlled mutation, might never be known.

For every useful mutation there were bound to be scores of useless or harmful ones. Mtengeni had been right: it had to be stopped while there was still normal stock left in the Park. He wondered again how to get in touch with the warden. He'd be damned if anything short of the threat of death would get him to walk on that foot, for a few days anyhow.

Ingwamza entered with a wooden dish full of a mess of some sort. Athelstan Cuff decided resignedly that he was expected to eat it. He couldn't tell by looking whether it was animal or vegetable in nature. After the first mouthful he was sure it was neither. Nothing in the animal and vegetable worlds could taste as awful as that. It was too bad Mqhavi hadn't been a Bamangwato; he'd have really known how to cook, and could have taught these monkeys. Still, he had to eat something to support life. He fell to with the wooden spoon they gave him, suppressing an occasional gag and watching the smaller solid particles closely. Sure enough, he had to smack two of them with the spoon to keep them from crawling out.

"How it is?" asked Ingwamza. Indlovu had gone out.

"Fine," lied Cuff. He was chasing a slimy piece of what he suspected was waterbuck tripe around the dish.

"I am glad. We'll feed you a lot of that. Do you like scorpions?"

"You mean to *eat*?"

"Of course. What else are they good for?"

He gulped. "No."

"I won't give you any then. You see I'm glad to know what my future husband likes."

"What?" He thought he had misunderstood her.

"I said, I am glad to know what you like, so I can please you after you are my husband."

Athelstan Cuff said nothing for sixty seconds. His naturally prominent eyes bulged even more as her words sank in. Finally he spoke.

"*Gluk*," he said.

"What's that?"

"*Gug. Gah*. My God. Let me out of here!" His voice jumped two octaves, and he tried to get up. Ingwamza caught his shoulders and pushed him gently, but firmly, back on his pallet. He struggled, but without visibly exerting herself the *'fene umfazi* held him as in a vise.

"You can't go," she said. "If you try to walk on that foot you will get sick."

His ruddy face was turning purple! "Let me up! Let me up, I say! I can't stand this!"

"Will you promise not to try to go out if I do? Father would be furious if I let you do anything unwise."

He promised, getting a grip on himself again. He already felt a bit foolish about his panic. He was in a nasty jam, certainly, but an official of His Majesty didn't act like a frightened schoolgirl at every crisis.

"What," he asked, "is this all about?"

"Father is so grateful to you for saving my life that he intends to bestow me on you in marriage, without even asking a bride price."

"But . . . but . . . I'm married already," he lied.

"What of it? I'm not afraid of your other wives. If they got fresh, I'd tear them in pieces like this." She bared her teeth and went through the motions of tearing several Mistresses Cuff in pieces. Athelstan Cuff shut his eyes at the horrid sight.

"Among my people," he said, "you're allowed only one wife."

"That's too bad," said Ingwamza. "That means that you couldn't go back to your people after you married me, doesn't it?"

Cuff sighed. These *'fene abantu* combined the mental outlook of uneducated Maxosa with physical equipment that would make a lion think twice before attacking one. He'd probably have to shoot his way out. He looked around the hut craftily. His rifle wasn't in sight. He didn't dare ask about it for fear of arousing suspicion.

"Is your father set on this plan?" he asked.

"Oh, yes, very. Father is a good *umntu,* but he gets set on ideas like this and nothing will make him change them. And he has a terrible temper. If you cross him when he has his heart set on something, he will tear you in pieces. *Small* pieces." She seemed to relish the phrase.

"How do *you* feel about it, Ingwamza?"

"Oh, I do everything father says. He knows more than any of us."

"Yes, but I mean you personally. Forget about your father for the moment."

She didn't quite catch on for a moment, but after further explanation she said: "I wouldn't mind. It would be a great thing for my people if one of us was married to a man."

Cuff silently thought that that went double for him.

Indlovu came in with two other *amafene abantu.* "Run along, Ingwamza," he said. The three baboon-men squatted around Athelstan Cuff and began questioning him about men and the world outside the Delta.

When Cuff stumbled over a phrase, one of the questioners, a scarred fellow named Sondlo, asked why he had difficulty. Cuff explained that Xosa wasn't his native language.

"Men do speak other languages?" asked Indlovu. "I remember now, the great Mqhavi once told me something to that effect. But he never taught me any other languages. Perhaps he and Heeky spoke one of these other languages, but I was too young when Heeky died to remember."

Cuff explained something about linguistics. He was immediately pressed to "say something in English." Then they wanted to learn English, right then, that afternoon.

Cuff finished his evening meal and looked without enthusiasm at his pallet. No artificial light, so these people rose and set with the sun. He stretched out. The straw rustled. He jumped up, bringing his injured foot down hard. He yelped, swore, and felt the bandage. Yes, he'd started it bleeding again. Oh, to hell with it. He attacked the straw, chasing out a mouse, six cockroaches, and uncounted smaller bugs. Then he stretched out again. Looking up, he felt his scalp prickle. A ten-inch centipede was methodically hunting its prey over the underside of the roof. If it missed its footing when it was right over him— He unbuttoned his shirt and pulled it up over his face. Then the mosquitoes attacked his midriff. His foot throbbed.

A step brought him up; it was Ingwamza.

"What is it now?" he asked.

"*Ndiya kuhlaha apha,*" she answered.

"Oh no, you're not going to stay here. We're not . . . well, anyway, it simply isn't done among my people."

"But Esselten, somebody must watch you in case you get sick. My father—"

"No, I'm sorry, but that's final. If you're going to marry me you'll have to learn how to behave among men. And we're beginning right now."

To his surprise and relief, she went without further

objection, albeit sulkily. He'd never have dared to try to put her out by force.

When she had gone, he crawled over to the door of the hut. The sun had just set, and the moon would follow it in a couple of hours. Most of the *'fene abantu* had retired. But a couple of them squatted outside their huts, in sight of his place, watchfully.

Heigh ho, he thought, they aren't taking any chances. Perhaps the old boy *is* grateful and all that rot. But I think my fiancée let the cat out when she said that about the desirability of hitching one of the tribe to a human being. Of course the poor things don't know that it wouldn't have any legal standing at all. But that fact wouldn't save me from a jolly unpleasant experience in the meantime. Suppose I haven't escaped by the time of the ceremony. Would I go through with it? *Br-r-r!* Of course not. I'm an Englishman and an officer of the Crown. But if it meant my life . . . I don't know. I'm dashed if I do. Perhaps I can talk them out of it . . . being careful not to get them angry in the process—

He was tied to the straw, and enormous centipedes were dropping off the ceiling onto his face. Then he was running through the swamp, with Ingwamza and her irate pa after him. His feet stuck in the mud so he couldn't move, and there was a light in his face. Mtengeni—good old George!—was riding a two-headed rhino. But instead of rescuing him, the warden said: "Mr. Cuff, you must do something about these Bechuana. Them, they are catching all my animals and painting them red with green stripes." Then he woke up.

It took him a second to realize that the light was from the setting moon, not the rising sun, and that he therefore had been asleep less than two hours. It took him another second to realize what had wakened him. The straw of the hut wall had been wedged apart, and through the gap a *'fene umntu* was crawling. While Cuff was still wondering why one of his hosts, or captors, should use this peculiar method of getting in, the baboon-man stood up. He looked enormous in the faint light.

"What is it?" asked Cuff.

"If you make a noise," said the stranger, "I will kill you."

"What? What's the idea? Why should you want to kill me?"

"You have stolen my Ingwamza."

"But . . . but—" Cuff was at a loss. Here the gal's old man would tear him in pieces—*small* pieces—if he didn't marry her, and a rival or something would kill him if he did. "Let's talk it over first," he said, in what he hoped was a normal voice. "Who are you, by the way?"

"My name is Cukata. I was to have married Ingwamza next month. And then you came."

"What . . . what—"

"I won't kill you. Not if you make no noise. I will just fix you so you won't marry Ingwamza." He moved toward the pile of straw.

Cuff didn't waste time inquiring into the horrid details. "Wait a minute," he said, cold sweat bedewing not merely his brow, but his whole torso. "My dear fellow, this marriage wasn't my idea. It was Indlovu's, entirely. I don't want to steal your girl. They just informed me that I was going to marry her, without asking me about it at all. I don't *want* to marry her. In fact there's nothing I want to do less."

The *'fene umntu* stood still for a moment, thinking. Then he said softly: "You wouldn't marry my Ingwamza if you had the chance? You think she is ugly?"

"Well—"

"By u-Qamata, that's an insult! Nobody shall think such thoughts of my Ingwamza! Now I will kill you for sure!"

"Wait, wait!" Cuff's voice, normally a pleasant low baritone, became a squeak. "That isn't it at all! She's beautiful, intelligent, industrious, all that a *'ntu* could want. But I can never marry her." Inspiration! Cuff went on rapidly. Never had he spoken Xosa so fluently. "You know that if lion mates with leopard, there are no offspring." Cuff wasn't sure that was so, but he took a chance. "It is that way with my people and yours. We are too different. There would be no issue to our marriage, and Indlovu would not have grandchildren by us to gladden his old age."

Cukata, after some thought, saw, or thought he did. "But," he said, "how can I prevent this marriage without killing you?"

"You could help me escape."

"So. Now that's an idea. Where do you want to go?"

"Do you know where the Hickey machine is?"

"Yes, though I have never been close to it. That is forbidden. About fifteen miles north of here, on the edge of the Chobe Swamp, is a rock. By the rock are three baobab trees, close together. Between the trees and the swamp are two houses. The machine is in one of those houses."

He was silent again. "You can't travel fast with that wounded foot. They would overtake you. Perhaps Indlovu would tear you in pieces, or perhaps he would bring you back. If he brought you back, we should fail. If he tore you in pieces, I should be sorry, for I like you, even if you are a feeble little *isipham-pham*." Cuff wished that the simian brain would get around to the point. "I have it. In ten minutes I shall whistle. You will then crawl out through this hole in the wall, making no noise. You understand?"

When Athelstan Cuff crawled out, he found Cukata in the alley between two rows of huts. There was a strong reptilian stench in the air. Behind the baboon-man was something large and black. It walked with a swaying motion. It brushed against Cuff, and he almost cried out at the touch of cold, leathery hide.

"This is the largest," said Cukata. "We hope some day to have a whole herd of them. They are fine for traveling across the swamps, because they can swim as well as run. And they grow much faster than the ordinary crocodile."

The thing was a crocodile—but such a crocodile! Though not much over fifteen feet in length, it had long, powerful legs that raised its body a good four feet off the ground, giving it a dinosaurian look. It rubbed against Cuff, and the thought occurred to him that it had taken an astonishing mutation indeed to give a brainless and voracious reptile an affection for human beings.

Cukata handed Cuff a knobkerry, and explained: "Whistle, loudly, when you want him to come. To start him, hit him on the tail with this. To stop him, hit him on the nose. To make him go to the left, hit him on the right side of the neck, not too hard. To make him go to the right, hit him—"

"On the left side of the neck, but not too hard," finished Cuff. "What does he eat?"

"Anything that is meat. But you needn't feed him for two or three days; he has been fed recently."

"Don't you use a saddle?"

"Saddle? What's that?"

"Never mind." Cuff climbed aboard, wincing as he settled onto the sharp dorsal ridges of the animal's hide.

"Wait," said Cukata. "The moon will be completely gone in a moment. Remember, I shall say that I know nothing about your escape, but that you got out and stole him yourself. His name Soga."

There were the baobab trees, and there were the houses. There were also a dozen elephants, facing the rider and his bizarre mount and spreading their immense ears. Athelstan Cuff was getting so blasé about freaks that he hardly noticed that two of the elephants had two trunks apiece; that another of them was colored a fair imitation of a Scotch tartan; that another of them had short legs like a hippopotamus, so that it looked like something out of a dachshund breeder's nightmare.

The elephants, for their part, seemed undecided whether to run or to attack, and finally compromised by doing nothing. Cuff realized when he was already past them that he had done a wickedly reckless thing in going so close to them unarmed except for the useless kerry. But somehow he couldn't get excited about mere elephants. His whole life for the past forty-eight hours had had a dreamlike quality. Maybe he was dreaming. Or maybe he had a charmed life. Or something. Though there was nothing dream-like about the throb in his foot, or the acute soreness in his gluteus maximus.

Soga, being a crocodile, bowed his whole body at every stride. First the head and tail went to the right and the body to the left; then the process was re-versed. Which was most unpleasant for his rider.

Cuff was willing to swear that he'd ridden at least fifty miles instead of the fifteen Cukata had men-tioned. Actually he had done about thirty, not having been able to follow a straight line and having to steer by stars and, when it rose, the sun. A fair portion of the thirty had been hugging Soga's barrel while the croc's great tail drove them through the water like a racing shell. No hippo or other crocs had bothered them; evidently they knew when they were well off.

Athelstan Cuff slid—almost fell—off, and hobbled up to the entrance of one of the houses. His practiced eye took in the roof cistern, the solar boiler, the steam-electric plant, the batteries, and finally the tube inside. He went in. Yes, by Jove, the tube was in operation after all these years. Hickey must have had something jolly unusual. Cuff found the main switch easily enough and pulled it. All that happened was that the little orange glow in the tube died.

The house was so silent it made Cuff uncomfort-able, except for the faint hum of the solar power plant. As he moved about, using the kerry for a crutch, he stirred up the dust which lay six inches deep on the floor. Maybe there were notebooks or something which ought to be collected. There had

88   SCIENCE FICTION BESTIARY

been, he soon discovered, but the termites had eaten
every scrap of paper, and even the imitation-leather
covers, leaving only the metal binding rings and
their frames. It was the same with the books.

Something white caught his eye. It was paper, lying
on a little metal-legged stand that the termites evidently hadn't thought well enough of to climb. He
limped toward it eagerly. But it was only a newspaper,
Umlindi we Nyanga—"The Monthly Watchman"—
published in East London. Evidently, Stanley H. Mqhavi had subscribed to it. It crumbled at Cuff's touch.

Oh, well, he thought, can't expect much. We'll
run along, and some of the bio-physicist chappies can
come in and gather up the scientific apparatus.

He went out, called Soga, and started east. He
figured that he could strike the old wagon road somewhere north of the Mababe, and get down to Mtengeni's main station that way.

Were those human voices? Cuff shifted uneasily on
his Indian fakir's seat. He had gone about four miles
after leaving Hickey's scientific station.

They were voices, but not human ones. They be-
longed to a dozen *'fene abantu*, who came loping
through the grass with old Indlovu at their head.

Cuff reached back and thumped Soga's tail. If he
could get the croc going all out, he might be able to
run away from his late hosts. Soga wasn't as fast as a
horse, but he could trot right along. Cuff was relieved
to see that they hadn't brought his rifle along. They
were armed with kerries and spears, like any of the
more savage *abantu*. Perhaps the fear of injuring
their pet would make them hesitate to throw things at
him. At least he hoped so.

A familiar voice caught up with him in a piercing yell of "Soga!" The croc slackened his pace and tried to turn his head. Cuff whacked him unmercifully. Indlovu's yell came again, followed by a whistle. The croc was now definitely off his stride. Cuff's efforts to keep him headed away from his proper masters resulted in his zigzagging erratically. The contrary directions confused and irritated him. He opened his jaws and hissed. The baboon-men were gaining rapidly.

So, thought Cuff, this is the end. I hate like hell to go out before I've had a chance to write my report. But mustn't show it. Not an Englishman and an officer of the Crown. Wonder what poor Mtengeni'll think.

Something went *whick* past him; a fraction of a second later, the crash of an elephant rifle reached him. A big puff of dust ballooned up in front of the baboon-men. They skittered away from it as if the dust and not the bullet that made it were something deadly. George Mtengeni appeared from behind the nearest patch of thorn scrub, and yelled, "Hold still there, or me, I'll blow your heads off." If the *'fene abantu* couldn't understand his English, they got his tone.

Cuff thought vaguely, good old George, he could shoot their ears off at that distance, but he has more sense than to kill any of them before he finds out. Cuff slid off Soga and almost fell in a heap.

The warden came up. "What . . . what in the heavens has been happening to you, Mr. Cuff? What are these?" He indicated the baboon-men.

"Joke," giggled Cuff. "Good joke on you, George. Been living in your dashed Park for years, and you never knew—Wait, I've got to explain something to these chaps. I say, Indlovu . . . hell, he doesn't know English. Got to use Xosa. You know Xosa, don't you George?" He giggled again.

"Why, me, I . . . I can follow it. It's much like Zulu. But my God, what happened to the seat of your pants?"

Cuff pointed a wavering finger at Soga's saw-toothed back. "Good old Soga. Should have had a saddle. Dashed outrage, not providing a saddle for His Majesty's representative."

"But you look as if you'd been skinned! Me, I've got to get you to a hospital . . . and what about your foot?"

"T'hell with the foot. 'Nother joke. Can't stand up, can't sit down. Jolly, what? Have to sleep on my stomach. But, Indlovu! I'm sorry I had to run away. I couldn't marry Ingwamza. Really. Because . . . because—" Athelstan Cuff swayed and collapsed in a small, ragged pile.

Peter Cuff's eyes were round. He asked the inevitable small-boy question: "What happened then?"

Athelstan Cuff was stuffing his pipe. "Oh, about what you'd expect. Indlovu was jolly vexed, I can tell you, but he didn't dare do anything with George standing there with the gun. He calmed down later after he understood what I had been driving at, and we became good friends. When he died, Cukata was elected chief in his place. I still get Christmas cards from him."

"Christmas cards from a baboon?"

"Certainly. If I get one next Christmas, I'll show it

to you. It's the same card every year. He's an economical fella, and he bought a hundred cards of the same pattern because he could get them at a discount."

"Were you all right?"

"Yes, after a month in the hospital. I still don't know why I didn't get sixteen kinds of blood poisoning. Fool's luck, I suppose."

"But what's that got to do with me being a 'dopted boy?"

"Peter!" Cuff gave the clicks represented in the Bantu languages by x and in English by *tsk*. "Isn't it obvious? That tube of Hickey's was on when I approached his house. So I got a full dose of the radiations. Their effect was to produce violent mutations in the germ-plasm. You know what that is, don't you? Well, I never dared have any children of my own after that, for fear they'd turn out to be some sort of monster. That didn't occur to me until afterward. It fair bowled me over, I can tell you, when I did think of it. I went to pieces, rather, and lost my job in South Africa. But now that I have you and your mother, I realize that it wasn't so important after all."

"Father—" Peter hesitated.

"Go on, old man."

"If you'd thought of the rays before you went to the house, would you have been brave enough to go ahead anyway?"

Cuff lit his pipe and looked off at nothing. "I've often wondered about that myself. I'm dashed if I know. I wonder . . . just what would have happened—"

The Preserving Machine

BY PHILIP K. DICK

Since 1952, science-fiction fans have eagerly welcomed every new story from the productive typewriter of Philip K. Dick. He appeared, at first, with what seemed like a hundred short stories at once, all of them original in concept and deft in execution. Then, a few years later, he turned to novels, making his debut with the impressive Solar Lottery *of 1955 and going on to such dark, disturbing books as* The Three Stigmata of Palmer Eldritch, Ubik, *and the Hugo-winning* The Man in the High Castle. *The story here, one of his early ones, shows how quickly Dick's skills developed. His recent work has the quality of nightmare; this elegantly-told story is dreamlike too, but it is a gentler sort of dream.*

Doc Labyrinth leaned back in his lawn chair, closing his eyes gloomily. He pulled his blanket up around his knees.

"Well?" I said. I was standing by the barbecue pit, warming my hands. It was a clear cold day. The sunny Los Angeles sky was almost cloud-free. Beyond Labyrinth's modest house a gently undulating expanse

of green stretched off until it reached the mountains
—a small forest that gave the illusion of wilderness
within the very limits of the city. "Well?" I said. "Then
the Machine did work the way you expected?"

Labyrinth did not answer. I turned around. The
old man was staring moodily ahead, watching an
enormous dun-colored beetle that was slowly climbing the side of his blanket. The beetle rose methodically, its face blank with dignity. It passed over the
top and disappeared down the far side. We were alone
again.

Labyrinth sighed and looked up at me. "Oh, it
worked well enough."

I looked after the beetle, but it was nowhere to be
seen. A faint breeze eddied around me, chill and thin
in the fading afternoon twilight. I moved nearer
the barbecue pit.

"Tell me about it," I said.

Doctor Labyrinth, like most people who read a
great deal and who have too much time on their
hands, had become convinced that our civilization
was going the way of Rome. He saw, I think, the same
cracks forming that had sundered the ancient world,
the world of Greece and Rome; and it was his con-
viction that presently our world, our society, would
pass away as theirs did, and a period of darkness
would follow.

Now Labyrinth, having thought this, began to
brood over all the fine and lovely things that would
be lost in the reshuffling of societies. He thought of
the art, the literature, the manners, the music, everything that would be lost. And it seemed to him that of
all these grand and noble things, music would probably be the most lost, the quickest forgotten.

Music is the most perishable of things, fragile and delicate, easily destroyed.

Labyrinth worried about this, because he loved music, because he hated the idea that some day there would be no more Brahms and Mozart, no more gentle chamber music that he could dreamily associate with powdered wigs and resined bows, and long, slender candles, melting away in the gloom.

What a dry and unfortunate world it would be, without music! How dusty and unbearable.

This is how he came to think of the Preserving Machine. One evening as he sat in his living-room in his deep chair, the gramophone on low, a vision came to him. He perceived in his mind a strange sight, the last score of a Schubert trio, the last copy, dog-eared, well-thumbed, lying on the floor of some gutted place, probably a museum.

A bomber moved overhead. Bombs fell, bursting the museum to fragments, bringing the walls down in a roar of rubble and plaster. In the debris the last score disappeared, lost in the rubbish, to rot and mold.

And then, in Doc Labyrinth's vision, he saw the score come burrowing out, like some buried mole. Quite like a mole, in fact, with claws and sharp teeth and a furious energy.

If music had that faculty, the ordinary, everyday instinct of survival which every worm and mole has, how different it would be! If music could be transformed into living creatures, animals with claws and teeth, then music might survive. If only a Machine could be built, a Machine to process musical scores into living forms.

But Doc Labyrinth was no mechanic. He made a few tentative sketches and sent them hopefully around to the research laboratories. Most of them were much too busy with war contracts, of course. But at last he found the people he wanted. A small midwestern university was delighted with his plans, and they were happy to start work on the Machine at once.

Weeks passed. At last Labyrinth received a postcard from the university. The Machine was coming along fine; in fact, it was almost finished. They had given it a trial run, feeding a couple of popular songs into it. The results? Two small mouse-like animals had come scampering out, rushing around the laboratory until the cat caught and ate them. But the Machine was a success.

It came to him shortly after, packed carefully in a wood crate, wired together and fully insured. He was quite excited as he set to work, taking the slats from it. Many fleeting notions must have coursed through his mind as he adjusted the controls and made ready for the first transformation. He had selected a priceless score to begin with, the score of the Mozart G Minor Quintet. For a time he turned the pages, lost in thought, his mind far away. At last he carried it to the Machine and dropped it in.

Time passed. Labyrinth stood before it, waiting nervously, apprehensive and not really certain what would greet him when he opened the compartment. He was doing a fine and tragic work, it seemed to him, preserving the music of the great composers for all eternity. What would his thanks be? What would he find? What form would this all take, before it was over?

There were many questions unanswered. The red

light of the Machine was glinting, even as he meditated. The process was over, the transformation had already taken place. He opened the door.

"Good Lord!" he said. "This is very odd."

A bird, not an animal, stepped out. The mozart bird was pretty, small and slender, with the flowing plumage of a peacock. It ran a little way across the room and then walked back to him, curious and friendly. Trembling, Doc Labyrinth bent down, his hand out. The mozart bird came near. Then, all at once, it swooped up into the air.

"Amazing," he murmured. He coaxed the bird gently, patiently, and at last it fluttered down to him. Labyrinth stroked it for a long time, thinking. What would the rest of them be like? He could not guess. He carefully gathered up the mozart bird and put it into a box.

He was even more surprised the next day when the beethoven beetle came out, stern and dignified. That was the beetle I saw myself, climbing along his red blanket, intent and withdrawn, on some business of its own.

After that came the schubert animal. The schubert animal was silly, an adolescent sheep-creature that ran this way and that, foolish and wanting to play. Labyrinth sat down right then and there and did some heavy thinking.

Just what *were* survival factors? Was a flowing plume better than claws, better than sharp teeth? Labyrinth was stumped. He had expected an army of stout badger creatures, equipped with claws and scales, digging, fighting, ready to gnaw and kick. Was he getting the right thing? Yet who could say what was good for survival?—the dinosaurs had been well armed, but there were none of them left. In any case the Machine was built; it was too late to turn back, now.

Labyrinth went ahead, feeding the music of many composers into the Preserving Machine, one after another, until the woods behind his house was filled with creeping, bleating things that screamed and crashed in the night. There were many oddities that came out, creations that startled and astonished him. The brahms insect had many legs sticking in all directions, a vast, platter-shaped centipede. It was low and flat, with a coating of uniform fur. The brahms insect liked to be by itself, and it went off promptly, taking great pains to avoid the wagner animal, who had come just before.

The wagner animal was large and splashed with deep colors. It seemed to have quite a temper, and Doc Labyrinth was a little afraid of it, as were the bach bugs, the round ball-like creatures, a whole flock of them, some large, some small, that had been obtained for the Forty-Eight Preludes and Fugues. And there was the stravinsky bird, made up of curious fragments and bits, and many others besides.

So he let them go, off into the woods, and away they went, hopping and rolling and jumping as best they could. But already a sense of failure hung over him. Each time a creature came out he was astonished; he did not seem to have control over the results at all. It was out of his hands, subject to some strong, invisible law that had subtly taken over, and this worried him greatly. The creatures were bending, changing before a deep, impersonal force, a force that Labyrinth could neither see nor understand. And it made him afraid.

Labyrinth stopped talking. I waited for a while but he did not seem to be going on. I looked around at him. The old man was staring at me in a strange, plaintive way.

"I don't really know much more," he said. "I haven't been back there for a long time, back in the woods. I'm afraid to. I know something is going on, but—"

"Why don't we both go and take a look?"

He smiled with relief. "You wouldn't mind, would you? I was hoping you might suggest that. This business is beginning to get me down." He pushed his blanket aside and stood up, brushing himself off. "Let's go then."

We walked around the side of the house and along a narrow path, into the woods. Everything was wild and chaotic, overgrown and matted, an unkempt, unattended sea of green. Doc Labyrinth went first, pushing the branches off the path, stooping and wriggling to get through.

"Quite a place," I observed. We made our way for a time. The woods were dark and damp; it was almost sunset now, and a light mist was descending on us, drifting down through the leaves above.

"No one comes here." The Doc stopped suddenly, looking around. "Maybe we'd better go and find my gun. I don't want anything to happen."

"You seem certain that things have got out of hand." I came up beside him and we stood together. "Maybe it's not as bad as you think."

Labyrinth looked around. He pushed some shrub-bery back with his foot. "They're all around us, every-where, watching us. Can't you feel it?"

I nodded absently. "What's this?" I lifted up a heavy, moldering branch, particles of fungus break-ing from it. I pushed it out of the way. A mound lay outstretched, shapeless and indistinct, half buried in the soft ground.

"What is it?" I said again. Labyrinth stared down, his face tight and forlorn. He began to kick at the mound aimlessly. I felt uncomfortable. "What is it, for heaven's sake?" I said. "Do you know?"

Labyrinth looked slowly up at me. "It's the schu-bert animal," he murmured. "Or it was, once. There isn't much left of it, any more."

The schubert animal—that was the one that had run and leaped like a puppy, silly and wanting to play. I bent down, staring at the mound, pushing a few leaves and twigs from it. It was dead all right. Its mouth was open, its body had been ripped wide. Ants and vermin were already working on it, toiling endlessly away. It had begun to stink.

"But what happened?" Labyrinth said. He shook his head. "What could have done it?"

There was a sound. We turned quickly.

For a moment we saw nothing. Then a bush moved, and for the first time we made out its form. It must have been standing there watching us all the time. The creature was immense, thin and extended, with bright, intense eyes. To me, it looked something like a coyote, but much heavier. Its coat was matted and thick, its muzzle hung partly open as it gazed at us silently, studying us as if astonished to find us there.

"The wagner animal," Labyrinth said thickly. "But it's changed. It's changed. I hardly recognize it."

The creature sniffed the air, its hackles up. Suddenly it moved back, into the shadows, and a moment later it was gone.

We stood for a while, not saying anything. At last Labyrinth stirred. "So, that's what it was," he said. "I can hardly believe it. But why? What—"

"Adaptation," I said. "When you toss an ordinary house cat out it becomes wild. Or a dog."

"Yes." He nodded. "A dog becomes a wolf again, to stay alive. The law of the forest. I should have expected it. It happens to everything."

I looked down at the corpse on the ground, and then around at the silent bushes. Adaptation—or maybe something worse. An idea was forming in my mind, but I said nothing, not right away.

"I'd like to see some more of them," I said. "Some of the others. Let's look around some more."

He agreed. We began to poke slowly through the grass and weeds, pushing branches and foliage out of the way. I found a stick, but Labyrinth got down on his hands and knees, reaching and feeling, staring nearsightedly down.

"Even children turn into beasts," I said. "You remember the wolf children of India? No one could believe they had been ordinary children."

Labyrinth nodded. He was unhappy, and it was not hard to understand why. He had been wrong, mistaken in his original idea, and the consequences of it were just now beginning to become apparent to him. Music would survive as living creatures, but he had forgotten the lesson of the Garden of Eden:

that once a thing has been fashioned it begins to exist on its own, and thus ceases to be the property of its creator to mold and direct as he wishes. God, watching man's development, must have felt the same sadness—and the same humiliation—as Labyrinth, to see His creatures alter and change to meet the needs of survival.

That his musical creatures should survive could mean nothing to him any more, for the very thing he had created them to prevent, the brutalization of beautiful things, was happening in *them*, before his own eyes. Doc Labyrinth looked up at me suddenly, his face full of misery. He had ensured their survival, all right, but in so doing he had erased any meaning, any value in it. I tried to smile a little at him, but he promptly looked away again.

"Don't worry so much about it," I said. "It wasn't much of a change for the wagner animal. Wasn't it pretty much that way anyhow, rough and temperamental? Didn't it have a proclivity towards violence—"

I broke off. Doc Labyrinth had leaped back, jerking his hand out of the grass. He clutched his wrist, shuddering with pain.

"What is it?" I hurried over. Trembling, he held his little old hand out to me. "What is it? What happened?"

I turned the hand over. All across the back of it were marks, red cuts that swelled even as I watched. He had been stung, stung or bitten by something in the grass. I looked down, kicking the grass with my foot.

There was a stir. A little golden ball rolled quickly

away, back towards the bushes. It was covered with spines like a nettle.

"Catch it!" Labyrinth cried. "Quick!"

I went after it, holding out my handkerchief, trying to avoid the spines. The sphere rolled frantically, trying to get away, but finally I got it into the handkerchief.

Labyrinth stared at the struggling handkerchief as I stood up. "I can hardly believe it," he said. "We'd better go back to the house."

"What is it?"

"One of the bach bugs. But it's changed. . . ."

We made our way back along the path, towards the house, feeling our way through the darkness. I went first, pushing the branches aside, and Labyrinth followed behind, moody and withdrawn, rubbing his hand from time to time.

We entered the yard and went up the back steps of the house, onto the porch. Labyrinth unlocked the door and we went into the kitchen. He snapped on the light and hurried to the sink to bathe his hand.

I took an empty fruit jar from the cupboard and carefully dropped the bach bug into it. The golden ball rolled testily around as I clamped the lid on. I sat down at the table. Neither of us spoke, Labyrinth at the sink, running cold water over his stung hand, I at the table, uncomfortably watching the golden ball in the fruit jar trying to find some way to escape.

"Well?" I said at last.

"There's no doubt." Labyrinth came over and sat down opposite me. "It's undergone some metamorphosis. It certainly didn't have poisoned spines to start with. You know, it's a good thing that I played my noah role carefully."

"What do you mean?"

"I made them all neuter. They can't reproduce. There will be no second generation. When these die, that will be the end of it."

"I must say I'm glad you thought of that."

"I wonder," Labyrinth murmured. "I wonder how it would sound, now, this way."

"What?"

"The sphere, the bach bug. That's the real test, isn't it? I could put it back through the Machine. We could see. Do you want to find out?"

"Whatever you say, Doc," I said. "It's up to you. But don't get your hopes up too far."

He picked up the fruit jar carefully and we walked downstairs, down the steep flights of steps to the cellar. I made out an immense column of dull metal rising up in the corner, by the laundry tubs. A strange feeling went through me. It was the Preserving Machine.

"So this is it," I said.

"Yes, this is it." Labyrinth turned the controls on and worked with them for a time. At last he took the jar and held it over the hopper. He removed the lid carefully, and the bach bug dropped reluctantly from the jar, into the Machine. Labyrinth closed the hopper after it.

"Here we go," he said. He threw the control and the Machine began to operate. Labyrinth folded his arms and we waited. Outside the night came on, shutting out the light, squeezing it out of existence. At last an indicator on the face of the Machine blinked red. The

Doc turned the control to OFF and we stood in silence, neither of us wanting to be the one who opened it.

"Well?" I said finally. "Which one of us is going to look?"

Labyrinth stirred. He pushed the slot-piece aside and reached into the Machine. His fingers came out grasping a slim sheet, a score of music. He handed it to me. "This is the result," he said. "We can go upstairs and play it."

We went back up, to the music room, Labyrinth sat down before the grand piano and I passed him back the score. He opened it and studied it for a moment, his face blank, without expression. Then he began to play.

I listened to the music. It was hideous. I have never heard anything like it. It was distorted, diabolical, without sense or meaning, except, perhaps, an alien, disconcerting meaning that should never have been there. I could believe only with the greatest effort that it had once been a Bach Fugue, part of a most orderly and respected work.

"That settles it," Labyrinth said. He stood up, took the score in his hands, and tore it to shreds.

As we made our way down the path to my car I said, "I guess the struggle for survival is a force bigger than any human ethos. It makes our precious morals and manners look a little thin."

Labyrinth agreed. "Perhaps nothing can be done, then, to save those manners and morals."

"Only time will tell," I said. "Even though this method failed, some other may work; something that we can't foresee or predict now may come along, some day."

I said good night and got into my car. It was pitch dark; night had fallen completely. I switched on my headlights and moved off down the road, driving into the utter darkness. There were no other cars in sight anywhere. I was alone, and very cold.

At the corner I stopped, slowing down to change gears. Something moved suddenly at the curb, something by the base of a huge sycamore tree, in the darkness. I peered out, trying to see what it was.

At the base of the sycamore tree a huge dun-colored beetle was building something, putting a bit of mud into place on a strange-awkward structure. I watched the beetle for a time, puzzled and curious, until at last it noticed me and stopped. The beetle turned abruptly and entered its building, snapping the door firmly shut behind it.

I drove away.

A Martian Odyssey

BY STANLEY G. WEINBAUM

*This story astonished science-fiction readers
when it appeared in 1934. Into a field of writing marked by gray prose and gray characters
came this glittering, lively story, carrying with
it the unforgettable Martian, Tweel, and an
assortment of other strange creatures. Weinbaum demonstrated that science fiction could
be fun, and demonstrated it so well that when
the Science Fiction Writers of America voted
in 1968 on the best short science-fiction
stories of all time, "A Martian Odyssey" finished in second place, just behind Isaac
Asimov's classic "Nightfall."*

*Unhappily, Weinbaum had little chance to
fulfill the brilliant promise of this, his first
published story. Within a year and a half of
its publication he was dead, only thirty-five
years old.*

Jarvis stretched himself as luxuriously as he
could in the cramped general quarters of the *Ares.*

"Air you can breathe!" he exulted. "It feels as thick
as soup after the thin stuff out there!" He nodded at
the Martian landscape stretching flat and desolate in

the light of the nearer moon, beyond the glass of the port.

The other three stared at him sympathetically—Putz, the engineer, Leroy, the biologist, and Harrison, the astronomer and captain of the expedition. Dick Jarvis was chemist of the famous crew, the *Ares* expedition, first human beings to set foot on the mysterious neighbor of the earth, the planet Mars. This, of course, was in the old days, less than twenty years after the mad American Doheny perfected the atomic blast at the cost of his life, and only a decade after the equally mad Cardoza rode on it to the moon. They were true pioneers, these four of the *Ares.* Except for a half dozen moon expeditions and the ill-fated de Lancey flight aimed at the seductive orb of Venus, they were the first men to feel other gravity than earth's, and certainly the first successful crew to leave the earth-moon system. And they deserved that success when one considers the difficulties and discomforts—the months spent in acclimatization chambers back on earth, learning to breathe the air as tenuous as that of Mars, the challenging of the void in the tiny rocket driven by the cranky reaction motors of the twenty-first century, and mostly the facing of an absolutely unknown world.

Jarvis stretched and fingered the raw and peeling tip of his frost-bitten nose. He sighed again contentedly.

"Well," exploded Harrison abruptly, "are we going to hear what happened? You set out all shipshape in an auxiliary rocket, we don't get a peep for ten days, and finally Putz here picks you out of a lunatic antheap with a freak ostrich as your pal! Spill it, man!"

"Speel?" queried Leroy perplexedly. "Speel what?"

"He means *'spiel,'*" explained Putz soberly. "It iss to tell."

Jarvis met Harrison's amused glance without the shadow of a smile. "That's right, Karl," he said in grave agreement with Putz. *"Ich spiel es!"* He grunted comfortably and began.

"According to orders," he said, "I watched Karl here take off toward the north, and then I got into my flying sweat-box and headed south. You'll remember, Cap—we had orders not to land, but just scout about for points of interest. I set the two cameras clicking and buzzed along, riding pretty high—about two thousand feet—for a couple of reasons. First, it gave the cameras a greater field, and second, the under-jets travel so far in this half-vacuum they call air here that they stir up dust if you move low."

"We know all that from Putz," grunted Harrison. "I wish you'd saved the films, though. They'd have paid the cost of this junket; remember how the public mobbed the first moon pictures?"

"The films are safe," retorted Jarvis. "Well," he resumed, "as I said, I buzzed along at a pretty good clip; just as we figured, the wings haven't much lift in this air at less than a hundred miles per hour, and even then I had to use the under-jets.

"So, with the speed and the altitude and the blurring caused by the under-jets, the seeing wasn't any too good. I could see enough, though, to distinguish that what I sailed over was just more of this grey plain that we'd been examining the whole week since our landing—same blobby growths and the same eternal carpet of crawling little plant-animals, or biopods, as Leroy calls them. So I sailed along, calling back my position every hour as instructed, and not knowing whether you heard me."

"I did!" snapped Harrison.

"A hundred and fifty miles south," continued Jarvis imperturbably, "the surface changed to a sort of low plateau, nothing but desert and orange-tinted sand. I figured that we were right in our guess, then, and this grey plain we dropped on was really the Mare Cimmerium, which would make my orange desert the region called Xanthus. If I were right, I ought to hit another grey plain, the Mare Chronium, in another couple of hundred miles, and then another orange desert, Thyle I or II. And so I did."

"Putz verified our position a week and a half ago!" grumbled the captain. "Let's get to the point."

"Coming!" remarked Jarvis. "Twenty miles into Thyle—believe it or not—I crossed a canal!"

"Putz photographed a hundred! Let's hear something new!"

"And did he also see a city?"

"Twenty of 'em, if you call those heaps of mud cities!"

"Well," observed Jarvis, "from here on I'll be telling a few things Putz didn't see!" He rubbed his tingling nose, and continued. "I knew that I had sixteen hours of daylight at this season, so eight hours— eight hundred miles—from here, I decided to turn back. I was still over Thyle, whether I or II I'm not sure, not more than twenty-five miles into it. And right there, Putz's pet motor quit!"

"Quit? How?" Putz was solicitous.

"The atomic blast got weak. I started losing altitude right away, and suddenly there I was with a

thump right in the middle of Thyle! Smashed my
nose on the window, too!" He rubbed the injured
member ruefully.

"Did you maybe try vashing der combustion chamber mit acid sulphuric?" inquired Putz. "Sometimes
der lead giffs a secondary radiation—"

"Naw!" said Jarvis disgustedly. "I wouldn't try that,
of course—not more than ten times! Besides, the
bump flattened the landing gear and busted off the
under-jets. Suppose I got the thing working—what
then? Ten miles with the blast coming right out of
the bottom and I'd have melted the floor from under
me!" He rubbed his nose again. "Lucky for me a
pound only weighs seven ounces here, or I'd have
been mashed flat!"

"I could have fixed!" ejaculated the engineer. "I
bet it vas not serious."

"Probably not," agreed Jarvis sarcastically. "Only
it wouldn't fly. Nothing serious, but I had my choice
of waiting to be picked up or trying to walk back—
eight hundred miles, and perhaps twenty days before
we had to leave! Forty miles a day! Well," he concluded, "I chose to walk. Just as much chance of being
picked up, and it kept me busy."

"We'd have found you," said Harrison.

"No doubt. Anyway, I rigged up a harness from
some seat straps, and put the water tank on my back,
took a cartridge belt and revolver, and some iron
rations, and started out."

"Water tank!" exclaimed the little biologist, Leroy.
"She weigh one-quarter ton!"

"Wasn't full. Weighed about two hundred and fifty
pounds earth-weight, which is eighty-five here. Then,

besides, my own personal two hundred and ten pounds is only seventy on Mars, so, tank and all, I grossed a hundred and fifty-five, or fifty-five pounds less than my everyday earth-weight. I figured on that when I undertook the forty-mile daily stroll. Oh—of course I took a thermo-skin sleeping bag for these wintry Martian nights.

"Off I went, bouncing along pretty quickly. Eight hours of daylight meant twenty miles or more. It got tiresome, of course—plugging along over a soft sand desert with nothing to see, not even Leroy's crawling biopods. But an hour or so brought me to the canal— just a dry ditch about four hundred feet wide, and straight as a railroad on its own company map.

"There'd been water in it sometime, though. The ditch was covered with what looked like a nice green lawn. Only, as I approached, the lawn moved out of my way!"

"Eh?" said Leroy.

"Yeah, it was a relative of your biopods. I caught one—a little grass-like blade about as long as my finger, with two thin, stemmy legs."

"He is where?" Leroy was eager.

"He is let go! I had to move, so I plowed along with the walking grass opening in front and closing behind. And then I was out on the orange desert of Thyle again.

"I plugged steadily along, cussing the sand that made going so tiresome, and, incidentally, cussing that cranky motor of yours, Karl. It was just before twilight that I reached the edge of Thyle, and looked down over the grey Mare Chronium. And I knew there was seventy-five miles of *that* to be walked over, and then a couple of hundred miles of that Xanthus desert, and about as much more Mare Cimmerium. Was I pleased? I started cussing you fellows for not picking me up!"

"We were trying, you sap!" said Harrison.

"That didn't help. Well, I figured I might as well use what was left of daylight in getting down the cliff that bounded Thyle. I found an easy place, and down I went. Mare Chronium was just the same sort of place as this—crazy leafless plants and a bunch of crawlers; I gave it a glance and hauled out my sleeping bag. Up to that time, you know, I hadn't seen anything worth worrying about on this half-dead world—nothing dangerous, that is."

"Did you?" queried Harrison.

"*Did I!* You'll hear about it when I come to it. Well, I was just about to turn in when suddenly I heard the wildest sort of shenanigans!"

"Vot iss shenanigans?" inquired Putz.

"He says, '*Je ne sais quoi*,'" explained Leroy. "It is to say, 'I don't know what.'"

"That's right," agreed Jarvis. "I didn't know what, so I sneaked over to find out. There was a racket like a flock of crows eating a bunch of canaries—whistles, cackles, caws, trills, and what have you. I rounded a clump of stumps, and there was Tweel!"

"Tweel?" said Harrison, and "Tveel?" said Leroy and Putz.

"That freak ostrich," explained the narrator. "At least, Tweel is as near as I can pronounce it without sputtering. He called it something like 'Trrrweerrlll.'"

"What was he doing?" asked the captain.

"He was being eaten! And squealing, of course, as anyone would."

"Eaten! By what?"

"I found out later. All I could see then was a bunch of black ropy arms tangled around what looked like, as Putz described it to you, an ostrich. I wasn't going to interfere, naturally; if both creatures were dangerous, I'd have one less to worry about.

"But the bird-like thing was putting up a good battle, dealing vicious blows with an eighteen-inch beak, between screeches. And besides, I caught a glimpse or two of what was on the end of those arms!" Jarvis shuddered. "But the clincher was when I noticed a little black bag or case hung about the neck of the bird-thing! It was intelligent! That or tame, I assumed. Anyway, it clinched my decision. I pulled out my automatic and fired into what I could see of its antagonist.

"There was a flurry of tentacles and a spurt of black corruption, and then the thing, with a disgusting sucking noise, pulled itself and its arms into a hole in the ground. The other let out a series of clacks, staggered around on legs about as thick as golf sticks, and turned suddenly to face me. I held my weapon ready, and the two of us stared at each other.

"The Martian wasn't a bird, really. It wasn't even bird-like, except just at first glance. It had a beak all right, and a few feathery appendages, but the beak wasn't really a beak. It was somewhat flexible; I could see the tip bend slowly from side to side; it was almost like a cross between a beak and a trunk. It had four-toed feet, and four-fingered things—hands, you'd have to call them, and a little roundish body, and a long neck ending in a tiny head—and that beak. It stood an inch or so taller than I, and—well, Putz saw it!"

The engineer nodded. "*Ja!* I saw!"

Jarvis continued. "So—we stared at each other. Finally the creature went into a series of clackings and twitterings and held out its hands toward me, empty. I took that as a gesture of friendship."

"Perhaps," suggested Harrison, "it looked at that nose of yours and thought you were its brother!"

"Huh! You can be funny without talking! Anyway, I put up my gun and said, 'Aw, don't mention it,' or something of the sort, and the thing came over and we were pals.

"By that time, the sun was pretty low and I knew that I'd better build a fire or get into my thermo-skin. I decided on the fire. I picked a spot at the base of the Thyle cliff, where the rock could reflect a little heat on my back. I started breaking off chunks of this desiccated Martian vegetation, and my companion caught the idea and brought in an armful. I reached for a match, but the Martian fished into his pouch and brought out something that looked like a glowing coal; one touch of it, and the fire was blazing—and you all know what a job we have starting a fire in this atmosphere!

"And that bag of his!" continued the narrator. "That was a manufactured article, my friends; press an end and she popped open—press the middle and she sealed so perfectly you couldn't see the line. Better than zippers.

"Well, we stared at the fire a while and I decided to attempt some sort of communication with the Martian. I pointed at myself and said 'Dick'; he caught the drift immediately, stretched a bony claw at me and repeated 'Tick.' Then I pointed at him, and he gave that whistle I called Tweel; I can't imitate his accent. Things were going smoothly; to emphasize the names, I repeated 'Dick,' and then, pointing at him, 'Tweel.'

"There we stuck! He gave some clacks that sounded negative, and said something like 'P-p-p-root.' And that was just the beginning; I was always 'Tick,' but as for him—part of the time he was 'Tweel,' and part of the time he was 'P-p-p-root,' and part of the time he was sixteen other noises!

"We just couldn't connect. I tried 'rock,' and I tried 'star,' and 'tree,' and 'fire,' and Lord knows what else, and try as I would, I couldn't get a single word! Nothing was the same for two successive minutes, and if that's a language, I'm an alchemist! Finally I gave it up and called him Tweel, and that seemed to do.

"But Tweel hung on to some of my words. He remembered a couple of them, which I suppose is a great achievement if you're used to a language you have to make up as you go along. But I couldn't get the hang of his talk; either I missed some subtle point or we just didn't *think* alike—and I rather believe the latter view.

"I've other reasons for believing that. After a while I gave up the language business, and tried mathematics. I scratched two plus two equals four on the ground, and demonstrated it with pebbles. Again Tweel caught the idea, and informed me that three plus three equals six. Once more we seemed to be getting somewhere.

"So, knowing that Tweel had at least a grammar school education, I drew a circle for the sun, pointing first at it, and then at the last glow of the sun. Then I sketched in Mercury, and Venus, and Mother Earth, and Mars, and finally, pointing to Mars, I swept my hand around in a sort of inclusive gesture to indicate that Mars was our current environment. I was working up to putting over the idea that my home was on the earth.

"Tweel understood my diagram all right. He poked his beak at it, and with a great deal of trilling and clucking, he added Deimos and Phobos to Mars, and then sketched in the earth's moon!

"Do you see what that proves? It proves that Tweel's race uses telescopes—that they're civilized!"

"Does not!" snapped Harrison. "The moon is visible from here as a fifth magnitude star. They could see its revolution with the naked eye."

"The moon, yes!" said Jarvis. "You've missed my point. Mercury isn't visible! And Tweel knew of Mercury because he placed the Moon at the *third* planet, not the second. If he didn't know Mercury, he'd put the earth second, and Mars third, instead of fourth! See?"

"Humph!" said Harrison.

"Anyway," proceeded Jarvis, "I went on with my lesson. Things were going smoothly, and it looked as if I could put the idea over. I pointed at the earth on my diagram, and then at myself, and then, to clinch it, I pointed to myself and then to the earth itself shining bright green almost at the zenith.

"Tweel set up such an excited clacking that I was certain he understood. He jumped up and down, and suddenly he pointed at himself and then at the sky, and then at himself and at the sky again. He pointed at his middle and then at Arcturus, at his head and then at Spica, at his feet and then at half a dozen stars, while I just gaped at him. Then, all of a sudden, he gave a tremendous leap. Man, what a hop! He shot straight up into the starlight, seventy-five feet if an inch! I saw him silhouetted against the sky, saw him turn and come down at me head first, and land smack on his beak like a javelin! There he stuck square in the center of my sun-circle in the sand—a bull's eye!"

"Nuts!" observed the captain. "Plain nuts!"

"That's what I thought, too! I just stared at him open-mouthed while he pulled his head out of the sand and stood up. Then I figured he'd missed my point, and I went through the whole blamed riga-marole again, and it ended the same way, with Tweel on his nose in the middle of my picture!"

"Maybe it's a religious rite," suggested Harrison.

"Maybe," said Jarvis dubiously. "Well, there we were. We could exchange ideas up to a certain point, and then—blooey! Something in us was different, unre-lated; I don't doubt that Tweel thought me just as screwy as I thought him. Our minds simply looked at the world from different viewpoints, and perhaps his viewpoint is as true as ours. But—we couldn't get together, that's all. Yet, in spite of all difficulties, I *liked* Tweel, and I have a queer certainty that he liked me."

"Nuts!" repeated the captain. "Just daffy!"

"Yeah? Wait and see. A couple of times I've thought that perhaps we—" He paused, and then resumed his narrative. "Anyway, I finally gave it up, and got into my thermo-skin to sleep. The fire hadn't kept me any too warm, but that damned sleeping bag did. Got stuffy five minutes after I closed myself in. I opened it a little and bingo! Some eighty-below-zero air hit my nose, and that's when I got this pleasant little frostbite to add to the bump I acquired during the crash of my rocket.

"I don't know what Tweel made of my sleeping. He sat around, but when I woke up, he was gone. I'd just crawled out of my bag, though, when I heard some twittering, and there he came, sailing down from that three-story Thyle cliff to alight on his beak beside me. I pointed to myself and toward the north, and he pointed at himself and toward the south, but when I loaded up and started away, he came along.

"Man, how he traveled! A hundred and fifty feet at a jump, sailing through the air stretched out like a spear, and landing on his beak. He seemed surprised at my plodding, but after a few moments he fell in beside me, only every few minutes he'd go into one of his leaps, and stick his nose into the sand a block ahead of me. Then he'd come shooting back at me; it made me nervous at first to see that beak of his coming at me like a spear, but he always ended in the sand at my side.

"So the two of us plugged along across the Mare Chronium. Same sort of place as this—same crazy plants and same little green biopods growing in the sand, or crawling out of your way. We talked—not that we understood each other, you know, but just for company. I sang songs, and I suspect Tweel did too; at least, some of his trillings and twitterings had a subtle sort of rhythm.

"Then, for variety, Tweel would display his smattering of English words. He'd point to an outcropping and say 'rock,' and point to a pebble and say it again; or he'd touch my arm and say 'Tick,' and then repeat it. He seemed terrifically amused that the same word meant the same thing twice in succession, or that the same word could apply to two different objects. It set me wondering if perhaps his language wasn't like the primitive speech of some earth people —you know, Captain, like the Negritoes, for instance, who haven't any generic words. No word for food or water or man—words for good food and bad food, or rain water and sea water, or strong man and weak man—but no names for general classes. They're too primitive to understand that rain water and sea water are just different aspects of the same thing. But that wasn't the case with Tweel; it was just that we were somehow mysteriously different—our minds were alien to each other. And yet—we *liked* each other!"

"Looney, that's all," remarked Harrison. "That's why you two were so fond of each other."

"Well, I like *you!*" countered Jarvis wickedly. "Anyway," he resumed, "don't get the idea that there was anything screwy about Tweel. In fact, I'm not so sure but that he couldn't teach our highly praised human intelligence a trick or two. Oh, he wasn't an intellectual superman, I guess; but don't overlook the point that he managed to understand a little of my mental workings, and I never even got a glimmering of his."

"Because he didn't have any!" suggested the captain, while Putz and Leroy blinked attentively.

"You can judge of that when I'm through," said Jarvis. "Well, we plugged along across the Mare Chronium all that day, and all the next. Mare

Chronium—Sea of Time! Say, I was willing to agree with Schiaparelli's name by the end of that march! Just that grey, endless plain of weird plants, and never a sign of any other life. It was so monotonous that I was even glad to see the desert of Xanthus toward the evening of the second day.

"I was fair worn out, but Tweel seemed as fresh as ever, for all I never saw him drink or eat. I think he could have crossed the Mare Chronium in a couple of hours with those block-long nose dives of his, but he stuck along with me. I offered him some water once or twice; he took the cup from me and sucked the liquid into his beak, and then carefully squirted it all back into the cup and gravely returned it.

"Just as we sighted Xanthus, or the cliffs that bounded it, one of those nasty sand clouds blew along, not as bad as the one we had here, but mean to travel against. I pulled the transparent flap of my thermo-skin bag across my face and managed pretty well, and I noticed that Tweel used some feathery appendages growing like a mustache at the base of his beak to cover his nostrils, and some similar fuzz to shield his eyes."

"He is a desert creature!" ejaculated the little biologist, Leroy.

"Huh? Why?"

"He drink no water—he is adapt' for sand storm—"

"Proves nothing! There's not enough water to waste anywhere on this desiccated pill called Mars. We'd call all of it desert on earth, you know." He paused. "Anyway, after the sand storm blew over, a little wind kept blowing in our faces, not strong enough to stir the sand. But suddenly things came drifting along from the Xanthus cliffs—small, transparent spheres, for all the world like glass tennis balls! But light—they were almost light enough to float even in this thin air—empty, too; at least, I cracked open a couple and nothing came out but a bad smell. I asked Tweel about them, but all he said was 'No, no, no,' which I took to mean that he knew nothing about them. So they went bouncing by like tumbleweeds, or like soap bubbles, and we plugged on toward Xanthus. Tweel pointed at one of the crystal balls once and said 'rock,' but I was too tired to argue with him. Later I discovered what he meant.

"We came to the bottom of the Xanthus cliffs finally, when there wasn't much daylight left. I decided to sleep on the plateau if possible; anything dangerous, I reasoned, would be more likely to prowl through the vegetation of the Mare Chronium than the sand of Xanthus. Not that I'd seen a single sign of menace, except the rope-armed black thing that had trapped Tweel, and apparently that didn't prowl at all, but lured its victims within reach. It couldn't lure me while I slept, especially as Tweel didn't seem to sleep at all, but simply sat patiently around all night. I wondered how the creature had managed to trap Tweel, but there wasn't any way of asking him. I found that out too, later; it's devilish!

"However, we were ambling around the base of the Xanthus barrier looking for an easy spot to climb. At least, I was. Tweel could have leaped it easily, for the cliffs were lower than Thyle—perhaps sixty feet. I found a place and started up, swearing at the water tank strapped to my back—it didn't bother me except when climbing—and suddenly I heard a sound that I thought I recognized!

"You know how deceptive sounds are in this thin

air. A shot sounds like the pop of a cork. But this sound was the drone of a rocket, and sure enough, there went our second auxiliary about ten miles to westward, between me and the sunset!"

"Vas me!" said Putz. "I hunt for you."

"Yeah; I knew that, but what good did it do me? I hung on to the cliff and yelled and waved with one hand. Tweel saw it too, and set up a trilling and twittering, leaping to the top of the barrier and then high into the air. And while I watched, the machine droned on into the shadows to the south.

"I scrambled to the top of the cliff. Tweel was still pointing and trilling excitedly, shooting up toward the sky and coming down head-on to stick upside down on his beak in the sand. I pointed toward the south and at myself, and he said, 'Yes—Yes—Yes'; but somehow I gathered that he thought the flying thing was a relative of mine, probably a parent. Perhaps I did his intellect an injustice; I think now that I did.

"I was bitterly disappointed by the failure to attract attention. I pulled out my thermo-skin bag and crawled into it, as the night chill was already apparent. Tweel stuck his beak into the sand and drew up his legs and arms and looked for all the world like one of those leafless shrubs out there. I think he stayed that way all night."

"Protective mimicry!" ejaculated Leroy. "See? He is desert creature!"

"In the morning," resumed Jarvis, "we started off again. We hadn't gone a hundred yards into Xanthus when I saw something queer! This is one thing Putz didn't photograph, I'll wager!

"There was a line of little pyramids—tiny ones, not

more than six inches high, stretching across Xanthus as far as I could see! Little buildings made of pygmy bricks, they were, hollow inside and truncated, or at least broken at the top and empty. I pointed at them and said 'What?' to Tweel, but he gave some negative twitters to indicate, I suppose, that he didn't know. So off we went, following the row of pyramids because they ran north, and I was going north.

"Man, we trailed that line for hours! After a while, I noticed another queer thing: they were getting larger. Same number of bricks in each one, but the bricks were larger.

"By noon they were shoulder high. I looked into a couple—all just the same, broken at the top and empty. I examined a brick or two as well; they were silica, and old as creation itself!"

"How you know?" asked Leroy.

"They were weathered—edges rounded. Silica doesn't weather easily even on earth, and in this climate—!"

"How old you think?"

"Fifty thousand—a hundred thousand years. How can I tell? The little ones we saw in the morning were older—perhaps ten times as old. Crumbling. How old would that make *them*? Half a million years? Who knows?" Jarvis paused a moment. "Well," he resumed, "we followed the line. Tweel pointed at them and said 'rock' once or twice, but he'd done that many times before. Besides, he was more or less right about these.

"I tried questioning him. I pointed at a pyramid and asked 'People?' and indicated the two of us. He set up a negative sort of clucking and said, 'No, no, no. No one-one-two. No two-two-four,' meanwhile rubbing his stomach. I just stared at him and he went through the business again. 'No one-one-two. No two-two-four.' I just gaped at him."

"That proves it!" exclaimed Harrison. "Nuts!"

"You think so?" queried Jarvis sardonically. "Well, I figured it out different! 'No one-one-two!' You don't get it, of course, do you?"

"Nope—nor do you!"

"I think I do! Tweel was using the few English words he knew to put over a very complex idea. What, let me ask, does mathematics make you think of?"

"Why—of astronomy. Or—or logic!"

"That's it! 'No one-one-two!' Tweel was telling me that the builders of the pyramids weren't people—or that they weren't intelligent, that they weren't reasoning creatures! Get it?"

"Huh! I'll be damned!"

"You probably will."

"Why," put in Leroy, "he rub his belly?"

"Why? Because, my dear biologist, that's where his brains are! Not in his tiny head—in his middle!"

"*C'est impossible!*"

"Not on Mars, it isn't! This flora and fauna aren't earthly; your biopods prove that!" Jarvis grinned and took up his narrative. "Anyway, we plugged along across Xanthus and in about the middle of the afternoon, something else queer happened. The pyramids ended."

"Ended!"

"Yeah; the queer part was that the last one—and now they were ten-footers—was capped! See? Whatever built it was still inside; we'd trailed 'em from their half-million-year-old origin to the present.

"Tweel and I noticed it about the same time. I yanked out my automatic (I had a clip of Boland explosive bullets in it) and Tweel, quick as a sleight-of-hand trick, snapped a queer little glass revolver out of his bag. It was much like our weapons, except that the grip was larger to accommodate his four-taloned hand. And we held our weapons ready while we sneaked up along the lines of empty pyramids.

"Tweel saw the movement first. The top tiers of bricks were heaving, shaking, and suddenly slid down the sides with a thin crash. And then—something—something was coming out!

"A long, silvery-grey arm appeared, dragging after it an armored body. Armored, I mean, with scales, silver-grey and dull-shining. The arm heaved the body out of the hole; the beast crashed to the sand.

"It was a nondescript creature—body like a big grey cask, arm and a sort of mouth-hole at one end; stiff, pointed tail at the other—and that's all. No other limbs, no eyes, ears, nose—nothing! The thing dragged itself a few yards, inserted its pointed tail in the sand, pushed itself upright, and just sat.

"Tweel and I watched it for ten minutes before it moved. Then, with a creaking and rustling like—oh, like crumpling stiff paper—its arm moved to the mouth-hole and out came a brick! The arm placed the brick carefully on the ground, and the thing was still again.

"Another ten minutes—another brick. Just one of Nature's bricklayers. I was about to slip away and move on when Tweel pointed at the thing and said 'rock'! I went 'huh?' and he said it again. Then, to the accompaniment of some of his trilling, he said, 'No—no—,' and gave two or three whistling breaths.

"Well, I got his meaning, for a wonder! I said, 'No breath?' and demonstrated the word. Tweel was ecstatic; he said, 'Yes, yes, yes! No, no, no breet!' Then he gave a leap and sailed out to land on his nose about one pace from the monster!

"I was startled, you can imagine! The arm was going up for a brick, and I expected to see Tweel caught and mangled, but—nothing happened! Tweel pounded on the creature, and the arm took the brick and placed it neatly beside the first. Tweel rapped on its body again, and said 'rock,' and I got up nerve enough to take a look myself.

"Tweel was right again. The creature *was* rock, and it didn't breathe!"

"How you know?" snapped Leroy, his black eyes blazing interest.

"Because I'm a chemist. The beast was made of silica! There must have been pure silicon in the sand, and it lived on that. Get it? We, and Tweel, and those plants out there, and even the biopods are *carbon* life; this thing lived by a different set of chemical reactions. It was silicon life!"

"*La vie silicieuse!*" shouted Leroy. "I have suspect, and now it is proof! I must go see! *Il faut que je—*"

"All right! All right!" said Jarvis. "You can go see. Anyhow, there the thing was, alive and yet not alive, moving every ten minutes, and then only to remove a brick. Those bricks were its waste matter. See, Frenchy? We're carbon, and our waste is carbon dioxide, and this thing is silicon, and *its* waste is silicon dioxide—silica. But silica is a solid, hence the bricks. And it builds itself in, and when it is covered, it moves over to a fresh place to start over. No wonder it creaked! A living creature half a million years old!"

"How you know how old?" Leroy was frantic.

"We trailed its pyramids from the beginning, didn't we? If this weren't the original pyramid builder, the series would have ended somewhere before we found him, wouldn't it?—ended and started over with the small ones. That's simple enough, isn't it?

"But he reproduces, or tries to. Before the third brick came out, there was a little rustle and out popped a whole stream of those little crystal balls. They're his spores, or eggs, or seeds—call 'em what you want. They went bouncing by across Xanthus just as they'd bounced by us back in the Mare Chronium. I've a hunch how they work, too—this is for your information, Leroy. I think the crystal shell of silica is no more than a protective covering, like an eggshell, and that the active principle is the smell inside. It's some sort of gas that attacks silicon, and if the shell is broken near a supply of that element, some reaction starts that ultimately develops into a beast like that one."

"You should try!" exclaimed the little Frenchman. "We must break one to see!"

"Yeah? Well, I did. I smashed a couple against the sand. Would you like to come back in ten thousand years to see if I planted some pyramid monsters? You'd most likely be able to tell by that time!" Jarvis paused and drew a deep breath. "Lord! That queer creature! Do you picture it? Blind, deaf, nerveless, brainless—just a mechanism, and yet—immortal! Bound to go on making bricks, building pyramids, as long as silicon and oxygen exist, and even afterwards it'll just stop. It won't be dead. If the accidents of a million years bring it its food again, there it'll be, ready to run again, while brains and civilizations are part of the past. A queer beast—yet I met a stranger one!"

"If you did, it must have been in your dreams!" growled Harrison.

"You're right!" said Jarvis soberly. "In a way, you're right. The dream-beast! That's the best name for it —and it's the most fiendish, terrifying creation one could imagine! More dangerous than a lion, more insidious than a snake!"

"Tell me!" begged Leroy. "I must go see!"

"Not *this* devil!" He paused again. "Well," he resumed, "Tweel and I left the pyramid creature and plowed along through Xanthus. I was tired and a little disheartened by Putz's failure to pick me up, and Tweel's trilling got on my nerves, as did his flying nosedives. So I just strode along without a word, hour after hour across that monotonous desert.

"Toward mid-afternoon we came in sight of a low dark line on the horizon. I knew what it was. It was a canal; I'd crossed it in the rocket and it meant that we were just one third of the way across Xanthus. Pleasant thought, wasn't it? And still, I was keeping up to schedule.

"We approached the canal slowly; I remembered that this one was bordered by a wide fringe of vegetation and that Mudheap City was on it.

"I was tired, as I said. I kept thinking of a good hot

meal, and then from that I jumped to reflections of how nice and home-like even Borneo would seem after this crazy planet, and from that, to thoughts of little old New York, and then to thinking about a girl I know there—Fancy Long. Know her?"

"Vision entertainer," said Harrison. "I've tuned her in. Nice blonde—dances and sings on the *Yerba Mate* hour."

"That's her," said Jarvis ungrammatically. "I know her pretty well—just friends, get me?—though she came down to see us off in the *Ares*. Well, I was thinking about her, feeling pretty lonesome, and all the time we were approaching that line of rubbery plants.

"And then—I said, 'What 'n Hell!' and stared. And there she was—Fancy Long, standing plain as day under one of those crack-brained trees, and smiling and waving just the way I remembered her when we left!"

"Now you're nuts, too!" observed the captain.

"Boy, I almost agreed with you! I stared and pinched myself and closed my eyes and then stared again—and every time, there was Fancy Long smiling and waving! Tweel saw something, too; he was trilling and clucking away, but I scarcely heard him. I was bounding toward her over the sand, too amazed even to ask myself questions.

"I wasn't twenty feet from her when Tweel caught me with one of his flying leaps. He grabbed my arm, yelling, 'No—no—no!' in his squeaky voice. I tried to shake him off—he was as light as if he were built of bamboo—but he dug his claws in and yelled. And finally some sort of sanity returned to me and I stopped less than ten feet from her. There she stood, looking as solid as Putz's head!"

"Vot?" said the engineer.

"She smiled and waved, and waved and smiled, and I stood there dumb as Leroy, while Tweel squeaked and chattered. I *knew* it couldn't be real, yet—there she was!

"Finally I said, 'Fancy! Fancy Long!' She just kept on smiling and waving, but looking as real as if I hadn't left her thirty-seven million miles away.

"Tweel had his glass pistol out, pointing it at her. I grabbed his arm, but he tried to push me away. He pointed at her and said, 'No breet! No breet!' and I understood that he meant that the Fancy Long thing wasn't alive. Man, my head was whirling!

"Still, it gave me the jitters to see him pointing his weapon at her. I don't know why I stood there watching him take careful aim, but I did. Then he squeezed the handle of his weapon; there was a little puff of steam, and Fancy Long was gone! And in her place was one of those writhing, black, rope-armed horrors like the one I'd saved Tweel from!

"The dream-beast! I stood there dizzy, watching it die while Tweel trilled and whistled. Finally he touched my arm, pointed at the twisting thing, and said, 'You one-one-two, he one-one-two.' After he'd repeated it eight or ten times, I got it. Do any of you?"

"*Oui!*" shrilled Leroy. "*Moi—je le comprends!* He mean you think of something, the beast he know, and you see it! *Un chien*—a hungry dog, he would see the big bone with meat! Or smell it—not?"

"Right!" said Jarvis. "The dream-beast uses its victim's longings and desires to trap its prey. The bird at nesting season would see its mate; the fox, prowling for its own prey, would see a helpless rabbit!"

"How he do?" queried Leroy.

"How do I know? How does a snake back on earth charm a bird into its very jaws? And aren't there deep-sea fish that lure their victims into their mouths? Lord!" Jarvis shuddered. "Do you see how insidious the monster is? We're warned now—but henceforth we can't trust even our eyes. You might see me—I might see one of you—and back of it may be nothing but another of those black horrors!"

"How'd your friend know?" asked the captain abruptly.

"Tweel? I wonder! Perhaps he was thinking of something that couldn't possibly have interested me, and when I started to run, he realized that I saw something different and was warned. Or perhaps the dream-beast can only project a single vision, and Tweel saw what I saw—or nothing. I couldn't ask him. But it's just another proof that his intelligence is equal to ours or greater."

"He's daffy, I tell you!" said Harrison. "What makes you think his intellect ranks with the human?"

"Plenty of things! First, the pyramid-beast. He hadn't seen one before; he said as much. Yet he recognized it as a dead-alive automaton of silicon."

"He could have heard of it," objected Harrison. "He lives around here, you know."

"Well how about the language? I couldn't pick up a single idea of his and he learned six or seven words of mine. And do you realize what complex ideas he put over with no more than those six or seven words? The pyramid-monster—the dream-beast! In a single phrase he told me that one was a harmless automaton and the other a deadly hypnotist. What about that?"

"Huh!" said the captain.

"*Huh* if you wish! Could you have done it knowing only six words of English? Could you go even further, as Tweel did, and tell me that another creature was of a sort of intelligence so different from ours that understanding was impossible—even more impossible than that between Tweel and me?"

"Eh? What was that?"

"Later. The point I'm making is that Tweel and his race are worthy of our friendship. Somewhere on Mars—and you'll find I'm right—is a civilization and culture equal to ours, and maybe more than equal. And communication is possible between them and us; Tweel proves that. It may take years of patient trial, for their minds are alien, but less alien than the next minds we encountered—if they *are* minds."

"The next ones? What next ones?"

"The people of the mud cities along the canals." Jarvis frowned, then resumed his narrative. "I thought the dream-beast and the silicon-monster were the strangest beings conceivable, but I was wrong. These creatures are still more alien, less understandable than either and far less comprehensible than Tweel, with whom friendship is possible, and even, by patience and concentration, the exchange of ideas.

"Well," he continued, "we left the dream-beast dying, dragging itself back into its hole, and we moved toward the canal. There was a carpet of that queer walking-grass scampering out of our way, and when we reached the bank, there was a yellow trickle of water flowing. The mound city I'd noticed from the rocket was a mile or so to the right and I was curious enough to want to take a look at it.

"It had seemed deserted from my previous glimpse of it, and if any creatures were lurking in it—well, Tweel and I were both armed. And by the way, that crystal weapon of Tweel's was an interesting device; I took a look at it after the dream-beast episode. It fired a little glass splinter, poisoned, I suppose, and I guess it held at least a hundred of 'em to a load. The propellant was steam—just plain steam!"

"Shteam!" echoed Putz. "From vot come, shteam?"

"From water, of course! You could see the water through the transparent handle and about a gill of another liquid, thick and yellowish. When Tweel squeezed the handle—there was no trigger—a drop of water and a drop of the yellow stuff squirted into the firing chamber, and the water vaporized—pop! —like that. It's not so difficult; I think we could develop the same principle. Concentrated sulphuric acid will heat water almost to boiling, and so will quicklime, and there's potassium and sodium—

"Of course, his weapon hadn't the range of mine, but it wasn't so bad in this thin air, and it *did* hold as many shots as a cowboy's gun in a Western movie. It was effective, too, at least against Martian life; I tried it out, aiming at one of the crazy plants, and darned if the plant didn't wither up and fall apart! That's why I think the glass splinters were poisoned.

"Anyway, we trudged along toward the mud-heap city and I began to wonder whether the city builders dug the canals. I pointed to the city and then at the canal, and Tweel said 'No—no—no!" and gestured toward the south. I took it to mean that some other race had created the canal system, perhaps Tweel's people. I don't know; maybe there's still another intelligent race on the planet, or a dozen others. Mars is a queer little world.

"A hundred yards from the city we crossed a sort of road—just a hard-packed mud trail, and then, all of a sudden, along came one of the mound builders!

"Man, talk about fantastic beings! It looked rather like a barrel trotting along on four legs with four other arms or tentacles. It had no head, just body and members and a row of eyes completely around it. The top end of the barrel-body was a diaphragm stretched as tight as a drum head, and that was all. It was pushing a little coppery cart and tore right past us like the proverbial bat out of Hell. It didn't even notice us, although I thought the eyes on my side shifted a little as it passed.

"A moment later another came along, pushing another empty cart. Same thing—it just scooted past us. Well, I wasn't going to be ignored by a bunch of barrels playing train, so when the third one approached, I planted myself in the way—ready to jump, of course, if the thing didn't stop.

"But it did. It stopped and set up a sort of drumming from the diaphragm on top. And I held out both hands and said, 'We are friends!' And what do you suppose the thing did?"

"Said, 'Pleased to meet you,' I'll bet!" suggested Harrison.

"I couldn't have been more surprised if it had! It drummed on its diaphragm, and then suddenly boomed out, 'We are v-r-r-riends!' and gave its pushcart a vicious poke at me! I jumped aside, and away it went while I stared dumbly after it.

"A minute later another one came hurrying along. This one didn't pause, but simply drummed out, 'We are v-r-r-riends!' and scurried by. How did it learn the phrase? Were all the creatures in some sort of communication with each other? Were they all part of some central organism? I don't know, though I think Tweel does.

"Anyway, the creatures went sailing past us, every one greeting us with the same statement. It got to be funny; I never thought to find so many friends on this God-forsaken ball! Finally I made a puzzled gesture to Tweel; I guess he understood, for he said, 'One-one-two—yes!—two-two-four—no!' Get it?"

"Sure," said Harrison. "It's a Martian nursery rhyme."

"Yeah! Well, I was getting used to Tweel's symbolism, and I figured it out this way. 'One-one-two—yes!' The creatures were intelligent. 'Two-two-four—no!' Their intelligence was not of our order, but something different and beyond the logic of two and two is four. Maybe I missed his meaning. Perhaps he meant that their minds were of low degree, able to figure out simple things—'One-one-two—yes!'—but not more difficult things—'Two-two-four—no!' But I think from what we saw later that he meant the other.

"After a few moments, the creatures came rushing back—first one, then another. Their pushcarts were full of stones, sand, chunks of rubbery plants, and such rubbish as that. They droned out their friendly greeting, which didn't really sound so friendly, and dashed on. The third one I assumed to be my first acquaintance and I decided to have another chat with him. I stepped into his path again and waited.

"Up he came, booming out his 'We are v-r-r-riends' and stopped. I looked at him; four or five of his eyes looked at me. He tried his password again and gave a shove on his cart, but I stood firm. And then the— the dashed creature reached out one of his arms, and two finger-like nippers tweaked my nose!"

"Haw!" roared Harrison. "Maybe the things have a sense of beauty!"

"Laugh!" grumbled Jarvis. "I'd already had a nasty bump and a mean frostbite on that nose. Anyway, I yelled 'Ouch!' and jumped aside and the creature dashed away; but from then on, their greeting was 'We are v-r-r-riends! Ouch!' Queer beasts!

"Tweel and I followed the road squarely up to the nearest mound. The creatures were coming and going, paying us not the slightest attention, fetching their loads of rubbish. The road simply dived into an opening, and slanted down like an old mine, and in and out darted the barrel-people, greeting us with their eternal phrase.

"I looked in; there was a light somewhere below, and I was curious to see it. It didn't look like a flame or torch, you understand, but more like a civilized light, and I thought that I might get some clue as to the creatures' development. So in I went and Tweel tagged along, not without a few trills and twitters, however.

"The light was curious; it sputtered and flared like an old arc light, but came from a single black rod set in the wall of the corridor. It was electric, beyond doubt. The creatures were fairly civilized, apparently.

"Then I saw another light shining on something that glittered and I went on to look at that, but it was only a heap of shiny sand. I turned toward the entrance to leave, and the Devil take me if it wasn't gone!

"I suppose the corridor had curved, or I'd stepped into a side passage. Anyway, I walked back in that direction I thought we'd come, and all I saw was more dim-lit corridor. The place was a labyrinth! There was nothing but twisting passages running every way, lit by occasional lights, and now and then a creature running by, sometimes with a pushcart, sometimes without.

"Well, I wasn't much worried at first. Tweel and I had only come a few steps from the entrance. But every move we made after that seemed to get us in deeper. Finally, I tried following one of the creatures with an empty cart, thinking he'd be going out for his rubbish, but he ran around aimlessly, into one passage and out another. When he started dashing around a pillar like one of these Japanese waltzing mice, I gave up, dumped my water tank on the floor, and sat down.

"Tweel was as lost as I. I pointed up and he said 'No—no—no!' in a sort of helpless trill. And we couldn't get any help from the natives. They paid no attention at all, except to assure us they were friends—ouch!

"Lord! I don't know how many hours or days we wandered around there! I slept twice from sheer exhaustion; Tweel never seemed to need sleep. We tried following only the upward corridors, but they'd run uphill a ways and then curve downwards. The temperature in that damned ant hill was constant; you couldn't tell night from day, and after my first sleep I didn't know whether I'd slept one hour or thirteen, so I couldn't tell from my watch whether it was midnight or noon.

"We saw plenty of strange things. There were machines running in some of the corridors, but they didn't seem to be doing anything—just wheels turning. And several times I saw two barrel-beasts with a little one growing between them, joined to both."

"Parthenogenesis!" exulted Leroy. "Parthenogenesis by budding like *les tulipes!*"

"If you say so, Frenchy," agreed Jarvis. "The things never noticed us at all, except, as I say, to greet us with 'We are v-r-r-riends! Ouch!' They seemed to have no home-life of any sort, but just scurried around with their pushcarts, bringing in rubbish. And finally I discovered what they did with it.

"We'd had a little luck with a corridor, one that slanted upwards for a great distance. I was feeling that we ought to be close to the surface when suddenly the passage debouched into a domed chamber the only one we'd seen. And man!—I felt like dancing when I saw what looked like daylight through a crevice in the roof.

"There was a—a sort of machine in the chamber, just an enormous wheel that turned slowly, and one of the creatures was in the act of dumping his rubbish below it. The wheel ground it with a crunch—sand, stones, plants, all into powder that sifted away somewhere. While we watched, others filed in, repeating the process, and that seemed to be all. No rhyme nor reason to the whole thing—but that's characteristic of this crazy planet. And there was another fact that's almost too bizarre to believe.

"One of the creatures, having dumped his load, pushed his cart aside with a crash and calmly shoved himself under the wheel! I watched him being crushed, too stupefied to make a sound, and a moment later, another followed him! They were perfectly methodical about it, too; one of the cartless creatures took the abandoned pushcart.

"Tweel didn't seem surprised; I pointed out the next suicide to him, and he just gave the most human-like shrug imaginable, as much as to say, 'What can I do about it?' He must have known more or less about these creatures.

"Then I saw something else. There was something beyond the wheel, something shining on a sort of low pedestal. I walked over; there was a little crystal about the size of an egg, fluorescing to beat Tophet. The light from it stung my hands and face, almost like a static discharge, and then I noticed another funny thing. Remember that wart I had on my left thumb? Look!" Jarvis extended his hand. "It dried up and fell off—just like that! And my abused nose— say, the pain went out of it like magic! The thing had the property of hard x-rays or gamma radiations, only more so; it destroyed diseased tissue and left healthy tissue unharmed!

"I was thinking what a present *that'd* be to take back to Mother Earth when a lot of racket interrupted. We dashed back to the other side of the wheel in time to see one of the pushcarts ground up. Some suicide had been careless, it seems.

"Then suddenly the creatures were booming and

drumming all around us and their noise was decidedly menacing. A crowd of them advanced toward us; we backed out of what I thought was the passage we'd entered by, and they came rumbling after us, some pushing carts and some not. Crazy brutes! There was a whole chorus of 'We are v-r-r-riends! Ouch!' I didn't like the 'ouch'; it was rather suggestive.

"Tweel had his glass gun out and I dumped my water tank for greater freedom and got mine. We backed up the corridor with the barrel-beasts following—about twenty of them. Queer thing—the ones coming in with loaded carts moved past us inches away without a sign.

"Tweel must have noticed that. Suddenly, he snatched out that glowing coal cigar-lighter of his and touched a cart-load of plant limbs. Puff! The whole load was burning—and the crazy beast pushing it went right along without a change of pace! It created some disturbance among our 'v-r-r-riends,' however—and then I noticed the smoke eddying and swirling past us, and sure enough, there was the entrance!

"I grabbed Tweel and out we dashed and after us our twenty pursuers. The daylight felt like Heaven, though I saw at first glance that the sun was all but set, and that was bad, since I couldn't live outside my thermo-skin bag in a Martian night—at least, without a fire.

"And things got worse in a hurry. They cornered us in an angle between two mounds, and there we stood. I hadn't fired nor had Tweel; there wasn't any use in irritating the brutes. They stopped a little distance away and began their booming about friendship and ouches.

"Then things got still worse! A barrel-brute came out with a pushcart and they all grabbed into it and came out with handfuls of foot-long copper darts —sharp-looking ones—and all of a sudden one sailed past my ear—zing! And it was shoot or die then.

"We were doing pretty well for a while. We picked off the ones next to the pushcart and managed to keep the darts at a minimum, but suddenly there was a thunderous booming of 'v-r-r-riends' and 'ouches,' and a whole army of 'em came out of their hole.

"Man! We were through and I knew it! Then I realized that Tweel wasn't. He could have leaped the mound behind us as easily as not. He was staying for me!

"Say, I could have cried if there'd been time! I'd liked Tweel from the first, but whether I'd have had gratitude to do what he was doing—suppose I *had* saved him from the first dream-beast—he'd done as much for me, hadn't he? I grabbed his arm, and said 'Tweel,' and pointed up, and he understood. He said, 'No—no—no, Tick!' and popped away with his glass pistol.

"What could I do? I'd be a goner anyway when the sun set, but I couldn't explain that to him. I said, 'Thanks, Tweel. You're a man!' and felt that I wasn't paying him any compliment at all. A man! There are mighty few men who'd do that.

"So I went 'bang' with my gun and Tweel went 'puff' with his, and the barrels were throwing darts and getting ready to rush us, and booming about being friends. I had given up hope. Then suddenly an angel dropped right down from Heaven in the shape of Putz, with his under-jets blasting the barrels into very small pieces!

"Wow! I let out a yell and dashed for the rocket; Putz opened the door and in I went, laughing and crying and shouting! It was a moment or so before I remembered Tweel; I looked around in time to see him rising in one of his nose dives over the mound and away.

"I had a devil of a job arguing Putz into following! By the time we got the rocket aloft, darkness was down; you know how it comes here—like turning off a light. We sailed out over the desert and put down once or twice. I yelled 'Tweel!' and yelled it a hundred times, I guess. We couldn't find him; he could travel like the wind and all I got—or else I imagined it— was a faint trilling and twittering drifting out of the south. He'd gone, and damn it! I wish—I wish he hadn't!"

The four men of the *Ares* were silent—even the sardonic Harrison. At last little Leroy broke the stillness.

"I should like to see," he murmured.

"Yeah," said Harrison. "And the wart-cure. Too bad you missed that; it might be the cancer cure they've been hunting for a century and a half."

"Oh, that!" muttered Jarvis gloomily. "That's what started the fight!" He drew a glistening object from his pocket.

"Here it is."

The Sheriff of Canyon Gulch

BY POUL ANDERSON AND GORDON R. DICKSON

Don't be fooled by the title of this one. It may sound like bang-bang horse opera, and in a sense it is, but it's also science fiction of the purest sort. When it first appeared in 1951, it introduced the science-fiction world to the critters known as "hokas," who aren't human but who would very much like to be. Five hoka adventures followed, and eventually the whole series was gathered into a single volume, Earthman's Burden.

The authors are two of science fiction's best-known figures, who were neighbors in Minnesota when they began work on the hoka stories. Poul Anderson, who has since deserted the frozen northlands for sunny California, is a three-time Hugo winner, celebrated for such novels as The High Crusade *and* Brain Wave. *Gordon Dickson, still a Minneapolitan, won a Hugo for his novella "Soldier, Ask Not," and a Nebula for his short story "Call Him Lord." He is a past president of the Science Fiction Writers of America.*

143

It had been a very near thing. Alexander Jones spent several minutes enjoying the simple pleasure of still being alive.

Then he looked around.

It could almost have been Earth—almost, indeed, his own North America. He stood on a great prairie whose dun grasses rolled away beneath a high windy sky. A flock of birds, alarmed by his descent, clamored upward; they were not so very different from the birds he knew. A line of trees marked the river, a dying puff of steam the final berth of his scoutboat. In the hazy eastern distance he saw dim blue hills. Beyond those, he knew, were the mountains, and then the enormous dark forests, and finally the sea near which the *Draco* lay. A hell of a long ways to travel.

Nevertheless, he was uninjured, and on a planet almost the twin of his own. The air, gravity, biochemistry, the late-afternoon sun, could only be told from those of home with sensitive instruments. The rotational period was approximately 24 hours, the sidereal year nearly 12 months, the axial tilt a neat but not gaudy 11½ degrees. The fact that two small moons were in the sky and a third lurking somewhere else, that the continental outlines were an alien scrawl, that a snake coiled on a nearby rock had wings, that he was about five hundred light-years from the Solar System—all this was mere detail. The veriest bagatelle. Alex laughed at it.

The noise jarred so loud in this emptiness that he decided a decorous silence was more appropriate to his status as an officer and, by Act of Parliament as ratified locally by the United States Senate, a gentleman. Therefore he straightened his high-collared blue naval tunic, ran a nervous hand down the creases of his white naval trousers, buffed his shining naval boots on the spilled-out naval parachute, and reached for his emergency kit.

He neglected to comb his rumpled brown hair, and his lanky form did not exactly snap to attention. But he was, after all, quite alone.

Not that he intended to remain in that possibly estimable condition. He shrugged the heavy pack-sack off his shoulders. It had been the only thing he grabbed besides the parachute when his boat failed, and the only thing he really needed. His hands fumbled it open and he reached in for the small but powerful radio which would bring help.

He drew out a book.

It looked unfamiliar, somehow . . . had they issued a new set of instructions since he was in boot camp? He opened it, looking for the section on Radios, Emergency, Use of. He read the first page he turned to:

"—apparently incredibly fortunate historical development was, of course, quite logical. The relative decline in politico-economic influence of the Northern Hemisphere during the later twentieth century, the shift of civilized dominance to a Southeast Asia–Indian Ocean region with more resources, did not, as alarmists at the time predicted, spell the end of Western civilization. Rather did it spell an upsurge of Anglo-Saxon democratic and libertarian influence, for the simple reason that this area, which now held the purse strings of Earth, was in turn primarily led by Australia and New Zealand, which nations retained their primordial loyalty to the British

Crown. The consequent renascence and renewed growth of the British Commonwealth of Nations, the shaping of its councils into a truly world—even interplanetary—government, climaxed as it was by the American Accession, has naturally tended to fix Western culture, even in small details of everyday life, in the mold of that particular time, a tendency which was accentuated by the unexpectedly early invention of the faster-than-light secondary drive and repeated contact with truly different mentalities, and has produced in the Solar System a social stability which our forefathers would have considered positively Utopian and which the Service, working through the Interbeing League, has as its goal to bring to all sentient races—"

"*Guk!*" said Alex.

He snapped the book shut. Its title leered up at him:

EMPLOYEES' ORIENTATION MANUAL
by Adalbert Parr, Chief Control Commissioner
Cultural Development Service
Foreign Ministry of the United Commonwealths
League City, N.Z., Sol III

"Oh, no!" said Alex.

Frantically, he pawed through the pack. There *must* be a radio . . . a ray thrower . . . a compass . . . one little can of beans?

He extracted some five thousand tightly bundled copies of CDS Form J-16-LKR, to be filled out in quadruplicate by applicant and submitted with attached Forms G-776802 and W-2-ZGU.

Alex's snub-nosed face sagged open. His blue eyes revolved incredulously. There followed a long, dreadful moment in which he could only think how utterly useless the English language was when it came to describing issue-room clerks.

"Oh, hell," said Alexander Jones.

He got up and began to walk.

He woke slowly with the sunrise and lay there for a while wishing he hadn't. A long hike on an empty stomach followed by an uneasy attempt to sleep on the ground, plus the prospect of several thousand kilometers of the same, is not conducive to joy. And those animals, whatever they were, that had been yipping and howling all night sounded so damnably *hungry.*

"He looks human."

"Yeah. But he ain't dressed like no human."

Alex opened his eyes with a wild surmise. The drawling voices spoke . . . English!

He closed his eyes again, immediately. "No," he groaned.

"He's awake, Tex." The voices were high-pitched, slightly unreal. Alex curled up into the embryonic position and reflected on the peculiar horror of a squeaky drawl.

"Yeah. Git up, stranger. These hyar parts ain't healthy right now, nohow."

"No," gibbered Alex. "Tell me it isn't so. Tell me I've gone crazy, but deliver me from its being real!"

"I dunno." The voice was uncertain. "He don't talk like no human."

Alex decided there was no point in wishing them

out of existence. They looked harmless, anyway—to
everything except his sanity. He crawled to his feet,
his bones seeming to grate against each other, and
faced the natives.

The first expedition, he remembered, had reported
two intelligent races, Hokas and Slissii, on this planet.
And these must be Hokas. For small blessings, give
praises! There were two of them, almost identical to
the untrained Terrestrial eye: about a meter tall,
tubby and golden-furred, with round blunt-muzzled
heads and small black eyes. Except for the stubby-
fingered hands, they resembled nothing so much as
giant teddy bears.

The first expedition had, however, said nothing
about their speaking English with a drawl. Or about
their wearing the dress of Earth's nineteenth-century
West.

All the American historical stereofilms he had ever
seen gabbled in Alex's mind as he assessed their costumes. They wore—let's see, start at the top and work
down and try to keep your reason in the process—
ten-gallon hats with brims wider than their own
shoulders, tremendous red bandanas, checked shirts
of riotous hues, levis, enormously flaring chaps, and
high-heeled boots with outsize spurs. Two sagging
cartridge belts on each plump waist supported heavy
Colt six-shooters which almost dragged on the ground.

One of the natives was standing before the Earthman, the other was mounted nearby, holding the
reins of the first one's—well—his animal. The beasts
were about the size of a pony, and had four hoofed
feet . . . also whiplike tails, long necks with beaked
heads, and scaly green hides. But of course, thought

Alex wildly, of course they bore Western saddles with lassos at the horns. Of course. Who ever heard of a cowboy without a lasso?

"Wa'l, I see yo're awake," said the standing Hoka. "Howdy, stranger, howdy." He extended his hand. "I'm Tex and my pardner here is Monty."

"Pleased to meet you," mumbled Alex, shaking hands in a dreamlike fashion. "I'm Alexander Jones."

"I dunno," said Monty dubiously. "He ain't named like no human."

"Are yo' human, Alexanderjones?" asked Tex.

The spaceman got a firm grip on himself and said, spacing his words with care: "I am Ensign Alexander Jones of the Terrestrial Interstellar Survey Service, attached to HMS *Draco*." Now it was the Hokas who looked lost. He added wearily: "In other words, I'm from Earth. I'm human. Satisfied?"

"I s'pose," said Monty, still doubtful. "But we'd better take yo' back to town with us an' let Slick talk to yo'. He'll know more about it. Cain't take no chances in these hyar times."

"Why not?" said Tex, with a surprising bitterness. "What we got to lose, anyhow? But come on, Alexanderjones, we'll go on to town. We shore don't want to be found by no Injun war parties."

"Injuns?" asked Alex.

"Shore. They're comin', you know. We'd better sashay along. My pony'll carry double."

Alex was not especially happy at riding a nervous reptile in a saddle built for a Hoka. Fortunately, the race was sufficiently broad in the beam for their seats to have spare room for a slim Earthman. The "pony" trotted ahead at a surprisingly fast and steady pace.

Reptiles on Toka—so-called by the first expedition from the word for "earth" in the language of the most advanced Hoka society—seemed to be more highly evolved than in the Solar System. A fully developed four-chambered heart and a better nervous system made them almost equivalent to mammals.

Nevertheless, the creature stank.

Alex looked around. The prairie was just as big and bare, his ship just as far away.

" 'Tain't none o' my business, I reckon," said Tex, "but how'd yo' happen to be hyar?"

"It's a long story," said Alex absentmindedly. His thoughts at the moment were chiefly about food. "The *Draco* was out on Survey, mapping new planetary systems, and our course happened to take us close to this star, your sun, which we knew had been visited once before. We thought we'd look in and check on conditions, as well as resting ourselves on an Earth-type world. I was one of the several who went out in scout-boats to skim over this continent. Something went wrong, my engines failed and I barely escaped with my life. I parachuted out, and as bad luck would have it, my boat crashed in a river. So—well—due to various other circumstances, I just had to start hiking back toward my ship."

"Won't yore pardners come after yo'?"

"Sure, they'll search—but how likely are they to find a shattered wreck on the bottom of a river, with half a continent to investigate? I could, perhaps have grubbed a big SOS in the soil and hoped it would be seen from the air, but what with the necessity of hunting food and all . . . well, I figured my best chance was to keep moving. But now I'm hungry enough to eat a . . . a buffalo."

"Ain't likely to have buffalo meat in town," said the Hoka imperturbably. "But we got good T-bone steaks."

"Oh," said Alex.

"Yo' wouldn't'a lasted long, hoofin' it," said Monty. "Ain't got no gun."

"No, thanks to—never mind!" said Alex. "I thought I'd try to make a bow and some arrows."

"Bow an' arrers—Say!" Monty squinted suspiciously at him. "What yo' been doin' around the Injuns?"

"I ain't—I haven't been near any Injuns, dammit!"

"Bows an' arrers is Injun weapons, stranger."

"I wish they was," mourned Tex. "We didn't have no trouble back when only Hokas had six-guns. But now the Injuns got 'em too, it's all up with us." A tear trickled down his button nose.

If the cowboys are teddy bears, thought Alex, *then who—or what—are the Indians?*

"It's lucky for yo' me an' Tex happened to pass by," said Monty. "We was out to see if we couldn't round up a few more steers afore the Injuns get here. No such luck, though. The greenskins done rustled 'em all."

Greenskins! Alex remembered a detail in the report of the first expedition: two intelligent races, the mammalian Hokas and the reptilian Slissii. And the Slissii, being stronger and more warlike, preyed on the Hokas—

"Are the Injuns Slissii?" he asked.

"Wa'l, they're ornery, at least," said Monty.

"I mean . . . well . . . are they big tall beings, bigger

than I am, but walking sort of stooped over . . . tails and fangs and green skins, and their talk is full of hissing noises?"

"Why, shore. What else?" Monty shook his head, puzzled. "If yo're a human, how come yo' don't even know what a Injun is?"

They had been plop-plopping toward a large and noisy dust cloud. As they neared, Alex saw the cause, a giant herd of—uh—

"Longhorn steers," explained Monty.

Well . . . yes . . . one long horn apiece, on the snout. But at least the red-haired, short-legged, barrel-bodied "cattle" were mammals. Alex made out brands on the flanks of some. The entire herd was being urged along by fast-riding Hoka cowboys.

"That's the X Bar X outfit," said Tex. "The Lone Rider decided to try an' drive 'em ahead o' the Injuns. But I'm afeered the greenskins'll catch up with him purty soon."

"He cain't do much else," answered Monty. "All the ranchers, just about, are drivin' their stock off the range. There just ain't any place short o' the Devil's Nose whar we can make a stand. I shore don't intend tryin' to stay in town an' hold off the Injuns, an' I don't think nobody else does either, in spite o' Slick an' the Lone Rider wantin' us to."

"Hey," objected Alex. "I thought you said the, er, Lone Rider was fleeing. Now you say he wants to fight. Which is it?"

"Oh, the Lone Rider what owns the X Bar X is runnin', but the Lone Rider o' the Lazy T wants to stay. So do the Lone Rider o' Buffalo Stomp, the Really Lone Rider, an' the Loneliest Rider, but I'll bet they changes their minds when the Injuns gets as close to them as the varmints is to us right now."

Alex clutched his head to keep it from flying off his shoulders. "How many Lone Riders are there, anyway?" he shouted.

"How should I know?" shrugged Monty. "I knows at least ten myself. I gotta say," he added exasperatedly, "that English shore ain't got as many names as the old Hoka did. It gets gosh-awful tiresome to have a hundred other Montys around, or yell for Tex an' be asked which one."

They passed the bawling herd at a jog trot and topped a low rise. Beyond it lay a village, perhaps a dozen small frame houses and a single rutted street lined with square-built false-fronted structures. The place was jammed with Hokas—on foot, mounted, in covered wagons and buggies—refugees from the approaching Injuns, Alex decided. As he was carried down the hill, he saw a clumsily lettered sign:

WELCOME TO CANYON GULCH
Pop. Weekdays 212
Saturdays 1000

"We'll take yo' to Slick," said Monty above the hubbub. "He'll know what to do with yo'."

They forced their ponies slowly through the swirling, pressing, jabbering throng. The Hokas seemed to be a highly excitable race, given to arm-waving and shouting at the top of their lungs. There was no organization whatsoever to the evacuation, which proceeded slowly with its traffic tie-ups, arguments, gossip exchange, and exuberant pistol shooting into the air. Quite a few ponies and wagons stood deserted before the saloons, which formed an almost solid double row along the street.

Alex tried to remember what there had been in the report of the first expedition. It was a brief report, the ship had only been on Toka for a couple of months. But—yes—the Hokas were described as friendly, merry, amazingly quick to learn . . . and hopelessly inefficient. Only their walled seacoast towns, in a state of bronze-age technology, had been able to stand off the Slissii; otherwise the reptiles were slowly but steadily conquering the scattered ursinoid tribes. A Hoka fought bravely when he was attacked, but shoved all thought of the enemy out of his cheerful mind whenever the danger was not immediately visible. It never occurred to the Hokas to band to-gether in a massed offensive against the Slissii; such a race of individualists could never have formed an army anyway.

A nice, but rather ineffectual little people. Alex felt somewhat smug about his own height, his dashing spaceman's uniform, and the fighting, slugging, per-severing human spirit which had carried man out to the stars. He felt like an elder brother.

He'd have to do something about this situation, give these comic-opera creatures a hand. Which might also involve a promotion for Alexander Braithwaite Jones, since Earth wanted a plentiful supply of planets with friendly dominant species, and the first report on the Injuns—Slissii, blast it!—made it unlikely that they could ever get along with mankind.

A. Jones, hero. Maybe then Tanni and I can—

He grew aware that a fat, elderly Hoka was gaping

at him, together with the rest of Canyon Gulch. This particular one wore a large metal star pinned to his vest.

"Howdy, sheriff," said Tex, and snickered.

"Howdy, Tex, old pal," said the sheriff obsequiously. "An' my good old sidekick Monty too. Howdy, howdy, gents! Who's this hyar stranger—not a *human*?"

"Yep, that's what he says. Whar's Slick?"

"Which Slick?"

"*The* Slick, yo'—yo' sheriff!"

The fat Hoka winced. "I think he's in the backroom o' the Paradise Saloon," he said. And humbly: "Uh, Tex . . . Monty . . . yo'll remember yore old pal come *ee*-lection day, won't yo'?"

"Reckon we might," said Tex genially. "Yo' been sheriff long enough."

"Oh, thank yo', boys, thank yo'! If only the others will have yore kind hearts—" The eddying crowd swept the sheriff away.

"What off Earth?" exclaimed Alex. "What the *hell* was he trying to get you to do?"

"Vote ag'in him come the next *ee*-lection, o' course," said Monty.

"Against him? But the sheriff . . . he runs the town . . . maybe?"

Tex and Monty looked bewildered. "Now I really wonder if yo're human after all," said Tex. "Why, the humans themselves taught us the sheriff is the dumbest man in town. Only we don't think it's fair a man should have to be called that all his life, so we chooses him once a y'ar."

"Buck there has been *ee*-lected sheriff three times runnin'," said Monty. "He's *really* dumb!"

"But who is this Slick?" cried Alex a trifle wildly.

"The town gambler, o' course."

"What have I got to do with a town gambler?"

Tex and Monty exchanged glances. "Look, now," said Monty with strained patience, "we done allowed for a lot with yo'. But when yo' don't even know what the officer is what runs a town, that's goin' just a little too far."

"Oh," said Alex. "A kind of city manager, then."

"Yo're plumb loco," said Monty firmly. "*Ever'body* knows a town is run by a town gambler!"

Slick wore the uniform of his office: tight pants, a black coat, a checked vest, a white shirt with wing collar and string tie, a diamond stickpin, a Derringer in one pocket and a pack of cards in the other. He looked tired and harried; he must have been under a tremendous strain in the last few days, but he welcomed Alex with eager volubility and led him into an office furnished in vaguely nineteenth-century style. Tex and Monty came along, barring the door against the trailing, chattering crowds.

"We'll rustle up some sandwiches for yo'," beamed Slick. He offered Alex a vile purple cigar of some local weed, lit one himself, and sat down behind the rolltop desk. "Now," he said, "when can we get help from yore human friends?"

"Not soon, I'm afraid," said Alex. "The *Draco* crew doesn't know about this. They'll be spending all their time flying around in search of me. Unless they chance to find me here, which isn't likely, they won't even learn about the Injun war."

"How long they figger to be here?"

"Oh, they'll wait at least a month before giving me up for dead and leaving the planet."

"We can get yo' to the seacoast in that time, by hard ridin', but it'd mean takin' a shortcut through some territory which the Injuns is between us and it." Slick paused courteously while Alex untangled that one. "Yo'd hardly have a chance to sneak through. So, it looks like the only way we can get yo' to yore friends is to beat the Injuns. Only we can't beat the Injuns without help from yore friends."

Gloom.

To change the subject, Alex tried to learn some Hoka history. He succeeded beyond expectations, Slick proving surprisingly intelligent and well informed.

The first expedition had landed thirty-odd years ago. At the time, its report had drawn little Earthly interest; there were so many new planets in the vastness of the galaxy. Only now, with the *Draco* as a forerunner, was the League making any attempt to organize this frontier section of space.

The first Earthmen had been met with eager admiration by the Hoka tribe near whose village they landed. The autochthones were linguistic adepts, and between their natural abilities and modern psychography had learned English in a matter of days. To them, the humans were almost gods, though like most primitives they were willing to frolic with their deities.

Came the fatal evening. The expedition had set up an outdoor stereoscreen to entertain itself with films. Hitherto the Hokas had been interested but rather puzzled spectators. Now, tonight, at Wesley's insistence, an old film was reshown. It was a Western.

Most spacemen develop hobbies on their long voyages. Wesley's was the old American West. But he looked at it through romantic lenses, he had a huge stack of novels and magazines but very little factual material.

The Hokas saw the film and went wild.

The captain finally decided that their delirious, ecstatic reaction was due to this being something they could understand. Drawing-room comedies and interplanetary adventures meant little to them in terms of their own experience, but here was a country like their own, heroes who fought savage enemies, great herds of animals, gaudy costumes—

And it occurred to the captain and to Wesley that this race could find very practical use for certain elements of the old Western culture. The Hokas had been farmers, scratching a meager living out of prairie soil never meant to be plowed; they went about on foot, their tools were bronze and stone—they could do much better for themselves, given some help.

The ship's metallurgists had had no trouble reconstructing the old guns, Colt and Derringer and carbine. The Hokas had to be taught how to smelt iron, make steel and gunpowder, handle lathes and mills; but here again, native quickness and psychographic instruction combined to make them learn easily. Likewise they leaped at the concept of domesticating the wild beasts they had hitherto herded.

Before the ship left, Hokas were breaking "ponies" to the saddle and rounding up "longhorns." They were making treaties with the more civilized agricultural and maritime cities of the coast, arranging to ship meat in exchange for wood, grain, and manufactured goods. And they were gleefully slaughtering every Slissii warband that came against them.

As a final step, just before he left, Wesley gave his collection of books and magazines to the Hokas.

None of this had been in the ponderous official report Alex read: only the notation that the ursinoids had been shown steel metallurgy, the use of chemical weapons, and the benefits of certain economic forms. It had been hoped that with this aid they could subdue the dangerous Slissii, so that if man finally started coming here regularly, he wouldn't have a war on his hands.

Alex could fill in the rest. Hoka enthusiasm had run wild. The new way of life was, after all, very practical and well adapted to the plains—so why not go all the way, be just like the human godlings in every respect? Talk English with the stereofilm accent, adopt human names, human dress, human mannerisms, dissolve the old tribal organizations and replace them with ranches and towns—it followed very naturally. And it was so much more fun.

The books and magazines couldn't circulate far; most of the new gospel went by word of mouth. Thus certain oversimplifications crept in.

Three decades passed. The Hokas matured rapidly; a second generation which had been born to Western ways was already prominent in the population. The past was all but forgotten. The Hokas spread westward across the plains, driving the Slissii before them.

Until, of course, the Slissii learned how to make firearms too. Then, with their greater military talent, they raised an army of confederated tribes and proceeded to shove the Hokas back. This time they would probably continue till they had sacked the very cities of the coast. The bravery of individual Hokas was no match for superior numbers better organized.

And one of the Injun armies was now roaring down on Canyon Gulch. It could not be many kilometers away, and there was nothing to stop it. The Hokas gathered their families and belongings from the isolated ranch houses and fled. But with typical inefficiency, most of the refugees fled no further than this town; then they stopped and discussed whether to make a stand or hurry onward, and meanwhile they had just one more little drink. . . .

"You mean you haven't even *tried* to fight?" asked Alex.

"What could we do?" answered Slick. "Half the folks 'ud be ag'in the idea an' wouldn't have nothin' to do with it. Half o' those what did come would each have their own little scheme, an' when we didn't follow it they'd get mad an' walk off. That don't leave none too many."

"Couldn't you, as the leader, think of some compromise—some plan which would satisfy everybody?"

"O' course not," said Slick stiffly. "My own plan is the only right one."

"Oh, Lord!" Alex bit savagely at the sandwich in his hand. The food had restored his strength and the fluid fire the Hokas called whiskey had given him a warm, courageous glow.

"The basic trouble is, your people just don't know how to arrange a battle," he said. "Humans do."

"Yo're a powerful fightin' outfit," agreed Slick.

There was an adoration in his beady eyes which Alex had complacently noticed on most of the faces in town. He decided he rather liked it. But a demi-god has his obligations.

"What you need is a leader whom everyone will follow without question," he went on. "Namely me."

"Yo' mean—" Slick drew a sharp breath. "Yo'?"

Alex nodded briskly. "Am I right, that the Injuns are all on foot? Yes? Good. Then I know, from Earth history, what to do. There must be several thousand Hoka males around, and they all have some kind of firearms. The Injuns won't be prepared for a fast, tight cavalry charge. It'll split their army wide open."

"Wa'l, I'll be hornswoggled," murmured Slick. Even Tex and Monty looked properly awed.

Suddenly Slick began turning handsprings about the office. "Yahoo!" he cried. "I'm a rootin', tootin' son of a gun, I was born with a pistol in each hand an' I teethed on rattlesnakes!" He did a series of cartwheels. "My daddy was a catamount and my mother was a alligator. I can run faster backward than anybody else can run forrad, I can jump over the outermost moon with one hand tied behind me, I can fill an inside straight every time I draw, an' if any sidewinder here says it ain't so I'll fill him so full o' lead they'll mine him!"

"What the hell?" gasped Alex, dodging.

"The old human war-cry," explained Tex, who had apparently resigned himself to his hero's peculiar ignorances.

"Let's go!" whooped Slick, and threw open the office door. A tumultuous crowd surged outside. The gambler filled his lungs and roared squeakily:

"Saddle yore hosses, gents, an' load yore six-guns! We got us a human, an' he's gonna lead us all out to wipe the Injuns off the range!"

The Hokas cheered till the false fronts quivered around them, danced, somersaulted, and fired their guns into the air. Alex shook Slick and wailed: "—no, no, you bloody fool, not *now!* We have to study the situation, send out scouts, make a plan—"

Too late. His impetuous admirers swept him out into the street. He couldn't be heard above the falsetto din, he tried to keep his footing and was only vaguely aware of anything else. Someone gave him a six-shooter, he strapped it on as if in a dream. Someone else gave him a lasso, and he made out the voice: "Rope yoreself a bronc, Earthman, an' let's go!"

"Rope—" Alex grew groggily aware that there was a corral just behind the saloon. The half-wild reptile ponies galloped about inside it, excited by the noise. Hokas were deftly whirling their lariats forth to catch their personal mounts.

"Go ahead!" urged the voice. "Ain't got no time to lose."

Alex studied the cowboy nearest him. Lassoing didn't look so hard. You held the rope here and here, then you swung the noose around your head like *this—*

He pulled and came crashing to the ground. Through whirling dust, he saw that he had lassoed himself.

Tex pulled him to his feet and dusted him off. "I . . . I don't ride herd at home," he mumbled. Tex made no reply.

"I got a bronc for yo'," cried another Hoka, reeling in his lariat. "A real spirited mustang!"

Alex looked at the pony. It looked back. It had an evilly glittering little eye. At the risk of making a snap judgment, he decided he didn't like it very much. There might be personality conflicts between him and it.

"Come on, let's git goin'!" cried Slick impatiently. He was astraddle a beast which still bucked and reared, but he hardly seemed to notice.

Alex shuddered, closed his eyes, wondered what he had done to deserve this, and wobbled over to the pony. Several Hokas had joined to saddle it for him. He climbed aboard. The Hokas released the animal. There was a personality conflict.

Alex had a sudden feeling of rising and spinning on a meteor that twisted beneath him. He grabbed for the saddle horn. The front feet came down with a ten-gee thump and he lost his stirrups. Something on the order of a nuclear shell seemed to explode in his vicinity.

Though it came up and hit him with unnecessary hardness, he had never known anything so friendly as the ground just then.

"Oof!" said Alex and lay still.

A shocked, unbelieving silence fell on the Hokas. The human hadn't been able to use a rope—now he had set a new record for the shortest time in a saddle —*what sort of human was this, anyway?*

Alex sat up and looked into a ring of shocked fuzzy faces. He gave them a weak smile. "I'm not a horseman either," he said.

"What the hell are yo', then?" stormed Monty. "Yo' cain't rope, you cain't ride, yo' cain't talk right, yo' cain't shoot—"

"Now hold on!" Alex climbed to somewhat un-
steady feet. "I admit I'm not used to a lot of things
here, because we do it differently on Earth. But I can
out-shoot any man . . . er, any Hoka of you any day in
the week and twice on Sundays!"

Some of the natives looked happy again, but Monty
only sneered. "Yeah?"

"Yeah. I'll prove it." Alex looked about for a suit-
able target. For a change, he had no worries. He was
one of the best ray-thrower marksmen in the Fleet.
"Throw up a coin. I'll plug it through the middle."

The Hokas began looking awed. Alex gathered that
they weren't very good shots by any standards but
their own. Slick beamed, took a silver dollar from his
pocket, and spun it into the air. Alex drew and fired.

Unfortunately, ray-throwers don't have recoil. Re-
volvers do.

Alex went over on his back. The bullet broke a
window in the Last Chance Bar & Grill.

The Hokas began to laugh. It was a bitter kind of
merriment.

"Buck!" cried Slick. "Buck . . . yo' thar, sheriff . . .
c'mere!"

"Yes, sir, Mister Slick, sir?"

"I don't think we need yo' for sheriff no longer,
Buck. I think we just found ourselves another one.
Gimme yore badge!"

When Alex regained his feet, the star gleamed on
his tunic. And, of course, his proposed counterat-
tack had been forgotten.

He mooched glumly into Pizen's Saloon. During the
past few hours, the town had slowly drained itself of

refugees as the Injuns came horribly closer; but there were still a few delaying for one more drink. Alex was looking for such company.

Being official buffoon wasn't too bad in itself. The Hokas weren't cruel to those whom the gods had afflicted. But—well—he had just ruined human prestige on this continent. The Service wouldn't appreciate that.

Not that he would be seeing much of the Service in the near future. He couldn't possibly reach the *Draco* now before she left—without passing through territory held by the same Injuns whose army was advancing on Canyon Gulch. It might be years till another expedition landed. He might even be marooned here for life. Though come to think of it, that wouldn't be a lot worse than the disgrace which would attend his return.

Gloom.

"Here, sheriff, let me buy yo' a drink," said a voice at his elbow.

"Thanks," said Alex. The Hokas did have the pleasant rule that the sheriff was always treated when he entered a saloon. He had been taking heavy advantage of the custom, though it didn't seem to lighten his depression much.

The Hoka beside him was a very aged specimen, toothless and creaky. "I'm from Childish way," he introduced himself. "They call me the Childish Kid. Howdy, sheriff."

Alex shook hands, dully.

They elbowed their way to the bar. Alex had to stoop under Hoka ceilings, but otherwise the rococo fittings were earnestly faithful to their fictional prototypes—including a small stage where three scantily clad Hoka females were going through a song-and-dance number while a bespectacled male pounded a rickety piano.

The Childish Kid leered. "I know those gals," he sighed. "Some fillies, hey? Stacked, don't yo' think?"

"Uh . . . yes," agreed Alex. Hoka females had four mammaries apiece. "Quite."

"Zunami an' Goda an' Torigi, that's their names. If I warn't so danged old—"

"How come they have, er, non-English names?" inquired Alex.

"We had to keep the old Hoka names for our wimmin," said the Childish Kid. He scratched his balding head. "It's bad enough with the men, havin' a hundred Hopalongs in the same county . . . but how the hell can yo' tell yore wimmin apart when they're all named Jane?"

"We have some named 'Hey, you' as well," said Alex grimly. "And a lot more called 'Yes, dear.' "

His head was beginning to spin. This Hoka brew was potent stuff.

Nearby stood two cowboys, arguing with alcoholic loudness. They were typical Hokas, which meant that to Alex their tubby forms were scarcely to be distinguished from each other. "I know them two, they're from my old outfit," said the Childish Kid. "That one's Slim, an' t'other's Shorty."

"Oh," said Alex.

Brooding over his glass, he listened to the quarrel for lack of anything better to do. It had degenerated to the name-calling stage. "Careful what yo' say, Slim," said Shorty, trying to narrow his round little eyes. "I'm a powerful dangerous hombre."

"You ain't no powerful dangerous hombre," sneered Slim.

"I am so too a powerful dangerous hombre!" squeaked Shorty.

"Yo're a fathead what ought to be kicked by a jackass," said Slim, "an' I'm just the one what can do it."

"When yo' call me that," said Shorty, "smile!"

"I said yo're a fathead what ought to be kicked by a jackass," repeated Slim, and smiled.

Suddenly the saloon was full of the roar of pistols. Sheer reflex threw Alex to the floor. A ricocheting slug whanged nastily by his ear. The thunder barked again and again. He hugged the floor and prayed.

Silence came. Reeking smoke swirled through the air. Hokas crept from behind tables and the bar and resumed drinking, casually. Alex looked for the corpses. He saw only Slim and Shorty, putting away their emptied guns.

"Wa'l, that's that," said Shorty. "I'll buy this round."

"Thanks, pardner," said Slim. "I'll get the next one."

Alex bugged his eyes at the Childish Kid. "Nobody was hurt!" he chattered hysterically.

"O' course not," said the ancient Hoka. "Slim an' Shorty is old pals." He spread his hands. "Kind o' a funny human custom, that. It don't make much sense that every man should sling lead at every other man once a month. But I reckon maybe it makes 'em braver, huh?"

"Uh-huh," said Alex.

Others drifted over to talk with him. Opinion seemed about equally divided over whether he wasn't a human at all or whether humankind simply wasn't what the legends had cracked it up to be. But in spite of their disappointment, they bore him no ill will and stood him drinks. Alex accepted thirstily. He couldn't think of anything else to do.

It might have been an hour later, or two hours or ten, that Slick came into the saloon. His voice rose over the hubbub: "A scout just brung me the latest word, gents. The Injuns ain't no more'n five miles away an' comin' fast. We'll all have to git a move on."

The cowboys swallowed their drinks, smashed their glasses, and boiled from the building in a wave of excitement. "Gotta calm the boys down," muttered the Childish Kid, "or we could git a riot." With great presence of mind, he shot out the lights.

"Yo' fool!" bellowed Slick. "It's broad daylight outside!"

Alex lingered aimlessly by the saloon, until the gambler tugged at his sleeve. "We're short o' cowhands an' we got a big herd to move," ordered Slick. "Get yoreself a *gentle* pony an' see if yo' can help."

"Okay," hiccoughed Alex. It would be good to know he was doing something useful, however little. Maybe he would be defeated at the next election.

He traced a wavering course to the corral. Someone led forth a shambling wreck of a mount, too old to be anything but docile. Alex groped after the stirrup. It evaded him. "C'mere," he said sharply. "C'mere, shtirrup. Ten-*shun!* For'ard marsh!"

"Here yo' are." A Hoka who flickered around the edges . . . ghost Hoka? Hoka Superior? the Hoka after Hoka? . . . assisted him into the saddle. "By Pecos Bill, yo're drunk as a skunk!"

"No," said Alex. "I am shober. It's all Toka whish ish drunk. So only drunks on Toka ish shober. Tha's right. Y'unnershtan'? Only shober men on Toka ish uh drunks—"

His pony floated through a pink mist in some or other direction. "I'm a lo-o-o-one cowboy!" sang Alex. "I'm thuh loneliesh lone cowboy in these here parts."

He grew amorphously aware of the herd. The cattle were nervous, they rolled their eyes and lowed and pawed the ground. A small band of Hokas galloped around them, swearing, waving their hats, trying to get the animals going in the right path.

"I'm an ol' cowhand, from thuh Rio Grande!" bawled Alex.

"Not so loud!" snapped a Tex-Hoka. "These critters are spooky enough as it is."

"You wanna get 'em goin', don'cha?" answered Alex. "We gotta get going. The greenskins are coming. Simple to get going. Like this. See?"

He drew his six-shooter, fired into the air, and let out the loudest screech he had in him. "Yahoo!"

"*Yo' crazy fool!*"

"Yahoo!" Alex plunged toward the herd, shooting and shouting. "Ride 'em, cowboy! Get along, little dogies! Yippee!"

The herd, of course, stampeded.

Like a red tide, it suddenly broke past the thin Hoka line. The riders scattered, there was death in those thousands of hoofs, their universe was filled with roaring and rushing and thunder. The earth shook!

"Yahoo!" caroled Alexander Jones. He rode behind the longhorns, still shooting. "Git along, git along! Hi-yo, Silver!"

"Oh, my God," groaned Slick. "Oh, my God! The tumbleweed-headed idiot's got 'em stampeded *straight toward the Injuns—*"

"After 'em!" shouted a Hopalong-Hoka. "Mebbe we can still turn the herd! We cain't let the Injuns git all that beef!"

"An' we'll have a little necktie party, too," said a Lone Rider-Hoka. "I'll bet that thar Alexanderjones is a Injun spy planted to do this very job."

The cowboys spurred their mounts. A Hoka-brain had no room for two thoughts at once. If they were trying to head off a stampede, the fact that they were riding full tilt toward an overwhelming enemy simply did not occur to them.

"Whoopee-ti-yi yo-o-o-o!" warbled Alex, somewhere in the storm of dust.

Caught by the peculiar time-sense of intoxication, he seemed almost at once to burst over a long low hill. And beyond were the Slissii.

The reptile warriors went afoot, not being built for riding—but they could outrun a Hoka pony. Their tyrannosaurian forms were naked, save for war paint and feathers such as primitives throughout the galaxy wear, but they were armed with guns as well as lances, bows, and axes. Their host formed a great compact mass, tightly disciplined to the rhythm of the thudding signal drums. There were thousands of them . . . and a hundred cowboys, at most, galloped blindly toward their ranks.

Alex saw none of this. Being behind the stampede, he didn't see it hit the Injun army.

Nobody really did. The catastrophe was just too big.

When the Hokas arrived on the scene, the Injuns —such of them as had not simply been mashed flat —were scattered over the entire visible prairie. Slick wondered if they would ever stop running.

"At 'em, boys!" he yelled. "Go mop 'em up!"

The Hoka band sped forward. A few small Injun groups sounded their war-hisses and tried to rally for a stand, but it was too late, they were too demoralized, the Hokas cut them down. Others were chased as they fled, lassoed and hog-tied by wildly cheering teddy bears.

Presently Tex rode up to Slick. Dragging behind his pony at a lariat's end was a huge Injun, still struggling and cursing. "I think I got their chief," he reported.

The town gambler nodded happily. "Yep, you have. He's wearin' a high chief's paint. Swell! With him for a hostage, we can make t'other Injuns talk turkey— not that they're gonna bother this hyar country for a long time to come."

As a matter of fact, Canyon Gulch has entered the military textbooks with Cannae, Waterloo, and Xfisthgung as an example of total and crushing victory.

Slowly, the Hokas began to gather about Alex. The old utter awe shone in their eyes.

"*He* done it," whispered Monty. "All the time he was playin' dumb, he knew a way to stop the Injuns—"

"Yo' mean, make 'em bite the dust," corrected Slick solemnly.

"Bite the dust," agreed Monty. "He done it single-handed! Gents, I reckon we should'a knowed better'n to go mistrustin' o' a . . . *human!*"

Alex swayed in the saddle. A violent sickness gathered itself within him. And he reflected that he had caused a stampede, lost an entire herd of cattle, sacrificed all Hoka faith in the Terrestrial race for all time to come. If the natives hanged him, he thought grayly, it was no more than he deserved.

He opened his eyes and looked into Slick's adoring face.

"Yo' saved us," said the little Hoka. He reached out and took the sheriff's badge off Alex's tunic. Then, gravely, he handed over his Derringer and playing cards. "Yo' saved us all, human. So, as long as yo're here, yo're the town gambler o' Canyon Gulch."

Alex blinked. He looked around. He saw the assembled Hokas, and the captive Slissii, and the trampled field of ruin . . . why, why—they had won!

Now he could get to the *Draco*. With human assistance, the Hoka race could soon force a permanent peace settlement on their ancient foes. And Ensign Alexander Braithwaite Jones was a hero.

"Saved you?" he muttered. His tongue still wasn't under very close control. "Oh. Saved you. Yes, I did, didn't I? Saved you. Nice of me." He waved a hand. "No, no. Don't mention it. *Noblesse oblige,* and all that sort of thing."

An acute pain in his unaccustomed gluteal muscles spoiled the effect. He groaned. "I'm walking back to town. I won't be able to sit down for a week as it is!"

And the rescuer of Canyon Gulch dismounted, missed the stirrup, and fell flat on his face.

"Yo' know," murmured someone thoughtfully, "maybe that's the way humans get off their hosses. Maybe we should all—"

Drop Dead

By Clifford D. Simak

Cliff Simak is sometimes thought to belong to science fiction's "class of '39," that group of talented writers who emerged virtually simultaneously just before the Second World War. His stories appeared in the same magazine as theirs, he was just as popular with the readers as they were, and he went on to achieve the same sort of long-term fame. But actually Simak had been an established writer for half a dozen years before Messrs. Asimov, Heinlein, Sturgeon, de Camp & Co. came along. His first stories appeared back in 1932, a couple of years before the debut of Stanley G. Weinbaum.

As he has been for most of his life, Simak is today a Minneapolis newspaperman who writes science fiction in his spare time. He remains active in the field, producing a novel almost every year, and his contributions have been honored by his selection as guest of honor at the 1971 World Science Fiction Convention in Boston. Many of his stories have dealt with the problems of explorers on alien worlds—as, for instance, the one offered here.

173

The critters were unbelievable. They looked like something from the maudlin pen of a well-alco-holed cartoonist.

One herd of them clustered in a semicircle in front of the ship, not jittery or belligerent—just looking at us. And that was strange. Ordinarily, when a space-ship sets down on a virgin planet, it takes a week at least for any life that might have seen or heard it to creep out of hiding and sneak a look around.

The critters were almost cow-size, but nohow as graceful as a cow. Their bodies were pushed together as if every blessed one of them had run full-tilt into a wall. And they were just as lumpy as you'd expect from a collision like that. Their hides were splashed with large squares of pastel color—the kind of color one never finds on any self-respecting animal: violet, pink, orange, chartreuse, to name only a few. The overall effect was of a checkerboard done by an old lady who made crazy quilts.

And that, by far, was not the worst of it.

From their heads and other parts of their anatomy sprouted a weird sort of vegetation, so that it appeared each animal was hiding, somewhat ineffectively, be-hind a skimpy thicket. To compound the situation and make it completely insane, fruits and vegetables —or what *appeared* to be fruits and vegetables— grew from the vegetation.

So we stood there, the critters looking at us and we looking back at them, and finally one of them walked forward until it was no more than six feet from us. It stood there for a moment, gazing at us soulfully, then dropped dead at our feet.

The rest of the herd turned around and trotted awkwardly away, for all the world as if they had done what they had come to do and now could go about their business.

Julian Oliver, our botanist, put up a hand and rubbed his balding head with an absent-minded motion.

"Another whatisit coming up!" he moaned. "Why couldn't it, for once, be something plain and simple?"

"It never is," I told him. "Remember that bush out on Hamal V that spent half its life as a kind of glorified tomato and the other half as grade A poison ivy?"

"I remember it," Oliver said sadly.

Max Weber, our biologist, walked over to the critter, reached out a cautious foot and prodded it.

"Trouble is," he said, "that Hamal tomato was Julian's baby and this one here is mine."

"I wouldn't say entirely yours," Oliver retorted. "What do you call that underbrush growing out of it?"

I came in fast to head off an argument. I had listened to those two quarreling for the past twelve years, across several hundred light-years and on a couple dozen planets. I couldn't stop it here, I knew, but at least I could postpone it until they had something vital to quarrel about.

"Cut it out," I said. "It's only a couple of hours till nightfall and we have to get the camp set up."

"But this critter," Weber said. "We can't just leave it here."

"Why not? There are millions more of them. This one will stay right here and even if it doesn't—"

"But it dropped dead!"

"So it was old and feeble."

"It wasn't. It was right in the prime of life."

"We can talk about it later," said Alfred Kemper, our bacteriologist. "I'm as interested as you two, but what Bob says is right. We have to get the camp set up."

"Another thing," I added, looking hard at all of them. "No matter how innocent this place may look, we observe planet rules. No eating anything. No drinking any water. No wandering off alone. No carelessness of any kind."

"There's nothing here," said Weber. "Just the herds of critters. Just the endless plains. No trees, no hills, no nothing."

He really didn't mean it. He knew as well as I did the reason for observing planet rules. He only wanted to argue.

"All right," I said, "which is it? Do we set up camp or do we spend the night up in the ship?"

That did it.

We had the camp set up before the sun went down, and by dusk we were all settled in. Carl Parsons, our ecologist, had the stove together and the supper started before the last tent peg was driven.

I dug out my diet kit and mixed up my formula and all of them kidded me about it, the way they always did.

It didn't bother me. Their jibes were automatic and I had automatic answers. It was something that had been going on for a long, long time. Maybe it was best that way, better if they'd disregarded my enforced eating habits.

I remember Carl was grilling steaks and I had to move away so I couldn't smell them. There's never a time when I wouldn't give my good right arm for a steak or, to tell the truth, any other kind of normal chow. This diet stuff keeps a man alive all right, but that's about the only thing that can be said of it.

I know ulcers must sound silly and archaic. Ask any medic and he'll tell you they don't happen any more. But I have a riddled stomach and the diet kit to prove they sometimes do. I guess it's what you might call an occupational ailment. There's a lot of never-ending worry playing nursemaid to planet survey gangs.

After supper, we went out and dragged the critter in and had a closer look at it.

It was even worse to look at close than from a distance.

There was no fooling about that vegetation. It was the real McCoy and it was part and parcel of the critter. But it seemed that it only grew out of certain of the color blocks in the critter's body.

We found another thing that practically had Weber frothing at the mouth. One of the color blocks had holes in it—it looked almost exactly like one of those peg sets that children use as toys. When Weber took out his jackknife and poked into one of the holes, he pried out an insect that looked something like a bee. He couldn't quite believe it, so he did some more probing and in another one of the holes he found another bee. Both of the bees were dead.

He and Oliver wanted to start dissection then and there, but the rest of us managed to talk them out of it.

We pulled straws to see who would stand first guard and, with my usual luck, I pulled the shortest straw. Actually there wasn't much real reason for standing guard, with the alarm system set to protect the camp, but it was regulation—there had to be a guard.

I got a gun and the others said good night and went to their tents, but I could hear them talking for a long time afterward. No matter how hardened you may get to this survey business, no matter how blasé, you hardly ever get much sleep the first night on any planet.

I sat on a chair at one side of the camp table, on which burned a lantern in lieu of the campfire we would have had on any other planet. But here we couldn't have a fire because there wasn't any wood.

I sat at one side of the table, with the dead critter lying on the other side of it, and I did some worrying, although it wasn't time for me to start worrying yet. I'm an agricultural economist and I don't begin my worrying until at least the first reports are in.

But sitting just across the table from where it lay, I couldn't help but do some wondering about that mixed-up critter. I didn't get anywhere except go around in circles and I was sort of glad when Talbott Fullerton, the Double Eye, came out and sat down beside me.

Sort of, I said. No one cared too much for Fullerton. I have yet to see the Double Eye I or anybody else ever cared much about.

"Too excited to sleep?" I asked him.

He nodded vaguely, staring off into the darkness beyond the lantern's light.

"Wondering," he said. "Wondering if this could be the planet."

"It won't be," I told him. "You're chasing an El Dorado, hunting down a fable."

"They found it once before," Fullerton argued stubbornly. "It's all there in the records."

"So was the Gilded Man. And the Empire of Prester John. Atlantis and all the rest of it. So was the old Northwest Passage back on ancient Earth. So were the Seven Cities. But nobody ever found any of those places because they weren't there."

He sat with the lamplight in his face and he had that wild look in his eyes and his hands were knotting into fists, then straightening out again.

"Sutter," he said unhappily, "I don't know why you do this—this mocking of yours. Somewhere in this universe there is immortality. Somewhere, somehow, it has been accomplished. And the human race must find it. We have the space for it now—all the space there is—millions of planets and eventually other galaxies. We don't have to keep making room for new generations, the way we would if we were stuck on a single world or a single solar system. Immortality, I tell you, is the next step for humanity!"

"Forget it," I said curtly, but once a Double Eye gets going, you can't shut him up.

"Look at this planet," he said. "An almost perfect Earth-type planet. Main-sequence sun. Good soil, good climate, plenty of water—an ideal place for a colony. How many years, do you think, before Man will settle here?"

"A thousand. Five thousand. Maybe more."

"That's right. And there are countless other planets like it, planets crying to be settled. But we won't settle them, because we keep dying off. And that's not all of it . . ."

Patiently, I listened to all the rest—the terrible waste of dying—and I knew every bit of it by heart. Before Fullerton, we'd been saddled by one Double Eye fanatic and, before him, yet another. It was regulation. Every planet-checking team, no matter what its purpose or its destination, was required to carry as supercargo an agent of Immortality Institute.

But this kid seemed just a little worse than the usual run of them. It was his first trip out and he was all steamed up with idealism. In all of them, though, burned the same intense dedication to the proposition that Man must live forever, and an equally unyielding belief that immortality could and would be found. For had not a lost spaceship found the answer centuries before—an unnamed spaceship on an unknown planet in a long-forgotten year!

It was a myth, of course. It had all the hallmarks of one and all the fierce loyalty that a myth can muster. It was kept alive by Immortality Institute, operating under a government grant and billions of bequests and gifts from hopeful rich and poor—all of whom, of course, had died or would die in spite of their generosity.

"What are you looking for?" I asked Fullerton, just a little wearily, for I was bored with it. "A plant? An animal? A people?"

And he replied, solemn as a judge: "That's something I can't tell you."

As if I gave a damn!

But I went on needling him. Maybe it was just something to while away my time. That and the fact that I disliked the fellow. Fanatics annoy me. They won't get off your ear.

"Would you know it if you found it?"

He didn't answer that one, but he turned haunted eyes on me.

I cut out the needling. Any more of it and I'd have had him bawling.

We sat around a while longer, but we did no talking.

He fished a toothpick out of his pocket and put it in his mouth and rolled it around, chewing at it moodily. I would have liked to reach out and slug him, for he chewed toothpicks all the time and it was an irritating habit that set me unreasonably on edge: I guess I was jumpy, too.

Finally he spit out the mangled toothpick and slouched off to bed.

I sat alone, looking up at the ship, and the lantern light was just bright enough for me to make out the legend lettered on it: *Caph VII—Ag Survey 286*, which was enough to identify us anywhere in the Galaxy.

For everyone knew Caph VII, the agricultural experimental planet, just as they would have known Alderbaran XII, the medical research planet, or Capella IX, the university planet, or any of the other special departmental planets.

Caph VII is a massive operation and the hundreds of survey teams like us were just a part of it. But we were the spearheads who went out to new worlds, some of them uncharted, some just barely charted, looking for plants and animals that might be developed on the experimental tracts.

Not that our team had found a great deal. We had discovered some grasses that did well on one of the

Eltanian worlds, but by and large we hadn't done anything that could be called distinguished. Our luck just seemed to run bad—like that Hamal poison ivy business. We worked as hard as any of the rest of them, but a lot of good that did.

Sometimes it was tough to take—when all the other teams brought in stuff that got them written up and earned them bonuses, while we came creeping in with a few piddling grasses or maybe not a thing at all.

It's a tough life and don't let anyone tell you different. Some of the planets turn out to be a fairly rugged business. At times, the boys come back pretty much the worse for wear, and there are times when they don't come back at all.

But right now it looked as though we'd hit it lucky —a peaceful planet, good climate, easy terrain, no hostile inhabitants and no dangerous fauna.

Weber took his time relieving me at guard, but finally he showed up.

I could see he still was goggle-eyed about the critter. He walked around it several times, looking it over.

"That's the most fantastic case of symbiosis I have ever seen," he said. "If it weren't lying over there, I'd say it was impossible. Usually you associate symbiosis with the lower, more simple forms of life."

"You mean that brush growing out of it?"

He nodded.

"And the bees?"

He gagged over the bees.

"How are you so sure it's symbiosis?"

He almost wrung his hands. "I *don't* know," he admitted.

I gave him the rifle and went to the tent I shared with Kemper. The bacteriologist was awake when I came in.

"That you, Bob?"

"It's me. Everything's all right."

"I've been lying here and thinking," he said. "This is a screwy place."

"The critters?"

"No, not the critters. The planet itself. Never saw one like it. It's positively naked. No trees. No flowers. Nothing. It's just a sea of grass."

"Why not?" I asked. "Where does it say you can't find a pasture planet?"

"It's too simple," he protested. "Too simplified. Too neat and packaged. Almost as if someone had said let's make a simple planet, let's cut out all the frills, let's skip all the biological experiments and get right down to basics. Just one form of life and the grass for it to eat."

"You're way out on a limb," I told him. "How do you know all this? There may be other life-forms. There may be complexities we can't suspect. Sure, all we've seen are the critters, but maybe that's because there are so many of them."

"To hell with you," he said and turned over on his cot.

Now there's a guy I liked. We'd been tent partners ever since he'd joined the team better than ten years before and we got along fine.

Often I had wished the rest could get along as well. But it was too much to expect.

The fighting started right after breakfast, when Oliver and Weber insisted on using the camp table for dissecting. Parsons, who doubled as cook, jumped straight down their throats. Why he did it, I don't know. He knew before he said a word that he was licked, hands down. The same thing had happened many times before and he knew, no matter what he did or said, they would use the table.

But he put up a good battle. "You guys go and find some other place to do your butchering! Who wants to eat on a table that's all slopped up?"

"But, Carl, where can we do it? We'll use only one end of the table."

Which was a laugh, because in half an hour they'd be sprawled all over it.

"Spread out a canvas," Parsons snapped back.

"You can't dissect on a canvas. You got to have—"

"Another thing. How long do you figure it will take? In a day or two, that critter is going to get ripe."

It went on like that for quite a while, but by the time I started up the ladder to get the animals, Oliver and Weber had flung the critter on the table and were at work on it.

Unshipping the animals is something not exactly in my line of duty, but over the years I'd taken on the job of getting them unloaded, so they'd be there and waiting when Weber or some of the others needed them to run off a batch of tests.

I went down into the compartment where we kept them in their cages. The rats started squeaking at me and the zartyls from Centauri started screeching at me and the punkins from Polaris made an unholy racket, because the punkins are hungry all the time. You just can't give them enough to eat. Turn them loose with food and they'd eat themselves to death.

It was quite a job to get them all lugged up to the port and to rig up a sling and lower them to the ground, but I finally finished it without busting a single cage. That was an accomplishment. Usually I smashed a cage or two and some of the animals escaped and then Weber would froth around for days about my carelessness.

I had the cages all set out in rows and was puttering with canvas flies to protect them from the weather when Kemper came along and stood watching me.

"I have been wandering around," he announced. From the way he said it, I could see he had the wind up.

But I didn't ask him, for then he'd never have told me. You had to wait for Kemper to make up his mind to talk.

"Peaceful place," I said and it was all of that. It was a bright, clear day and the sun was not too warm. There was a little breeze and you could see a long way off. And it was quiet. Really quiet. There wasn't any noise at all.

"It's a lonesome place," said Kemper.

"I don't get you," I answered patiently.

"Remember what I said last night? About this planet being too simplified?"

He stood watching me put up the canvas, as if he might be considering how much more to tell me. I waited.

Finally, he blurted it. "Bob, there are no insects!"

"What have insects—"

"You know what I mean," he said. "You go out on Earth or any Earthlike planet and lie down in the grass and watch. You'll see the insects. Some of them on the ground and others on the grass. There'll be all kinds of them."

"And there aren't any here?"

He shook his head. "None that I could see. I wandered around and lay down and looked in a dozen different places. Stands to reason a man should find some insects if he looked all morning. It isn't natural, Bob."

I kept on with my canvas and I don't know why it was, but I got a little chilled about there not being any insects. Not that I care a hoot for insects, but as Kemper said, it was unnatural, although you come to expect the so-called unnatural in this planet-checking business.

"There are the bees," I said.

"What bees?"

"The ones that are in the critters. Didn't you see any?"

"None," he said. "I didn't get close to any critter herds. Maybe the bees don't travel very far."

"Any birds?"

"I didn't see a one," he said. "But I was wrong about the flowers. The grass has tiny flowers."

"For the bees to work on."

Kemper's face went stony. "That's right. Don't you see the pattern of it, the planned—"

"I see it," I told him.

He helped me with the canvas and we didn't say much more. When we had it done, we walked into camp.

Parsons was cooking lunch and grumbling at Oliver and Weber, but they weren't paying much attention to him. They had the table littered with different parts they'd carved out of the critter and they were looking slightly numb.

"No brain," Weber said to us accusingly, as if we

might have made off with it when he wasn't looking. "We can't find a brain and there's no nervous
system."

"It's impossible," declared Oliver. "How can a
highly organized, complex animal exist without a
brain or nervous system?"

"Look at that butcher shop!" Parsons yelled wrath-
fully from the stove. "You guys will have to eat
standing up!"

"Butcher shop is right," Weber agreed. "As near as
we can figure out, there are at least a dozen different
kinds of flesh—some fish, some fowl, some good red
meat. Maybe a little lizard, even."

"An all-purpose animal," said Kemper. "Maybe we
found something finally."

"If it's edible," Oliver added. "If it doesn't poison
you. If it doesn't grow hair all over you."

"That's up to you," I told him. "I got the cages down
and all lined up. You can start killing off the little
cusses to your heart's content."

Weber looked ruefully at the mess on the table.

"We did just a rough exploratory job," he explained. "We ought to start another one from
scratch. You'll have to get in on that next one,
Kemper."

Kemper nodded glumly.

Weber looked at me. "Think you can get us one?"

"Sure," I said. "No trouble."

It wasn't.

Right after lunch, a lone critter came walking
up, as if to visit us. It stopped about six feet from
where we sat, gazed at us soulfully, then obligingly
dropped dead.

During the next few days, Oliver and Weber barely took time out to eat and sleep. They sliced and probed. They couldn't believe half the things they found. They argued. They waved their scalpels in the air to emphasize their anguish. They almost broke down and wept. Kemper filled box after box with slides and sat hunched, half petrified, above his microscope.

Parsons and I wandered around while the others worked. He dug up some soil samples and tried to classify the grasses and failed, because there weren't any grasses—there was just one type of grass. He made notes on the weather and ran an analysis of the air and tried to pull together an ecological report without a lot to go on.

I looked for insects and I didn't find any except the bees and I never saw those unless I was near a critter herd. I watched for birds and there were none. I spent two days investigating a creek, lying on my belly and staring down into the water, and there were no signs of life. I hunted up a sugar sack and put a hoop in the mouth of it and spent another two days seining. I didn't catch a thing—not a fish, not even a crawdad, not a single thing.

By that time, I was ready to admit that Kemper had guessed right.

Fullerton walked around, too, but we paid no attention to him. All the Double Eyes, every one of them, always were looking for something no one else could see. After a while, you got pretty tired of them. I'd spent twenty years getting tired of them.

The last day I went seining, Fullerton stumbled onto me late in the afternoon. He stood up on the bank and watched me working in a pool. When I looked up, I had the feeling he'd been watching me for quite a little while.

"There's nothing there," he said.

The way he said it, he made it sound as if he'd known all along there was nothing there and that I was a fool for looking.

But that wasn't the only reason I got sore.

Sticking out of his face, instead of the usual toothpick, was a stem of grass, and he was rolling it around in his lips and chewing it the way he chewed the toothpicks.

"Spit out that grass!" I shouted at him. "You fool, spit it out!"

His eyes grew startled and he spit out the grass.

"It's hard to remember," he mumbled. "You see, it's my first trip out and—"

"It could be your last one, too," I told him brutally. "Ask Weber sometime, when you have a moment, what happened to the guy who pulled a leaf and chewed it. Absent-minded, sure. Habit, certainly. He was just as dead as if he'd committed suicide."

Fullerton stiffened up.

"I'll keep it in mind," he said.

I stood there, looking up at him, feeling a little sorry that I'd been so tough with him.

But I had to be. There were so many absent-minded, well-intentioned ways a man could kill himself.

"You find anything?" I asked.

"I've been watching the critters," he said. "There was something funny that I couldn't quite make out at first . . ."

"I can list you a hundred funny things."

"That's not what I mean, Sutter. Not the patch-work color or the bushes growing out of them. There was something else. I finally got it figured out. *There aren't any young.*"

Fullerton was right, of course. I realized it now, after he had told me. There weren't any calves or whatever you might call them. All we'd seen were adults. And yet that didn't necessarily mean there *weren't* any calves. It just meant we hadn't seen them. And the same, I knew, applied as well to in-sects, birds and fish. They all might be on the planet, but we just hadn't managed to find them yet.

And then, belatedly, I got it—the inference, the hope, the half-crazy fantasy behind this thing that Fullerton had found, or imagined he'd found.

"You're downright loopy," I said flatly.

He stared back at me and his eyes were shining like a kid's at Christmas.

He said: "It had to happen sometime, Sutter, somewhere."

I climbed up the bank and stood beside him. I looked at the net I still held in my hands and threw it back into the creek and watched it sink.

"Be sensible," I warned him. "You have no evi-dence. Immortality wouldn't work that way. It couldn't. That way, it would be nothing but a dead end. Don't mention it to anyone. They'd ride you without mercy all the way back home."

I don't know why I wasted time on him. He stared back at me stubbornly, but still with that awful light of hope and triumph on his face.

"I'll keep my mouth shut," I told him curtly. "I won't say a word."

"Thanks, Sutter," he answered. "I appreciate it a lot."

I knew from the way he said it that he could murder me with gusto.

We trudged back to camp.

The camp was all slicked up.

The dissecting mess had been cleared away and the table had been scrubbed so hard that it gleamed. Parsons was cooking supper and singing one of his obscene ditties. The other three sat around in their camp chairs and they had broken out some liquor and were human once again.

"All buttoned up?" I asked, but Oliver shook his head.

They poured a drink for Fullerton and he accepted it, a bit ungraciously, but he did take it. That was some improvement on the usual Double Eye.

They didn't offer me any. They knew I couldn't drink it.

"What have we got?" I asked.

"It could be something good," said Oliver. "It's a walking menu. It's an all-purpose animal, for sure. It lays eggs, gives milk, makes honey. It has six different kinds of red meat, two of fowl, one of fish and a couple of others we can't identify."

"Lays eggs," I said. "Gives milk. Then it reproduces."

"Certainly," said Weber. "What did you think?"

"There aren't any young."

Weber grunted. "Could be they have nursery areas. Certain places instinctively set aside in which to rear their young."

"Or they might have instinctive birth control," suggested Oliver. "That would fit in with the perfectly balanced ecology Kemper talks about."

Weber snorted. "Ridiculous!"

"Not so ridiculous," Kemper retorted. "Not half so ridiculous as some other things we found. Not one-tenth as ridiculous as no brain or nervous system. Not any more ridiculous than my bacteria."

"Your bacteria!" Weber said. He drank down half a glass of liquor in a single gulp to make his disdain emphatic.

"The critters swarm with them," Kemper went on. "You find them everywhere throughout the entire animal. Not just in the bloodstream, not in restricted areas, but in the entire organism. And all of them the same. Normally it takes a hundred different kinds of bacteria to make a metabolism work, but here there's only one. And that one, by definition, must be general purpose—it must do all the work that the hundred other species do."

He grinned at Weber. "I wouldn't doubt but right there are your brains and nervous systems—the bacteria doubling in brass for both systems."

Parsons came over from the stove and stood with his fists planted on his hips, a steak fork grasped in one hand and sticking out at a tangent from his body.

"If you ask me," he announced, "there ain't no such animal. The critters are all wrong. They can't be made that way."

"But they are," said Kemper.

"It doesn't make sense! One kind of life. One kind of grass for it to eat. I'll bet that if we could take a census, we'd find the critter population is at exact

capacity—just so many of them to the acre, figured
down precisely to the last mouthful of grass. Just
enough for them to eat and no more. Just enough
so the grass won't be overgrazed. Or undergrazed,
for that matter."

"What's wrong with that?" I asked, just to needle
him.

I thought for a minute he'd take the steak fork
to me.

"What's *wrong* with it?" he thundered. "Nature's
never static, never standing still. But here it's standing still. Where's the competition? Where's the
evolution?"

"That's not the point," said Kemper quietly. "The
fact is that that's the way it is. The point is *why*?
How did it happen? How was it planned? *Why* was
it planned?"

"Nothing's planned," Weber told him sourly. "You
know better than to talk like that."

Parsons went back to his cooking. Fullerton had
wandered off somewhere. Maybe he was discouraged
from hearing about the eggs and milk.

For a time, the four of us just sat.

Finally Weber said: "The first night we were here,
I came out to relieve Bob at guard and I said to
him . . ."

He looked at me. "You remember, Bob?"

"Sure. You said symbiosis."

"And now?" asked Kemper.

"I don't know. It simply couldn't happen. But if it
did—if it *could*—this critter would be the most beau-
tifully logical example of symbiosis you could dream
up. Symbiosis carried to its logical conclusion. Like,

long ago, all the life-forms said let's quit this feuding, let's get together, let's cooperate. All the plants and animals and fish and bacteria got together—"

"It's far-fetched, of course," said Kemper. "But, by and large, it's not anything unheard of, merely carried further, that's all. Symbiosis is a recognized way of life and there's nothing—"

Parsons let out a bellow for them to come and get it, and I went to my tent and broke out my diet kit and mixed up a mess of goo. It was a relief to eat in private, without the others making cracks about the stuff I had to choke down.

I found a thin sheaf of working notes on the small wooden crate I'd set up for a desk. I thumbed through them while I ate. They were fairly sketchy and sometimes hard to read, being smeared with blood and other gook from the dissecting table. But I was used to that. I worked with notes like that all the blessed time. So I was able to decipher them.

The whole picture wasn't there, of course, but there was enough to bear out what they'd told me and a good deal more as well.

For example, the color squares that gave the critters their crazy-quiltish look were separate kinds of meat or fish or fowl or unknown food, whatever it might be. Almost as if each square were the present-day survivor of each ancient symbiont—if, in fact, there was any basis to this talk of symbiosis.

The egg-laying apparatus was described in some biologic detail, but there seemed to be no evidence of recent egg production. The same was true of the lactation system.

There were, the notes said in Oliver's crabbed writing, five kinds of fruit and three kinds of vegetables to be derived from the plants growing from the critters.

I shoved the notes to one side and sat back on my chair, gloating just a little.

Here was diversified farming with a vengeance! You had meat and dairy herds, fish pond, aviary, poultry yard, orchard and garden rolled into one, all in the body of a single animal that was a complete farm in itself!

I went through the notes hurriedly again and found what I was looking for. The food product seemed high in relation to the gross weight of the animal. Very little would be lost in dressing out.

That is the kind of thing an ag economist has to consider. But that isn't all of it, by any means. What if a man couldn't eat the critter? Suppose the critters couldn't be moved off the planet because they died if you took them from their range?

I recalled how they'd just walked up and died; that in itself was another headache to be filed for future worry.

What if they could only eat the grass that grew on this one planet? And if so, could the grass be grown elsewhere? What kind of tolerance would the critter show to different kinds of climate? What was the rate of reproduction? If it was slow, as was indicated, could it be stepped up? What was the rate of growth?

I got up and walked out of the tent and stood for a while outside. The little breeze that had been blowing had died down at sunset and the place was quiet. Quiet because there was nothing but the critters to make any noise and we had yet to hear them make a single sound. The stars blazed overhead and there were so many of them that they lighted up the countryside as if there were a moon.

I walked over to where the rest of the men were sitting.

"It looks like we'll be here for a while," I said. "Tomorrow we might as well get the ship unloaded."

No one answered me, but in the silence I could sense the half-hidden satisfaction and the triumph. At last we'd hit the jackpot! We'd be going home with something that would make those other teams look pallid. *We'd* be the ones who got the notices and bonuses.

Oliver finally broke the silence. "Some of our animals aren't in good shape. I went down this afternoon to have a look at them. A couple of the pigs and several of the rats."

He looked at me accusingly.

I flared up at him. "Don't look at me! I'm not their keeper. I just take care of them until you're ready to use them."

Kemper butted in to head off an argument. "Before we do any feeding, we'll need another critter."

"I'll lay you a bet," said Weber.

Kemper didn't take him up.

It was just as well he didn't, for a critter came in, right after breakfast, and died with a *savoir faire* that was positively marvelous. They went to work on it immediately.

Parsons and I started unloading the supplies. We put in a busy day. We moved all the food except the emergency rations we left in the ship. We slung down a refrigerating unit Weber had been yelling for, to keep the critter products fresh. We unloaded a lot of equipment and some silly odds and ends that I knew we'd have no use for, but that some of the others wanted broken out. We put up tents and we lugged and pushed and hauled all day. Late in the afternoon, we had it all stacked up and under canvas and were completely bushed.

Kemper went back to his bacteria. Weber spent hours with the animals. Oliver dug up a bunch of grass and gave the grass the works. Parsons went out on field trips, mumbling and fretting.

Of all of us, Parsons had the job that was most infuriating. Ordinarily the ecology of even the simplest of planets is a complicated business and there's a lot of work to do. But here was almost nothing. There was no competition for survival. There was no dog eat dog. There were just critters cropping grass.

I started to pull my report together, knowing that it would have to be revised and rewritten again and again. But I was anxious to get going. I fairly itched to see the pieces fall together—although I knew from the very start some of them wouldn't fit. They almost never do.

Things went well. Too well, it sometimes seemed to me.

There were incidents, of course, like when the punkins somehow chewed their way out of their cage and disappeared.

Weber was almost beside himself.

"They'll come back," said Kemper. "With that appetite of theirs, they won't stay away for long."

And he was right about that part of it. The punkins

were the hungriest creatures in the Galaxy. You could never feed them enough to satisfy them. And they'd eat anything. It made no difference to them, just so there was a lot of it.

And it was that very factor in their metabolism that made them invaluable as research animals.

The other animals thrived on the critter diet. The carnivorous ones ate the critter-meat and the vegetarians chomped on critter-fruit and critter-vegetables. They all grew sleek and sassy. They seemed in better health than the control animals, which continued their regular diet. Even the pigs and rats that had been sick got well again and as fat and happy as any of the others.

Kemper told us, "This critter stuff is more than just a food. It's a medicine. I can see the signs: 'Eat Critter and Keep Well!' "

Weber grunted at him. He was never one for joking and I think he was a worried man. A thorough man, he'd found too many things that violated all the tenets he'd accepted as the truth. No brain or nervous system. The ability to die at will. The lingering hint of wholesale symbiosis. And the bacteria.

The bacteria, I think, must have seemed to him the worst of all.

There was, it now appeared, only one type involved. Kemper had hunted frantically and had discovered no others. Oliver found it in the grass. Parsons found it in the soil and water. The air, strangely enough, seemed to be free of it.

But Weber wasn't the only one who worried. Kemper worried, too. He unloaded most of it just before our bedtime, sitting on the edge of his cot and trying to talk the worry out of himself while I worked on my reports.

And he'd picked the craziest point imaginable to pin his worry on.

"You can explain it all," he said, "if you are only willing to concede on certain points. You can explain the critters if you're willing to believe in a symbiotic arrangement carried out on a planetary basis. You can believe in the utter simplicity of the ecology if you're willing to assume that, given space and time enough, anything can happen within the bounds of logic.

"You can visualize how the bacteria might take the place of brains and nervous systems if you're ready to say this is a bacterial world and not a critter world. And you can even envision the bacteria—all of them, every single one of them—as forming one gigantic linked intelligence. And if you accept that theory, then the voluntary deaths become understandable, because there's no actual death involved—it's just like you or me trimming off a hangnail. And if this is true, then Fullerton has found immortality, although it's not the kind he was looking for and it won't do him or us a single bit of good.

"But the thing that worries me," he went on, his face all knotted up with worry, "is the seeming lack of anything resembling a defense mechanism. Even assuming that the critters are no more than fronting for a bacterial world, the mechanism should be there as a simple matter of precaution. Every living thing we know of has some sort of way to defend itself or to escape potential enemies. It either fights or runs and hides to preserve its life."

He was right, of course. Not only did the critters have no defense, they even saved one the trouble of going out to kill them.

"Maybe we are wrong," Kemper concluded. "Maybe life, after all, is not as valuable as we think it is. Maybe it's not a thing to cling to. Maybe it's not worth fighting for. Maybe the critters, in their dying, are closer to the truth than we."

It would go on like that, night after night, with Kemper talking around in circles and never getting anywhere. I think most of the time he wasn't talking to me, but talking to himself, trying by the very process of putting it in words to work out some final answer.

And long after we had turned out the lights and gone to bed, I'd lie on my cot and think about all that Kemper said, and I thought in circles, too. I wondered why all the critters that came in and died were in the prime of life. Was the dying a privilege that was accorded only to the fit? Or were all the critters in the prime of life? Was there really some cause to believe they might be immortal?

I asked a lot of questions, but there weren't any answers.

We continued with our work. Weber killed some of his animals and examined them and there were no signs of ill effect from the critter diet. There were traces of critter bacteria in their blood, but no sickness, reaction or antibody formation. Kemper kept on with his bacterial work. Oliver started a whole series of experiments with the grass. Parsons just gave up.

The punkins didn't come back and Parsons and Fullerton went out and hunted for them, but without success.

I worked on my report and the pieces fell together better than I had hoped they would.

It began to look as though we had the situation well nailed down.

We were all feeling pretty good. We could almost taste that bonus.

But I think that, in the back of our minds, all of us were wondering if we could get away scot free. I know I had mental fingers crossed. It just didn't seem quite possible that something wouldn't happen.

And, of course, it did.

We were sitting around after supper, with the lantern lighted, when we heard the sound. I realized afterward that we had been hearing it for some time before we paid attention to it. It started so soft and so far away that it crept upon us without alarming us. At first, it sounded like a sighing, as if a gentle wind were blowing through a little tree, and then it changed into a rumble, but a far-off rumble that had no menace in it. I was just getting ready to say something about thunder and wondering if our stretch of weather was about to break when Kemper jumped up and yelled.

I don't know what he yelled. Maybe it wasn't a word at all. But the way he yelled brought us to our feet and sent us at a dead run for the safety of the ship. Even before we got there, in the few seconds it took to reach the ladder, the character of the sound had changed and there was no mistaking what it was —the drumming of hoofs heading straight for camp.

They were almost on top of us when we reached the ladder and there wasn't time or room for all of us to use it. I was the last in line and I saw I'd never make it and a dozen possible escape plans flickered through my mind. But I knew they wouldn't work fast enough. Then I saw the rope, hanging where I'd left it after the unloading job, and I made a jump for it. I'm no rope-climbing expert, but I shinnied up it with plenty of speed. And right behind me came Weber, who was no rope-climber, either, but who was doing rather well.

I thought of how lucky it had been that I hadn't found the time to take down the rig and how Weber had ridden me unmercifully about not doing it. I wanted to shout down and point it out to him, but I didn't have the breath.

We reached the port and tumbled into it. Below us, the stampeding critters went grinding through the camp. There seemed to be millions of them. One of the terrifying things about it was how silently they ran. They made no outcry of any kind; all you could hear was the sound of their hoofs pounding on the ground. It seemed almost as if they ran in some blind fury that was too deep for outcry.

They spread for miles, as far as one could see on the starlit plains, but the spaceship divided them and they flowed to either side of it and then flowed back again, and beyond the spaceship there was a little sector that they never touched. I thought how we could have been safe staying on the ground and huddling in that sector, but that's one of the things a man never can foresee.

The stampede lasted for almost an hour. When it was all over, we came down and surveyed the damage. The animals in their cages, lined up between the ship and the camp, were safe. All but one of the sleeping tents were standing. The lantern still burned brightly on the table. But everything else was gone. Our food supply was trampled in the ground. Much of the equipment was lost and wrecked. On either side of the camp, the ground was churned up like a half-plowed field. The whole thing was a mess.

It looked as if we were licked.

The tent Kemper and I used for sleeping still stood, so our notes were safe. The animals were all right. But that was all we had—the notes and animals.

"I need three more weeks," said Weber. "Give me just three weeks to complete the tests."

"We haven't got three weeks," I answered. "All our food is gone."

"The emergency rations in the ship?"

"That's for going home."

"We can go a little hungry."

He glared at us—at each of us in turn—challenging us to do a little starving.

"I can go three weeks," he said, "without any food at all."

"We could eat critter," suggested Parsons. "We could take a chance."

Weber shook his head. "Not yet. In three weeks, when the tests are finished, then maybe we will know. Maybe we won't need those rations for going home. Maybe we can stock up on critters and eat our heads off all the way to Caph."

I looked around at the rest of them, but I knew, before I looked, the answer I would get.

"All right," I said. "We'll try it."

"It's all right for you," Fullerton retorted hastily. "You have your diet kit."

Parsons reached out and grabbed him and shook

him so hard that he went cross-eyed. "We don't talk like that about those diet kits."

Then Parsons let him go.

We set up double guards, for the stampede had wrecked our warning system, but none of us got much sleep. We were too upset.

Personally, I did some worrying about why the critters had stampeded. There was nothing on the planet that could scare them. There were no other animals. There was no thunder or lightning—as a matter of fact, it appeared that the planet might have no boisterous weather ever. And there seemed to be nothing in the critter makeup, from our observation of them, that would set them off emotionally.

But there must be a reason and a purpose, I told myself. And there must be, too, in their dropping dead for us. But was the purpose intelligence or instinct?

That was what bothered me most. It kept me awake all night long.

At daybreak, a critter walked in and died for us happily.

We went without our breakfast and, when noon came, no one said anything about lunch, so we skipped that, too.

Late in the afternoon, I climbed the ladder to get some food for supper. There wasn't any. Instead, I found five of the fattest punkins you ever laid your eyes on. They had chewed holes through the packing boxes and the food was cleaned out. The sacks were limp and empty. They'd even managed to get the lid off the coffee can somehow and had eaten every bean.

The five of them sat contentedly in a corner, blinking smugly at me. They didn't make a racket, as they usually did. Maybe they knew they were in the wrong or maybe they were just too full. For once, perhaps, they'd gotten all they could eat.

I just stood there and looked at them and I knew how they'd gotten on the ship. I blamed myself, not them. If only I'd found the time to take down the unloading rig, they'd never gotten in. But then I remembered how that dangling rope had saved my life and Weber's and I couldn't decide whether I'd done right or wrong.

I went over to the corner and picked the punkins up. I stuffed three of them in my pockets and carried the other two. I climbed down from the ship and walked up to camp. I put the punkins on the table.

"Here they are," I said. "They were in the ship. That's why we couldn't find them. They climbed up the rope."

Weber took one look at them. "They look well fed. Did they leave anything?"

"Not a scrap. They cleaned us out entirely."

The punkins were quite happy. It was apparent they were glad to be back with us again. After all, they'd eaten everything in reach and there was no further reason for their staying in the ship.

Parsons picked up a knife and walked over to the critter that had died that morning.

"Tie on your bibs," he said.

He carved out big steaks and threw them on the table and then he lit his stove. I retreated to my tent as soon as he started cooking, for never in my life have I smelled anything as good as those critter steaks.

I broke out the kit and mixed me up some goo and sat there eating it, feeling sorry for myself.

Kemper came in after a while and sat down on his cot.

"Do you want to hear?" he asked me.

"Go ahead," I invited him resignedly.

"It's wonderful. It's got everything you've ever eaten backed clear off the table. We had three different kinds of red meat and a slab of fish and something that resembled lobster, only better. And there's one kind of fruit growing out of that bush in the middle of the back . . ."

"And tomorrow you drop dead."

"I don't think so," Kemper said. "The animals have been thriving on it. There's nothing wrong with them."

It seemed that Kemper was right. Between the animals and men, it took a critter a day. The critters didn't seem to mind. They were johnny-on-the-spot. They walked in promptly, one at a time, and keeled over every morning.

The way the man and animals ate was positively indecent. Parsons cooked great platters of different kinds of meat and fish and fowl and what-not. He prepared huge bowls of vegetables. He heaped other bowls with fruit. He racked up combs of honey and the men licked the platters clean. They sat around with belts unloosened and patted their bulging bellies and were disgustingly contented.

I waited for them to break out in a rash or to start

turning green with purple spots or grow scales or something of the sort. But nothing happened. They thrived, just as the animals were thriving. They felt better than they ever had.

Then, one morning, Fullerton turned up sick. He lay on his cot flushed with fever. It looked like Centaurian virus, although we'd been inoculated against that. In fact, we'd been inoculated and immunized against almost everything. Each time, before we blasted off on another survey, they jabbed us full of booster shots.

I didn't think much of it. I was fairly well convinced, for a time at least, that all that was wrong with him was overeating.

Oliver, who knew a little about medicine, but not much, got the medicine chest out of the ship and pumped Fullerton full of some new antibiotic that came highly recommended for almost everything.

We went on with our work, expecting he'd be on his feet in a day or two.

But he wasn't. If anything, he got worse.

Oliver went through the medicine chest, reading all the labels carefully, but didn't find anything that seemed to be the proper medication. He read the first-aid booklet. It didn't tell him anything except how to set broken legs or apply artificial respiration and simple things like that.

Kemper had been doing a lot of worrying, so he had Oliver take a sample of Fullerton's blood and then prepared a slide. When he looked at the blood through the microscope, he found that it swarmed with bacteria from the critters. Oliver took some more blood samples and Kemper prepared more slides, just to double-check, and there was no doubt about it.

By this time, all of us were standing around the table watching Kemper and waiting for the verdict. I know the same thing must have been in the mind of each of us.

It was Oliver who put it into words. "Who is next?" he asked.

Parsons stepped up and Oliver took the sample.

We waited anxiously.

Finally Kemper straightened.

"You have them, too," he said to Parsons. "Not as high a count as Fullerton."

Man after man stepped up. All of us had the bacteria, but in my case the count was low.

"It's the critter," Parsons said. "Bob hasn't been eating any."

"But cooking kills—" Oliver started to say.

"You can't be sure. These bacteria would have to be highly adaptable. They do the work of thousands of other microorganisms. They're a sort of handy-man, a jack-of-all-trades. They can acclimatize. They can meet new situations. They haven't weakened the strain by becoming specialized."

"Besides," said Parsons, "we don't cook all of it. We don't cook the fruit, and most of you guys raise hell if a steak is more than singed."

"What I can't figure out is why it should be Fullerton," Weber said. "Why should his count be higher? He started on the critter the same time as the rest of us."

I remembered that day down by the creek.

"He got a head start on the rest of you," I explained. "He ran out of toothpicks and took to chewing grass stems. I caught him at it."

I know it wasn't very comforting. It meant that in another week or two, all of them would have as high a count as Fullerton. But there was no sense not telling them. It would have been criminal not to. There was no place for wishful thinking in a situation like that.

"We can't stop eating critter," said Weber. "It's all the food we have. There's nothing we can do."

"I have a hunch," Kemper replied, "it's too late anyhow."

"If we started home right now," I said, "there's my diet kit . . ."

They didn't let me finish making my offer. They slapped me on the back and pounded one another and laughed like mad.

It wasn't funny. They just needed something they could laugh at.

"It wouldn't do any good," said Kemper. "We've already had it. Anyhow, your diet kit wouldn't last us all the way back home."

"We could have a try at it," I argued.

"It may be just a transitory thing," Parsons said. "Just a bit of fever. A little upset from a change of diet."

We all hoped that, of course.

But Fullerton got no better.

Weber took blood samples of the animals and they had a bacterial count almost as high as Fullerton's—much higher than when he'd taken it before.

Weber blamed himself. "I should have kept closer check. I should have taken tests every day or so."

"What difference would it have made?" demanded Parsons. "Even if you had, even if you'd found a lot of bacteria in the blood, we'd still have eaten critter. There was no other choice."

"Maybe it's not the bacteria," said Oliver. "We may be jumping at conclusions. It may be something else that Fullerton picked up."

Weber brightened up a bit. "That's right. The animals still seem to be okay."

They were bright and chipper, in the best of health.

We waited. Fullerton got neither worse nor better.

Then, one night, he disappeared.

Oliver, who had been sitting with him, had dozed off for a moment. Parsons, on guard, had heard nothing.

We hunted for him for three full days. He couldn't have gone far, we figured. He had wandered off in a delirium and he didn't have the strength to cover any distance.

But we didn't find him.

We did find one queer thing, however. It was a ball of some strange substance, white and fresh-appearing. It was about four feet in diameter. It lay at the bottom of a little gully, hidden out of sight, as if someone or something might have brought it there and hidden it away.

We did some cautious poking at it and we rolled it back and forth a little and wondered what it was, but we were hunting Fullerton and we didn't have the time to do much investigating. Later on, we agreed, we would come back and get it and find out what it was.

Then the animals came down with the fever, one after another—all except the controls, which had been eating regular food until the stampede had destroyed the supply. After that, of course, all of them ate critter.

By the end of two days, most of the animals were down.

Weber worked with them, scarcely taking time to rest. We all helped as best we could.

Blood samples showed a greater concentration of bacteria. Weber started a dissection, but never finished it. Once he got the animal open, he took a quick look at it and scraped the whole thing off the table into a pail. I saw him, but I don't think any of the others did. We were pretty busy.

I asked him about it later in the day, when we were alone for a moment. He briskly brushed me off.

I went to bed early that night because I had the second guard. It seemed I had no more than shut my eyes when I was brought upright by a racket that raised goose pimples on every inch of me.

I tumbled out of bed and scrabbled around to find my shoes and get them on. By that time, Kemper had dashed out of the tent.

There was trouble with the animals. They were fighting to break out, chewing the bars of their cages and throwing themselves against them in a blind and terrible frenzy. And all the time they were squealing and screaming. To listen to them set your teeth on edge.

Weber dashed around with a hypodermic. After what seemed hours, we had them full of sedative. A few of them broke loose and got away, but the rest were sleeping peacefully.

I got a gun and took over guard duty while the other men went back to bed.

I stayed down near the cages, walking back and forth because I was too tense to do much sitting down. It seemed to me that between the animals' frenzy to escape and Fullerton's disappearance, there was a parallel that was too similar for comfort.

I tried to review all that had happened on the planet and I got bogged down time after time as I tried to make the picture dovetail. The trail of thought I followed kept turning back to Kemper's worry about the critters' lack of a defense mechanism.

Maybe, I told myself, they had a defense mechanism, after all—the slickest, smoothest, trickiest one Man ever had encountered.

As soon as the camp awoke, I went to our tent to stretch out for a moment, perhaps to catch a catnap. Worn out, I slept for hours.

Kemper woke me.

"Get up, Bob!" he said. "For the love of God, get up!"

It was late afternoon and the last rays of the sun were streaming through the tent flap. Kemper's face was haggard. It was as if he'd suddenly grown old since I'd seen him less than twelve hours before.

"They're encysting," he gasped. "They're turning into cocoons or chrysalises or . . ."

I sat up quickly. "That one we found out there in the field!"

He nodded.

"Fullerton?" I asked.

"We'll go out and see, all five of us, leaving the camp and animals alone."

We had some trouble finding it because the land was so flat and featureless that there were no landmarks.

But finally we located it, just as dusk was setting in.

The ball had split in two—not in a clean break, in a jagged one. It looked like an egg after a chicken has been hatched.

And the halves lay there in the gathering darkness, in the silence underneath the sudden glitter of the stars—a last farewell and a new beginning and a terrible alien fact.

I tried to say something, but my brain was so numb that I was not entirely sure just what I should say. Anyhow, the words died in the dryness of my mouth and the thickness of my tongue before I could get them out.

For it was not only the two halves of the cocoon—it was the marks within that hollow, the impression of what had been there, blurred and distorted by the marks of what it had become.

We fled back to camp.

Someone, I think it was Oliver, got the lantern lighted. We stood uneasily, unable to look at one another, knowing that the time was past for all dissembling, that there was no use of glossing over or denying what we'd seen in the dim light in the gully.

"Bob is the only one who has a chance," Kemper finally said, speaking more concisely than seemed possible. "I think he should leave right now. Someone must get back to Caph. Someone has to tell them."

He looked across the circle of lantern light at me.

"Well," he said sharply, "get going! What's the matter with you?"

"You were right," I said, not much more than whispering. "Remember how you wondered about a defense mechanism?"

"They have it," Weber agreed. "The best you can find. There's no beating them. They don't fight you. They absorb you. They make you into them. No wonder there are just the critters here. No wonder the planet's ecology is simple. They have you pegged and measured from the instant you set foot on the planet. Take one drink of water. Chew a single grass stem. Take one bite of critter. Do any one of these things and they have you cold."

Oliver came out of the dark and walked across the lantern-lighted circle. He stopped in front of me.

"Here are your diet kit and notes," he said.

"But I can't run out on you!"

"Forget us!" Parsons barked at me. "We aren't human any more. In a few more days . . ."

He grabbed the lantern and strode down the cages and held the lantern high, so that we could see.

"Look," he said.

There were no animals. There were just the cocoons and the little critters and the cocoons that had split in half.

I saw Kemper looking at me and there was, of all things, compassion on his face.

"You don't want to stay," he told me. "If you do, in a day or two, a critter will come in and drop dead for you. And you'll go crazy all the way back home —wondering which one of us it was."

He turned away then. They all turned away from me and suddenly it seemed I was all alone.

Weber had found an axe somewhere and he started

walking down the row of cages, knocking off the bars to let the little critters out.

I walked slowly over to the ship and stood at the foot of the ladder, holding the notes and the diet kit tight against my chest.

When I got there, I turned around and looked back at them and it seemed I couldn't leave them.

I thought of all we'd been through together, and when I tried to think of specific things, the only thing I could think about was how they always kidded me about the diet kit.

And I thought of the times I had to leave and go off somewhere and eat alone so that I couldn't smell the food. I thought of almost ten years of eating that damn goo and that I could never eat like a normal human because of my ulcerated stomach.

Maybe *they* were the lucky ones, I told myself. If a man got turned into a critter, he'd probably come out with a whole stomach and never have to worry about how much or what he ate. The critters never ate anything except the grass, but maybe, I thought, that grass tasted just as good to them as a steak or a pumpkin pie would taste to me.

So I stood there for a while and I thought about it. Then I took the diet kit and flung it out into the darkness as far as I could throw it and I dropped the notes to the ground.

I walked back into the camp and the first man I saw was Parsons.

"What have you got for supper?" I asked him.

The Gnurrs Come from the Voodvork Out

BY R. BRETNOR

"R. Bretnor" sounds like a pseudonym, but it isn't. It is the by-line of one Reginald Bretnor, who lives on the West Coast and who since 1950 has been making infrequent but choice contributions to science fiction. This adventure of Papa Schimmelhorn and his friends was his first experiment in science fiction, and the success of that experiment is shown by the long list of anthology appearances the story has achieved. It is a pleasure to make that list a trifle longer herewith.

*W*hen Papa Schimmelhorn heard about the war with Bobovia, he bought a box-lunch, wrapped his secret weapon in brown paper, and took the first bus straight to Washington. He showed up at the main gate of the Secret Weapons Bureau shortly before midday, complete with box-lunch, beard, and bassoon.

That's right—*bassoon*. He had unwrapped his secret weapon. It looked like a bassoon. The difference didn't show.

Corporal Jerry Colliver, on duty at the gate, didn't know there was a difference. All he knew was that the Secret Weapons Bureau was a mock-up, put there to keep the crackpots out of everybody's hair, and that it was a lousy detail, and that there was the whole afternoon to go before his date with Katie.

"Goot morning, soldier boy!" bellowed Papa Schimmelhorn, waving the bassoon.

Corporal Colliver winked at the two Pfc's who were sunning themselves with him on the guardhouse steps. "Come back Chris'mus, Santa," he said. "We're closed for inventory."

"No!" Papa Schimmelhorn was annoyed. "I cannot stay so long from vork. Also, I haff here a zecret veapon. Ledt me in."

The Corporal shrugged. Orders were orders. Crazy or not, you had to let 'em in. He reached back and pressed the loony-button, to alert the psychos just in case. Then, keys jangling, he walked up to the gate. "A secret weapon, huh?" he said, unlocking it. "Guess you'll have the war all won and over in a week."

"A veek?" Papa Schimmelhorn roared with laughter. "Soldier boy, you vait! It iss ofer in two days! I am a chenius!"

As he stepped through, Corporal Colliver remembered regulations and asked him sternly if he had any explosives on or about his person.

"Ho-ho-ho! It iss nodt necessary to haff exblosives to vin a var! Zo all right, you zearch me!"

The corporal searched him. He searched the box-lunch, which contained one devilled egg, two pressed-ham sandwiches, and an apple. He examined the bassoon, shaking it and peering down it to make sure that it was empty.

"Okay, Pop," he said, when he had finished. "You can go on in. But you better leave your flute here."

"It iss nodt a fludt," Papa Schimmelhorn corrected him. "It iss a *gnurr-pfeife*. And I must take it because it iss my zecret veapon."

The Corporal, who had been looking forward to an hour or so of trying to tootle *Comin' Through the Rye,* shrugged philosophically. "Barney," he said to one of the Pfc's, "take this guy to Section Eight."

As the soldier went off with Papa Schimmelhorn in tow, he pressed the loony-button twice more just for luck. "Don't it beat all," he remarked to the other Pfc, "the way we gotta act like these nuts was top brass or something?"

Corporal Colliver, of course, didn't know that Papa Schimmelhorn had spoken only gospel truth. He didn't know that Papa Schimmelhorn really was a genius, or that the gnurrs would end the war in two days, or that Papa Schimmelhorn would win it.

Not then, he didn't.

At ten minutes past one, Colonel Powhattan Fairfax Pollard was still mercifully unaware of Papa Schimmelhorn's existence.

Colonel Pollard was long and lean and leathery. He wore Peal boots, spurs, and one of those plum-colored shirts which had been fashionable at Fort Huachuca in the 'twenties. He did not believe in secret weapons. He didn't even believe in atomic bombs and tanks, recoilless rifles and attack aviation. He believed in horses.

The Pentagon had called him back out of retirement to command the Secret Weapons Bureau, and he had been the right man for the job. In the four months of his tenure, only one inventor—a man with singularly sound ideas regarding packsaddles— had been sent on to higher echelons.

Colonel Pollard was seated at his desk, dictating to his blond WAC secretary from an open copy of Lieutenant-General Wardrop's *Modern Pigsticking*. He was accumulating material for a work of his own, to be entitled *Sword and Lance in Future Warfare*. Now, in the middle of a quotation outlining the virtues of the Bengal spear, he broke off abruptly. "Miss Hooper!" he announced. "A thought has occurred to me!"

Katie Hooper sniffed. If he had to be formal, why couldn't he just say *sergeant*? Other senior officers had always addressed her as *my dear* or *sweetheart*, at least when they were alone. *Miss* Hooper, indeed! She sniffed again, and said, "Yes, sir."

Colonel Pollard snorted, apparently to clear his mind. "I can state it as a principle," he began, "that the mania for these so-called scientific weapons is a grave menace to the security of the United States. Flying in the face of the immutable science of war, we are building one unproved weapon after another, counter-weapons against these weapons, counter-counter-weapons, and—and so on. Armed to the teeth with theories and delusions, we soon may stand defenseless, impotent—Did you hear me, Miss Hooper? *Impotent*—"

Miss Hooper snickered and said, "Yessir."

"—against the onrush of some Attila," shouted the Colonel, "some modern Genghis Khan, as yet unborn, who will sweep away our tinkering technicians like chaff, and carve his empire with cavalry—yes, *cavalry*, I say!—with horse and sword!"

"Yessir," said his secretary.

"Today," the Colonel thundered, "we have no cavalry! A million mounted moujiks could—"

But the world was not destined to find out just what a million mounted moujiks could or could not do. The door burst open. From the outer office, there came a short, sharp squeal. A plump young officer catapulted across the room, braked to a halt before the Colonel's desk, saluted wildly.

"*Oooh!*" gasped Katie Hooper, staring with vast blue eyes.

The Colonel's face turned suddenly to stone.

And the young officer caught his breath long enough to cry, "My God, it—it's happened, sir!"

Lieutenant Hanson was no combat soldier; he was a scientist. He had made no appointment. He had entered without knocking, in a most unmilitary manner. And—and—

"MISTER!" roared Colonel Pollard. "WHERE ARE YOUR TROUSERS?"

For Lieutenant Hanson obviously was wearing none. Nor was he wearing socks or shoes. And the tattered tails of his shirt barely concealed his shredded shorts.

"SPEAK UP, DAMMIT!"

Vacantly, the Lieutenant glanced at his lower limbs and back again. He began to tremble. "They— they *ate* them!" he blurted. "That's what I'm trying to tell you! Lord knows how he does it! He's about eighty, and he's a—a foreman in a cuckoo-clock factory! But it's the perfect weapon! And it works, it works, *it works!*" He laughed hysterically. "The gnurrs come from the voodvork out!" he sang, clapping his hands. "The voodvork out, the—"

Here Colonel Pollard rose from his chair, vaulted his desk, and tried to calm Lieutenant Hanson by shaking him vigorously. "Disgraceful!" he shouted in his ear. "Turn your back!" he ordered the blushing Katie Hooper. "NONSENSE!" he bellowed when the Lieutenant tried to chatter something about gnurrs.

And, "Vot iss nonzense, soldier boy?" enquired Papa Schimmelhorn from the doorway.

Colonel Pollard let go of the Lieutenant. He flushed a deep red cordovan. For the first time in his military career, words failed him.

The Lieutenant pointed unsteadily at Colonel Pollard. "Gnurrs iss nonzense!" he giggled. "*He* says so!"

"Ha!" Papa Schimmelhorn glared. "I show you, soldier boy!"

The Colonel erupted. "Soldier boy? SOLDIER BOY? *Stand at attention when I speak to you! ATTENTION, DAMN YOU!*"

Papa Schimmelhorn, of course, paid no attention whatsoever. He raised his secret weapon to his lips, and the first bars of *Come to the Church in the Wildwood* moaned around the room.

"Mister Hanson!" raged the Colonel. "Arrest that man! Take that thing away from him! I'll prefer charges! I'll—"

At this point, the gnurrs came from the voodvork out.

It isn't easy to describe a gnurr. Can you imagine a mouse-colored, mouse-sized critter shaped like a wild boar, but sort of *shimmery*? With thumbs fore and aft, and a pink, naked tail, and yellow eyes several sizes too large? And with three sets of sharp teeth in its face? You can? Well, that's about it—except that nobody has ever seen *a* gnurr. They don't come that way. When the gnurrs come from the voodvork out, they come *all over*—like lemmings, only more so—millions and millions and millions of them.

And they come eating.

The gnurrs came from the voodvork out just as Papa Schimmelhorn reached ". . . the church in the vale." They covered half the floor, and ate up half the carpet, before he finished "No scene is so dear to my childhood." Then they advanced on Colonel Pollard.

Mounting his desk, the Colonel started slashing around with his riding crop. Katie Hooper climbed a filing case, hoisted her skirt, and screamed. Lieutenant Hanson, secure in his nether nakedness, held his ground and guffawed insubordinately.

Papa Schimmelhorn stopped tootling to shout, "Don'dt vorry, soldier boy!" He started in again, playing something quite unrecognizable—something that didn't sound like a tune at all.

Instantly, the gnurrs halted. They looked over their shoulders apprehensively. They swallowed the remains of the Colonel's chair cushion, shimmered brightly, made a queasy sort of creaking sound, and turning tail, vanished into the wainscoting.

Papa Schimmelhorn stared at the Colonel's boots, which were surprisingly intact, and muttered, "Hmm-m, *zo!*" He leered appreciatively at Katie Hooper, who promptly dropped her skirt. He thumped himself on the chest, and announced, "They are vunderful, my gnurrs!" to the world at large.

"Wh—?" The Colonel showed evidences of profound psychic trauma. "Where did they go?"

"Vere they came from," replied Papa Schimmelhorn.

"Where's *that*?"

"It iss yesterday."

"That—that's absurd!" The Colonel stumbled down and fell into his chair. "They weren't here yesterday!"

Papa Schimmelhorn regarded him pityingly. "Of course nodt! They *vere* nodt here yesterday because yesterday vas then today. They *are* here yesterday, ven yesterday is yesterday already. It iss different."

Colonel Pollard wiped his clammy brow, and cast an appealing glance at Lieutenant Hanson.

"Perhaps I can explain, sir," said the Lieutenant, whose nervous system apparently had benefited by the second visit of the gnurrs. "May I make my report?"

"Yes, yes, certainly." Colonel Pollard clutched gladly at the straw. "Ah—sit down."

Lieutenant Hanson pulled up a chair, and—as Papa Schimmelhorn walked over to flirt with Katie— he began to talk in a low and very serious voice.

"It's absolutely incredible," he said. "All the routine tests show that he's at best a high grade moron. He quit school when he was eleven, served his apprenticeship, and worked as a clockmaker till he was in his fifties. After that, he was a janitor in the Geneva Institute of Higher Physics until just a few years ago. Then he came to America and got his present job. But it's the Geneva business that's important. They've been concentrating on extensions of Einstein's and Minkowski's work. He must have overheard a lot of it."

"But if he is a moron—" The Colonel had heard of Einstein, and knew that he was very deep indeed "—what good would it do him?"

"That's just the point, sir! He's a moron on the conscious level, but subconsciously he's a genius. Somehow, part of his mind absorbed the stuff, integrated it, and came up with this bassoon thing. It's got a weird little L-shaped crystal in it, impinging on the reed, and when you blow, the crystal vibrates. We don't know why it works—but it sure does!"

"You mean the—uh—the fourth dimension?"

"Precisely. Though we've left yesterday behind, the gnurrs have not. They're there *now*. When a day becomes our yesterday, it becomes their today."

"But—but how does he get rid of them?"

"He says he plays the same tune backwards, and reverses the effect. Damn' lucky, if you ask me!"

Papa Schimmelhorn, who had been encouraging Katie Hooper to feel his biceps, turned around. "You vait!" he laughed uproariously. "Soon, vith my *gnurr-pfeife* I broadcast to the enemy! Ve vin the var!"

The Colonel shied. "The thing's untried, unproven! It—er—requires further study—field service—acid test."

"We haven't time, sir. We'd lose the element of surprise!"

"We will make a regular report through channels," declared the Colonel. "It's a damn' machine, isn't it? They're unreliable. Always have been. It would be contrary to the principles of war."

And then Lieutenant Hanson had an inspiration. "But, sir," he argued, "we won't be fighting with the *gnurr-pfeife*! The gnurrs will be our real weapon, and they're not machines—they're animals! The greatest generals used animals in war! The gnurrs aren't interested in living creatures, but they'll devour just about anything else—wool, cotton, leather, even plastics—and their numbers are simply astronomical. If I were you, I'd get through to the Secretary right away!"

For an instant, the Colonel hesitated—but only for an instant. "Hanson," he said decisively, "you've got a point there—a very sound point!"

And he reached for the telephone.

It took less than twenty-four hours to organize *Operation Gnurr*. The Secretary of Defense, after conferring with the President and the Chiefs of Staff, personally rushed over to direct preliminary tests of Papa Schimmelhorn's secret weapon. By nightfall, it was known that the gnurrs could:

a. completely blanket everything within two hundred yards of the *gnurr-pfeife* in less than twenty seconds;

b. strip an entire company of infantry, supported by chemical weapons, to the skin in one minute and eighteen seconds;

c. ingest the contents of five Quartermaster warehouses in just over two minutes;

and,

d. come from the voodvork out when the *gnurr-pfeife* was played over a carefully shielded shortwave system.

It had also become apparent that there were only three effective ways to kill a gnurr—by shooting him to death, drenching him with liquid fire, or dropping an atomic bomb on him—and that there were entirely too many gnurrs for any of these methods to be worth a hoot.

By morning, Colonel Powhattan Fairfax Pollard— because he was the only senior officer who had ever seen a gnurr, and because animals were known to be right up his alley—had been made a lieutenant-general and given command of the operation. Lieutenant Hanson, as his aide, had suddenly found himself a major. Corporal Colliver had become a master-sergeant, presumably for being there when the manna fell. And Katie Hooper had had a brief but strenuous date with Papa Schimmelhorn.

Nobody was satisfied. Katie complained that Papa Schimmelhorn and the gnurrs had the same idea in mind, only his technique was different. Jerry Colliver, who had been dating Katie regularly, griped that the old buzzard with the muscles had sent his Hooper rating down to zero. Major Hanson had awakened to the possibility of somebody besides the enemy tuning in on the Papa Schimmelhorn Hour.

Even General Pollard was distressed—

"I could overlook everything, Hanson," he said sourly, "except his calling me 'soldier boy.' I won't stand for it! The science of war cannot tolerate indiscipline. I spoke to him about it, and all he said was, 'It iss all right, soldier boy. You can call me Papa.'"

Major Hanson disciplined his face, and said, "Well, why not call him Papa, sir? After all, it's just such human touches as these that make history."

"Ah, yes—History." The General paused reflectively. "Hmm, perhaps so, perhaps so. They always called Napoleon 'the little Corporal.' "

"The thing that really bothers me, General, is how we're going to get through without our own people listening in. I guess they must've worked out something on it, or they wouldn't have scheduled the—the offensive for five o'clock. That's only four hours off."

"Now that you mention it," said General Pollard, coming out of his reverie, "a memorandum did come through—Oh, Miss Hooper, bring me that memo from G-I, will you?—Thank you. Here it is. It seems that they have decided to—er—scramble the broadcast."

"*Scramble* it, sir?"

"Yes, yes. And I've issued operational orders accordingly. You see, Intelligence reported several weeks ago that the enemy knows how to unscramble anything we transmit that way. When Mr. Schimmelhorn goes on the air, we will scramble him, but we will not transmit the code key to our own people. It is assumed that from five to fifteen enemy monitors will hear him. His playing of the tune will constitute Phase One. When it is over, the microphones will be switched off, and he will play it backwards. That will be Phase Two, to dispose of such gnurrs as appear locally."

"Seems sound enough." Major Hanson frowned. "And it's pretty smart, if everything goes right. But what if it doesn't? Hadn't we better have an ace up our sleeve?"

He frowned again. Then, as the General didn't seem to have any ideas on the subject, he went about his duties. He made a final inspection of the special sound-proof room in which Papa Schimmelhorn would tootle. He allocated its observation windows—one to the President, the Secretary, and General Pollard; one to the Chiefs of Staff; another to Intelligence liaison; and the last to the functioning staff of Operation Gnurr, himself included. At ten minutes to five, when everything was ready, he was still worrying.

"Look here," he whispered to Papa Schimmelhorn, as he escorted him to the fateful door. "What are we going to do if your gnurrs really get loose here? You couldn't play them back into the voodvork in a month of Sundays!"

"Don'dt vorry, soldier boy!" Papa Schimmelhorn gave him a resounding slap on the back. "I haff yet vun trick I do nodt tell you!"

And with that vague assurance, he closed the door behind him.

"*Ready?*" called General Pollard tensely, at one minute to five.

"*Ready!*" echoed Sergeant Colliver.

In front of Papa Schimmelhorn, a red light flashed on. The tension mounted. The seconds ticked away. The General's hand reached for a sabre-hilt that wasn't there. At five exactly—

"*CHARGE!*" the General cried.

And Papa Schimmelhorn started tootling *Come to the Church in the Wildwood*.

The gnurrs, of course, came from the voodvork out.

The gnurrs came from the voodvork out, and a hungry gleam was in their yellow eyes. They carpeted the floor. They started piling up. They surged against thc massive legs of Papa Schimmelhorn, their tiny electric-razor sets of teeth going like all get out. His trousers vanished underneath the flood—his checkered coat, his tie, his collar, the fringes of his beard. And Papa Schimmelhorn, all undismayed, lifted his big bassoon out of gnurrs' way and tootled on. "Come, come, come, come. Come to the church in the vildvood. . . ."

Of course, Major Hanson couldn't hear the *gnurr-pfeife*—but he had sung the song in Sunday school, and now the words resounded in his brain. Verse after verse, chorus after chorus—The awful thought struck him that Papa Schimmelhorn would be over-whelmed, sucked under, drowned in gnurrs . . .

And then he heard the voice of General Pollard, no longer steady—

"*R-ready, Phase Two?*"

"*R-ready!*" replied Sergeant Colliver.

A green light flashed in front of Papa Schimmel-horn.

For a moment, nothing changed. Then the gnurrs hesitated. Apprehensively, they glanced over their hairy shoulders. They shimmered. They started to recede. Back, back, back they flowed, leaving Papa Schimmelhorn alone, triumphant, and naked as a jaybird.

The door was opened, and he emerged—to be con-gratulated and re-clothed, and (much to Sergeant Colliver's annoyance) to turn down a White House dinner invitation in favor of a date with Katie. The active phases of Operation Gnurr were over.

In far-away Bobovia, however, chaos reigned. Later it was learned that eleven inquisitive enemy monitors had unscrambled the tootle of the *gnurr-*

pfeife, and that tidal waves of gnurrs had inundated the enemy's eleven major cities. By seven fifteen, except for a few hysterical outlying stations, Bobovia was off the air. By eight, Bobovian military activity had ceased in every theatre. At twenty after ten, an astounded Press learned that the surrender of Bobovia could be expected momentarily. . . . The President had received a message from the Bobovian Marshalissimo, asking permission to fly to Washington with his Chief of Staff, the members of his Cabinet, and several relatives. And would His Excellency the President—the Marshalissimo had radioed—be so good as to have someone meet them at the airport with nineteen pairs of American trousers, new or used?

VE Day wasn't in it. Neither was VJ Day. As soon as the papers hit the streets—BOBOVIA SURRENDERS!—ATOMIC MICE DEVOUR ENEMY!—SWISS GENIUS' STRATEGY WINS WAR!—the crowds went wild. From Maine to Florida, from California to Cape Cod, the lights went on, sirens and bells and auto horns resounded through the night, millions of throats were hoarse from singing *Come to the Church in the Wildwood.*

Next day, after massed television cameras had let the entire nation in on the formal signing of the surrender pact, General Pollard and Papa Schimmelhorn were honored at an impressive public ceremony.

Papa Schimmelhorn received a vote of thanks from both Houses of Congress. He was awarded academic honors by Harvard, Princeton, M.I.T., and a number of denominational colleges down in Texas. He spoke briefly about cuckoo-clocks, the gnurrs, and

Katie Hooper—and his remarks were greeted by a thunder of applause.

General Pollard, having been presented with a variety of domestic and foreign decorations, spoke at some length on the use of animals in future warfare. He pointed out that the horse, of all animals, was best suited to normal military purposes, and he discussed in detail many of the battles and campaigns in which it had been tried and proven. He was just starting in on swords and lances when the abrupt arrival of Major Hanson cut short the whole affair.

Hanson raced up with sirens screaming. He left his escort of MP's and ran across the platform. Pale and panting, he reached the President—and, though he tried to whisper, his voice was loud enough to reach the General's ear. *"The—the gnurrs!"* he choked. *"They're in Los Angeles!"*

Instantly, the General rose to the occasion. "Attention, please!" he shouted at the microphone. "This ceremony is now over. You may consider yourselves —er—ah—DISMISSED!"

Before his audience could react, he had joined the knot of men around the President, and Hanson was briefing them on what had happened. "It was a research unit! They'd worked out a descrambler—new stuff—better than the enemy's. They didn't know. Tried it out on Papa here. Cut a record. Played it back today! Los Angeles is overrun!"

There were long seconds of despairing silence. Then, "Gentlemen," said the President quietly, "we're in the same boat as Bobovia."

The General groaned.

But Papa Schimmelhorn, to everyone's surprise, laughed boisterously. "Oh-ho-ho-ho! Don'dt vorry, soldier boy! You trust old Papa Schimmelhorn. All ofer, in Bobovia, iss gnurrs! Ve haff them only in Los Angeles, vere it does nodt matter! Also, I haff a trick I did nodt tell!" He winked a cunning wink. "Iss vun thing frightens gnurrs—"

"In God's name—*what?*" exclaimed the Secretary.

"Horzes," said Papa Schimmelhorn. "It iss the smell."

"Horses? Did you say *horses?*" The General pawed the ground. His eyes flashed fire. "CAVALRY!" he thundered. "We must have CAVALRY!"

No time was wasted. Within the hour, Lieutenant-General Powhattan Fairfax Pollard, the only senior cavalry officer who knew anything about gnurrs, was promoted to the rank of General of the Armies, and given supreme command. Major Hanson became a brigadier, a change of status which left him slightly dazed. And Sergeant Colliver (reflecting ruefully that he was now making more than enough to marry on) received his warrant.

General Pollard took immediate and decisive action. The entire Air Force budget for the year was commandeered. Anything even remotely resembling a horse, saddle, bridle, or bale of hay was shipped westward in requisitioned trains and trucks. Former cavalry officers and non-com's, ordered to instant duty regardless of age and wear-and-tear, were flown by disgruntled pilots to assembly points in Oregon, Nevada, and Arizona. Anybody and everybody who had ever so much as seen a horse was drafted into service. Mexico sent over several regiments on a lend-lease basis.

The Press had a field day. NUDE HOLLYWOOD STARS FIGHT GNURRS! headlined many a full front page of photographs. *Life* devoted a special issue to General of the Armies Pollard, Jeb Stuart, Marshal Ney, Belisarius, the Charge of the Light Brigade at Balaklava, and AR 50-45, School of the Soldier Mounted Without Arms. The *Journal-American* reported, on reliable authority, that the ghost of General Custer had been observed entering the Officer's Club at Fort Riley, Kansas.

On the sixth day, General Pollard had ready in the field the largest cavalry force in all recorded history. Its discipline and appearance left much to be desired. Its horsemanship was, to say the very least, uneven. Still, its morale was high, and—

"Never again," declared the General to correspondents who interviewed him at his headquarters in Phoenix, "must we let politicians and long-haired theorists persuade us to abandon the time-tried principles of war, and trust our national destiny to—to *gadgets.*"

Drawing his sabre, the General indicated his operations map. "Our strategy is simple," he announced. "The gnurr forces have by-passed the Mohave Desert in the south, and are invading Arizona. In Nevada, they have concentrated against Reno and Virginia City. Their main offensive, however, appears to be aimed at the Oregon border. As you know, I have more than two million mounted men at my disposal —some three hundred divisions. In one hour, they will move forward. We will force the gnurrs to retreat in three main groups—in the south, in the center, in the north. Then, when the terrain they hold has been sufficiently restricted, Papa—er, that is, Mister —Schimmelhorn will play his instrument over mobile public address systems."

With that, the General indicated that the interview was at an end, and, mounting a splendid bay gelding presented to him by the citizens of Louisville, rode off to emplane for the theatre of operations.

Needless to say, his conduct of the War Against the Gnurrs showed the highest degree of initiative and energy, and a perfect grasp of the immutable principles of strategy and tactics. Even though certain envious elements in the Pentagon afterwards referred to the campaign as "Polly's Round-up," the fact remained that he was able to achieve total victory in five weeks—months before Bobovia even thought of promising its Five Year Plan for retrousering its population. Inexorably, the terror-stricken gnurrs were driven back. Their queasy creaking could be heard for miles. At night, their shimmering lighted up the sky. In the south, where their deployment had been confined by deserts, three tootlings in reverse sufficed to bring about their downfall. In the center, where the action was heavier than anticipated, seventeen were needed. In the north, a dozen were required to do the trick. In each instance, the sound was carried over an area of several hundred square miles by huge loudspeaker units mounted in escort wagons or carried in pack. Innumerable cases of personal heroism were recorded—and Jerry Colliver, after having four pairs of breeches shot out from under him, was personally commissioned in the field by General Pollard.

Naturally, a few gnurrs made their escape—but

the felines of the state, who had been mewing with frustration, made short work of them. As for the numerous gay instances of indiscipline which occurred as the victorious troops passed through the quite literally denuded towns, these were soon forgiven and forgotten by the joyous populace.

Secretly, to avoid the rough enthusiasm of admiring throngs, General Pollard and Papa Schimmelhorn flew back to Washington—and three full regiments with drawn sabres were needed to clear a way for them. Finally, though, they reached the Pentagon. They walked toward the General's office arm in arm, and at the door they paused.

"Papa," said General Pollard, pointing at the *gnurrpfeife* with awe, "we have made History! And, by God, we'll make more of it!"

"*Ja!*" said Papa Schimmelhorn, with an enormous wink. "But tonight, soldier boy, ve vill make vhoopee! I haff a date vith Katie. For you she has a girl friend."

General Pollard hesitated. "Wouldn't it—wouldn't it be bad for—er—discipline?"

"Don'dt vorry, soldier boy! Ve don'dt tell anybody!" laughed Papa Schimmelhorn—and threw the door open.

There stood the General's desk. There, at its side, stood Brigadier-General Hanson, looking worried. Against one wall stood Lieutenant Jerry Colliver, smirking loathsomely, with a possessive arm around Katie Hooper's waist. And in the General's chair sat a very stiff old lady, in a very stiff black dress, tapping a very stiff umbrella on the blotting pad.

As soon as she saw Papa Schimmelhorn, she stopped tapping and pointed the umbrella at him.

"*So!*" she hissed. "You think you get avay? To spoil Cousin Anton's beaudtiful bassoon, and play vith mices, and passes at female soldier-girls to make?"

She turned to Katie Hooper, and they exchanged a feminine glance of triumph and understanding. "Iss lucky that you phone, so I find out," she said. "You are nice girl. You can see under the sheep's clothings."

She rose. As Katie blushed, she strode across the room, and grabbed the *gnurr-pfeife* from Papa Schimmelhorn. Before anyone could stop her, she stripped it of its reed—and crushed the L-shaped crystal underfoot. "Now," she exclaimed, "iss no more gnurrs and people-vithout-trousers-monkeyshines!"

While General Pollard stared in blank amazement and Jerry Colliver snickered gloatingly, she took poor Papa Schimmelhorn firmly by the ear. "So ve go home!" she ordered, steering him for the door. "Vere iss no soldier-girls, and the house needs painting!"

Looking crestfallen, Papa Schimmelhorn went without resistance. "Gootbye!" he called unhappily. "I must go home vith Mama."

But as he passed by General Pollard, he winked his usual wink. "Don'dt vorry, soldier boy!" he whispered. "I get avay again—I am a chenius!"

Collecting Team

BY ROBERT SILVERBERG

One way to write a science-fiction story is to take a standard, familiar theme and turn it upside down. For example, there's the one about the Earthmen who venture out to distant worlds to collect zoological specimens, like "Bring 'em Back Alive" Frank Buck of yesteryear. That story's been told a thousand times—but what if we twist things about just a bit. . . ?

From fifty thousand miles up, the situation looked promising. It was a middle-sized, brown-and-green, inviting-looking planet, with no sign of cities or any other such complications. Just a pleasant sort of place, the very sort we were looking for to redeem what had been a pretty futile expedition.

I turned to Clyde Holdreth, who was staring reflectively at the thermocouple.

"Well? What do you think?"

"Looks fine to me. Temperature's about seventy down there—nice and warm, and plenty of air. I think it's worth a try."

Lee Davison came strolling out from the storage

hold, smelling of animals, as usual. He was holding one of the blue monkeys we picked up on Alpheraz, and the little beast was crawling up his arm. "Have we found something, gentlemen?"

"We've found a planet," I said. "How's the storage space in the hold?"

"Don't worry about that. We've got room for a whole zooful more, before we get filled up. It hasn't been a very fruitful trip."

"No," I agreed. "It hasn't. Well? Shall we go down and see what's to be seen?"

"Might as well," Holdreth said. "We can't go back to Earth with just a couple of blue monkeys and some anteaters, you know."

"I'm in favor of a landing too," said Davison. "You?"

I nodded. "I'll set up the charts, and you get your animals comfortable for deceleration."

Davison disappeared back into the storage hold, while Holdreth scribbled furiously in the logbook, writing down the co-ordinates of the planet below, its general description, and so forth. Aside from being a collecting team for the zoological department of the Bureau of Interstellar Affairs, we also double as a survey ship, and the planet down below was listed as *unexplored* on our charts.

I glanced out at the mottled brown-and-green ball spinning slowly in the viewport, and felt the warning twinge of gloom that came to me every time we made a landing on a new and strange world. Repressing it, I started to figure out a landing orbit. From behind me came the furious chatter of the blue monkeys as Davison strapped them into their acceleration cradles, and under that the deep, unmusical honking of the Rigelian anteaters, noisily bleating their displeasure.

The planet was inhabited, all right. We hadn't had the ship on the ground more than a minute before the local fauna began to congregate. We stood at the viewport and looked out in wonder.

"This is one of those things you dream about," Davison said, stroking his little beard nervously. "Look at them! There must be a thousand different species out there."

"I've never seen anything like it," said Holdreth.

I computed how much storage space we had left and how many of the thronging creatures outside we would be able to bring back with us. "How are we going to decide what to take and what to leave behind?"

"Does it matter?" Holdreth said gaily. "This is what you call an embarrassment of riches, I guess. We just grab the dozen most bizarre creatures and blast off—and save the rest for another trip. It's too bad we wasted all that time wandering around near Rigel."

"We *did* get the anteaters," Davison pointed out. They were his finds, and he was proud of them.

I smiled sourly. "Yeah. We got the anteaters there." The anteaters honked at that moment, loud and clear. "You know, that's one set of beasts I think I could do without."

"Bad attitude," Holdreth said. "Unprofessional."

"Whoever said I was a zoologist, anyway? I'm just a spaceship pilot, remember. And if I don't like the way those anteaters talk—and smell—I see no reason why I—"

"Say, look at that one," Davison said suddenly.

I glanced out the viewport and saw a new beast emerging from the thick-packed vegetation in the background. I've seen some fairly strange creatures since I was assigned to the zoological department, but this one took the grand prize.

It was about the size of a giraffe, moving on long, wobbly legs and with a tiny head up at the end of a preposterous neck. Only it had six legs and a bunch of writhing snakelike tentacles as well, and its eyes, great violet globes, stood out nakedly on the ends of two thick stalks. It must have been twenty feet high. It moved with exaggerated grace through the swarm of beasts surrounding our ship, pushed its way smoothly toward the vessel, and peered gravely in at the viewport. One purple eye stared directly at me, the other at Davison. Oddly, it seemed to me as if it were trying to tell us something.

"Big one, isn't it?" Davison said finally.

"I'll bet you'd like to bring one back, too."

"Maybe we can fit a young one aboard," Davison said. "If we can find a young one." He turned to Holdreth. "How's that air analysis coming? I'd like to get out there and start collecting. God, that's a crazy-looking beast!"

The animal outside had apparently finished its inspection of us, for it pulled its head away and, gathering its legs under itself, squatted near the ship. A small doglike creature with stiff spines running along its back began to bark at the big creature, which took no notice. The other animals, which came in all shapes and sizes, continued to mill around the ship, evidently very curious about the newcomer to their world. I could see Davison's eyes

thirsty with the desire to take the whole kit and ca-
boodle back to Earth with him. I knew what was
running through his mind. He was dreaming of the
umpteen thousand species of extraterrestrial wild-
life roaming around out there, and to each one he
was attaching a neat little tag: *Something-or-other
davisoni.*

"The air's fine," Holdreth announced abruptly,
looking up from his test-tubes. "Get your butterfly
nets and let's see what we can catch."

There was something I didn't like about the place.
It was just too good to be true, and I learned long
ago that nothing ever is. There's always a catch
someplace.

Only this seemed to be on the level. The planet
was a bonanza for zoologists, and Davison and Holdreth were having the time of their lives, hip-deep in
obliging specimens.

"I've never seen anything like it," Davison said for
at least the fiftieth time, as he scooped up a small
purplish squirrel-like creature and examined it curiously. The squirrel stared back, examining Davison
just as curiously.

"Let's take some of these," Davison said. "I like
them."

"Carry 'em on in, then," I said, shrugging. I didn't
care which specimens they chose, so long as they
filled up the storage hold quickly and let me blast off
on schedule. I watched as Davison grabbed a pair of
the squirrels and brought them into the ship.

Holdreth came over to me. He was carrying a sort
of dog with insect-faceted eyes and gleaming, furless
skin. "How's this one, Gus?"

"Fine," I said bleakly. "Wonderful."

He put the animal down—it didn't scamper away, just sat there smiling at us—and looked at me. He ran a hand through his fast-vanishing hair. "Listen, Gus, you've been gloomy all day. What's eating you?"

"I don't like this place," I said.

"Why? Just on general principles?"

"It's too *easy*, Clyde. Much too easy. These animals just flock around here waiting to be picked up."

Holdreth chuckled. "And you're used to a struggle, aren't you? You're just angry at us because we have it so simple here!"

"When I think of the trouble we went through just to get a pair of miserable vile-smelling anteaters, and—"

"Come off it, Gus. We'll load up in a hurry, if you like. But this place is a zoological gold mine!"

I shook my head. "I don't like it, Clyde. Not at all."

Holdreth laughed again and picked up his faceted-eyed dog. "Say, know where I can find another of these, Gus?"

"Right over there," I said, pointing. "By that tree. With its tongue hanging out. It's just waiting to be carried away."

Holdreth looked and smiled. "What do you know about that!" He snared his specimen and carried both of them inside.

I walked away to survey the grounds. The planet was too flatly incredible for me to accept on face value, without at least a look-see, despite the blithe way my two companions were snapping up specimens.

For one thing, animals just don't exist this way—in

big miscellaneous quantities, living all together happily. I hadn't noticed more than a few of each kind, and there must have been five hundred different species, each one stranger-looking than the next. Nature doesn't work that way.

For another, they all seemed to be on friendly terms with one another, though they acknowledged the unofficial leadership of the giraffe-like creature. Nature doesn't work *that* way, either. I hadn't seen one quarrel between the animals yet. That argued that they were all herbivores, which didn't make sense ecologically.

I shrugged my shoulders and walked on.

Half an hour later, I knew a little more about the geography of our bonanza. We were on either an immense island or a peninsula of some sort, because I could see a huge body of water bordering the land some ten miles off. Our vicinity was fairly flat, except for a good-sized hill from which I could see the terrain.

There was a thick, heavily-wooded jungle not too far from the ship. The forest spread out all the way toward the water in one direction, but ended abruptly in the other. We had brought the ship down right at the edge of the clearing. Apparently most of the animals we saw lived in the jungle.

On the other side of our clearing was a low, broad plain that seemed to trail away into a desert in the distance; I could see an uninviting stretch of barren sand that contrasted strangely with the fertile jungle to my left. There was a small lake to the side. It was, I saw, the sort of country likely to attract a varied fauna, since there seemed to be every sort of habitat within a small area.

And the fauna! Although I'm a zoologist only by osmosis, picking up both my interest and my knowledge second-hand from Holdreth and Davison, I couldn't help but be astonished by the wealth of strange animals. They came in all different shapes and sizes, colors and odors, and the only thing they all had in common was their friendliness. During the course of my afternoon's wanderings a hundred animals must have come marching boldly right up to me, given me the once-over, and walked away. This included half a dozen kinds that I hadn't seen before, plus one of the eye-stalked, intelligent-looking giraffes and a furless dog. Again, I had the feeling that the giraffe seemed to be trying to communicate.

I didn't like it. I didn't like it at all.

I returned to our clearing, and saw Holdreth and Davison still buzzing madly around, trying to cram as many animals as they could into our hold.

"How's it going?" I asked.

"Hold's all full," Davison said. "We're busy making our alternate selections now." I saw him carrying out Holdreth's two furless dogs and picking up instead a pair of eight-legged penguinish things that uncomplainingly allowed themselves to be carried in. Holdreth was frowning unhappily.

"What do you want *those* for, Lee? Those dog-like ones seem much more interesting, don't you think?"

"No," Davison said. "I'd rather bring along these two. They're curious beasts, aren't they? Look at the muscular network that connects the—"

"Hold it, fellows," I said. I peered at the animal in

Davison's hands and glanced up. "This *is* a curious beast," I said. "It's got eight legs."

"You becoming a zoologist?" Holdreth asked, amused.

"No—but I am getting puzzled. Why should this one have eight legs, some of the others here six, and some of the others only four?"

They looked at me blankly, with the scorn of professionals.

"I mean, there ought to be some sort of logic to evolution here, shouldn't there? On Earth we've developed a four-legged pattern of animal life; on Venus, they usually run to six legs. But have you ever seen an evolutionary hodgepodge like this place before?"

"There are stranger setups," Holdreth said. "The symbiotes on Sirius Three, the burrowers of Mizar—but you're right, Gus. This *is* a peculiar evolutionary dispersal. I think we ought to stay and investigate it fully."

Instantly I knew from the bright expression on Davison's face that I had blundered, had made things worse than ever. I decided to take a new tack.

"I don't agree," I said. "I think we ought to leave with what we've got, and come back with a larger expedition later."

Davison chuckled. "Come on, Gus, don't be silly! This is a chance of a lifetime for us—why should we call in the whole zoological department on it?"

I didn't want to tell them I was afraid of staying longer. I crossed my arms. "Lee, I'm the pilot of this ship, and you'll have to listen to me. The schedule calls for a brief stopover here, and we have to leave. Don't tell me I'm being silly."

"But you are, man! You're standing blindly in the path of scientific investigation, of—"

"Listen to me, Lee. Our food is calculated on a pretty narrow margin, to allow you fellows more room for storage. And this is strictly a collecting team. There's no provision for extended stays on any one planet. Unless you want to wind up eating your own specimens, I suggest you allow us to get out of here."

They were silent for a moment. Then Holdreth said, "I guess we can't argue with that, Lee. Let's listen to Gus and go back now. There's plenty of time to investigate this place later, when we can take longer."

"But—oh, all right," Davison said reluctantly. He picked up the eight-legged penguins. "Let me stash these things in the hold, and we can leave." He looked strangely at me, as if I had done something criminal.

As he started into the ship, I called to him.

"What is it, Gus?"

"Look here, Lee. I don't *want* to pull you away from here. It's simply a matter of food," I lied, masking my nebulous suspicions.

"I know how it is, Gus." He turned and entered the ship.

I stood there thinking about nothing at all for a moment, then went inside myself to begin setting up the blastoff orbit.

I got as far as calculating the fuel expenditure when I noticed something. Feedwires were dangling crazily down from the control cabinet. Somebody had wrecked our drive mechanism, but thoroughly.

For a long moment, I stared stiffly at the sabotaged drive. Then I turned and headed into the storage hold.

"Davison?"

"What is it, Gus?"

"Come out here a second, will you?"

I waited, and a few minutes later he appeared, frowning impatiently. "What do you want, Gus? I'm busy and I—" His mouth dropped open. *"Look at the drive!"*

"You look at it," I snapped. "I'm sick. Go get Holdreth, on the double."

While he was gone I tinkered with the shattered mechanism. Once I had the cabinet panel off and could see the inside, I felt a little better; the drive wasn't damaged beyond repair, though it had been pretty well scrambled. Three or four days of hard work with a screwdriver and solderbeam might get the ship back into functioning order.

But that didn't make me any less angry. I heard Holdreth and Davison entering behind me, and I whirled to face them.

"All right, you idiots. Which one of you did this?"

They opened their mouths in protesting squawks at the same instant. I listened to them for a while, then said, "One at a time!"

"If you're implying that one of us deliberately sabotaged the ship," Holdreth said, "I want you to know—"

"I'm not implying anything. But the way it looks to me, you two decided you'd like to stay here a while longer to continue your investigations, and figured the easiest way of getting me to agree was to wreck the drive." I glared hotly at them. "Well, I've got news for you. I can fix this, and I can fix it in a couple of days. So go on—get about your business! Get all the zoologizing you can in, while you still have time. I—"

Davison laid a hand gently on my arm. "Gus," he said quietly, *"We didn't do it.* Neither of us."

Suddenly all the anger drained out of me and was replaced by raw fear. I could see that Davison meant it.

"If you didn't do it, and Holdreth didn't do it, and *I* didn't do it—then who did?"

Davison shrugged.

"Maybe it's one of us who doesnt' know he's doing it," I suggested. "Maybe—" I stopped. "Oh, that's nonsense. Hand me that tool-kit, will you, Lee?"

They left to tend to the animals, and I set to work on the repair job, dismissing all further speculations and suspicions from my mind, concentrating solely on joining Lead A to Input A and Transistor F to Potentiometer K, as indicated. It was slow, nerve-harrowing work, and by mealtime I had accomplished only the barest preliminaries. My fingers were starting to quiver from the strain of small-scale work, and I decided to give up the job for the day and get back to it tomorrow.

I slept uneasily, my nightmares punctuated by the moaning of the accursed anteaters and the occasional squeals, chuckles, bleats, and hisses of the various other creatures in the hold. It must have been four in the morning before I dropped off into a really sound sleep, and what was left of the night passed swiftly. The next thing I knew, hands were shaking me, and I was looking up into the pale, tense faces of Holdreth and Davison.

I pushed my sleep-stuck eyes open and blinked. "Huh? What's going on?"

Holdreth leaned down and shook me savagely. "Get up, Gus!"

I struggled to my feet slowly. "Hell of a thing to do, wake a fellow up in the middle of the—"

I found myself being propelled from my cabin and led down the corridor to the control room. Blearily, I followed where Holdreth pointed, and then I woke up in a hurry.

The drive was battered again. Someone—or *something*—had completely undone my repair job of the night before.

If there had been bickering among us, it stopped. This was past the category of a joke now; it couldn't be laughed off, and we found ourselves working together as a tight unit again, trying desperately to solve the puzzle before it was too late.

"Let's review the situation," Holdreth said, pacing nervously up and down the control cabin. "The drive has been sabotaged twice. None of us knows who did it, and on a conscious level each of us is convinced *he* didn't do it."

He paused. "That leaves us with two possibilities. Either, as Gus suggested, one of us is doing it unaware of it even himself, or someone else is doing it while we're not looking. Neither possibility is a very cheerful one."

"We can stay on guard, though," I said. "Here's what I propose: first, have one of us awake at all times—sleep in shifts, that is, with somebody guarding the drive until I get it fixed. Two—jettison all the animals aboard ship."

"What?"

"He's right," Davison said. "We don't know what we may have brought aboard. They don't seem to be intelligent, but we can't be sure. That purple-eyed baby giraffe, for instance—suppose he's been hypnotizing us into damaging the drive ourselves? How can we tell?"

"Oh, but—" Holdreth started to protest, then stopped and frowned soberly. "I suppose we'll have to admit the possibility," he said, obviously unhappy about the prospect of freeing our captives. "We'll empty out the hold, and you see if you can get the drive fixed. Maybe later we'll recapture them all, if nothing further develops."

We agreed to that, and Holdreth and Davison cleared the ship of its animal cargo while I set to work determinedly at the drive mechanism. By nightfall, I had managed to accomplish as much as I had the day before.

I sat up as watch the first shift, aboard the strangely quiet ship. I paced around the drive cabin, fighting the great temptation to doze off, and managed to last through until the time Holdreth arrived to relieve me.

Only—when he showed up, he gasped and pointed at the drive. It had been ripped apart a third time.

Now we had no excuse, no explanation. The expedition had turned into a nightmare.

I could only protest that I had remained awake my entire spell on duty, and that I had seen no one and no thing approach the drive panel. But that was hardly a satisfactory explanation, since it either cast guilt on me as the saboteur or implied that some unseen external power was repeatedly wrecking the drive. Neither hypothesis made sense, at least to me.

By now we had spent four days on the planet, and food was getting to be a major problem. My carefully budgeted flight schedule called for us to be two days out on our return journey to Earth by now. But we still were no closer to departure than we had been four days ago.

The animals continued to wander around outside, nosing up against the ship, examining it, almost fondling it, with those damned pseudo-giraffes staring soulfully at us always. The beasts were as friendly as ever, little knowing how the tension was growing within the hull. The three of us walked around like zombies, eyes bright and lips clamped. We were scared—all of us.

Something was keeping us from fixing the drive.

Something didn't want us to leave this planet.

I looked at the bland face of the purple-eyed giraffe staring through the viewport, and it stared mildly back at me. Around it was grouped the rest of the local fauna, the same incredible hodgepodge of improbable genera and species.

That night, the three of us stood guard in the control-room together. The drive was smashed anyway. The wires were soldered in so many places by now that the control panel was a mass of shining alloy, and I knew that a few more such sabotagings and it would be impossible to patch it together any more—if it wasn't so already.

The next night, I just didn't knock off. I continued soldering right on after dinner (and a pretty skimpy

dinner it was, now that we were on close rations)
and far on into the night.

By morning, it was as if I hadn't done a thing.

"I give up," I announced, surveying the damage.
"I don't see any sense in ruining my nerves trying to
fix a thing that won't stay fixed."

Holdreth nodded. He looked terribly pale. "We'll
have to find some new approach."

I yanked open the food closet and examined our
stock. Even figuring in the synthetics we would have
fed to the animals if we hadn't released them, we
were low on food. We had overstayed even the safety
margin. It would be a hungry trip back—if we ever
did get back.

I clambered through the hatch and sprawled down
on a big rock near the ship. One of the furless dogs
came over and nuzzled in my shirt. Davison stepped
to the hatch and called down to me.

"What are you doing out there, Gus?"

"Just getting a little fresh air. I'm sick of living
aboard that ship." I scratched the dog behind his
pointed ears, and looked around.

The animals had lost most of their curiosity about
us, and didn't congregate the way they used to. They
were meandering all over the plain, nibbling at little
deposits of a white doughy substance. It precipitated
every night. "Manna," we called it. All the animals
seemed to live on it.

I folded my arms and leaned back.

We were getting to look awfully lean by the eighth
day. I wasn't even trying to fix the ship any more; the
hunger was starting to get me. But I saw Davison
puttering around with my solderbeam.

"What are you doing?"

"I'm going to repair the drive," he said. "You don't want to, but we can't just sit around, you know." His nose was deep in my repair guide, and he was fumbling with the release on the solderbeam.

I shrugged. "Go ahead, if you want to." I didn't care what he did. All I cared about was the gaping emptiness in my stomach, and about the dimly grasped fact that somehow we were stuck here for good.

"Gus?"

"Yeah?"

"I think it's time I told you something. I've been eating the manna for four days. It's good. It's nourishing stuff."

"You've been eating—the manna? Something that grows on an alien world? You crazy?"

"What else can we do? Starve?"

I smiled feebly, admitting that he was right. From somewhere in the back of the ship came the sounds of Holdreth moving around. Holdreth had taken this thing worse than any of us. He had a family back on Earth, and he was beginning to realize that he wasn't ever going to see them again.

"Why don't you get Holdreth?" Davison suggested. "Go out there and stuff yourselves with the manna. You've got to eat something."

"Yeah. What can I lose?" Moving like a mechanical man, I headed toward Holdreth's cabin. We would go out and eat the manna and cease being hungry, one way or another.

"Clyde?" I called. "Clyde?"

I entered his cabin. He was sitting at his desk, shaking convulsively, staring at the two streams of blood that trickled in red spurts from his slashed wrists.

"Clyde!"

He made no protest as I dragged him toward the infirmary cabin and got tourniquets around his arms, cutting off the bleeding. He just stared dully ahead, sobbing.

I slapped him and he came around. He shook his head dizzily, as if he didn't know where he was.

"I—I—"

"Easy, Clyde. Everything's all right."

"It's *not* all right," he said hollowly. "I'm still alive. Why didn't you let me die? Why didn't you—"

Davison entered the cabin. "What's been happening, Gus?"

"It's Clyde. The pressure's getting him. He tried to kill himself, but I think he's all right now. Get him something to eat, will you?"

We had Holdreth straightened around by evening. Davison gathered as much of the manna as he could find, and we held a feast.

"I wish we had nerve enough to kill some of the local fauna," Davison said. "Then we'd have a feast—steaks and everything!"

"The bacteria," Holdreth pointed out quietly. "We don't dare."

"I know. But it's a thought."

"No more thoughts," I said sharply. "Tomorrow morning we start work on the drive panel again. Maybe with some food in our bellies we'll be able to keep awake and see what's happening here."

Holdreth smiled. "Good. I can't wait to get out of

this ship and back to a normal existence. God, I just can't wait!"

"Let's get some sleep," I said. "Tomorrow we'll give it another try. We'll get back," I said with a confidence I didn't feel.

The following morning I rose early and got my tool-kit. My head was clear, and I was trying to put the pieces together without much luck. I started toward the control cabin.

And stopped.

And looked out the viewport.

I went back and awoke Holdreth and Davison. "Take a look out the port," I said hoarsely.

They looked. They gaped.

"It looks just like my house," Holdreth said. "My house on Earth."

"With all the comforts of home inside, I'll bet." I walked forward uneasily and lowered myself through the hatch. "Let's go look at it."

We approached it, while the animals frolicked around us. The big giraffe came near and shook its head gravely. The house stood in the middle of the clearing, small and neat and freshly painted.

I saw it now. During the night, invisible hands had put it there. Had assembled and built a cozy little Earth-type house and dropped it next to our ship for us to live in.

"Just like my house," Holdreth repeated in wonderment.

"It should be," I said. "They grabbed the model from your mind, as soon as they found out we couldn't live on the ship indefinitely."

Holdreth and Davison asked as one, "What do you mean?"

BOOKS BY ROBERT SILVERBERG

Revolt on Alpha C
Lost Race of Mars
Time of the Great Freeze
Conquerors from the Darkness
Planet of Death
The Gate of Worlds
The Calibrated Alligator
Needle in a Timestack
To Open the Sky
Thorns
The Masks of Time
The Time Hoppers
Hawksbill Station
To Live Again
Recalled to Life
Starman's Quest
Tower of Glass
Earthmen and Strangers (*editor*)
Voyagers in Time (*editor*)
Men and Machines (*editor*)
Tomorrow's Worlds (*editor*)
Worlds of Maybe (*editor*)
Mind to Mind (*editor*)

The Science Fiction Bestiary